JESSICA
RULES
THE
DARK SIDE

Jessica Rules the Dark Side

Beth Fantaskey

HARCOURT

HOUGHTON MIFFLIN HARCOURT

Boston   New York   2012

Harcourt is an imprint of Houghton Mifflin Harcourt Publishing Company.

www.hmhbooks.com

The text was set in Adobe Garamond.

Library of Congress Cataloging-in-Publication Data
Fantaskey, Beth.
Jessica rules the dark side / Beth Fantaskey.
p. cm.
Summary: Eighteen-year-old vampire princess Jessica Packwood is in for the fight of
her life—and her husband's—when Lucius is accused of a horrible crime and Jessica,
trying to prove herself worthy of the throne, faces betrayal by those closest to her.
ISBN 978-0-547-39309-4
[1. Vampires—Fiction. 2. Courts and courtiers—Fiction. 3. Kings, queens,
rulers, etc.—Fiction. 4. Betrayal—Fiction. 5. Romania—Fiction.] I. Title.
PZ7.F222285Jeh 2012
[Fic]—dc22
2011009593

Manufactured in the United States of America
DOC 10 9 8 7 6 5 4 3 2
4500345089

For my three powerful princesses,
Paige, Julia, and Hope

"If you are reading this, Antanasia, it means that fate has unfolded as your father and I intended, and you have found your way home. I hope that your existence up to this point has been a happy one—and that you are prepared for the challenges and risks to come . . ."

To read about Jessica and Lucius's wedding, go to
www.bethfantaskey.com

Mr. and Mrs. Ned Packwood
Request the honour of your presence
at the marriage of their daughter

Antanasia Jessica Packwood

to

Lucius Valeriu Vladescu

Son of
Mr. and Mrs. Valeriu Vladescu

Saturday, the tenth of July
Vladescu Castle

Prologue

"MOTHER?"

The snow swirls around her, and she stands with her back to me, her body enveloped in a bright red cloak. Crimson . . . Mihaela's color. The queen who once ruled the Dragomirs looks like a splash of blood against the expanse of white, and yet she is as strong and substantial as the jagged Carpathian rocks that rise out of the lonely Romanian mountain where we always meet.

I step toward her, not understanding. Why doesn't she turn to greet me? "Mother?"

And then Mihaela Dragomir does turn, her face obscured by the cloak. And in her hands she holds an object, something she presses against her chest the way a nun would cradle a cross. But Mihaela is no humble, pious sister, and that thing . . . It is no holy relic.

The stake . . . The bloodstained stake . . .

Lucius's stake, which he used to destroy his uncle—and which he'd once nearly used to—

"No! Never!"

Thrashing, fighting off something that seemed to press against my chest, I struggled to sit up and opened my eyes to see firelight flickering against stone, and for a second I wasn't sure where I was.

Gradually, though, my surroundings sank in. I was in Lucius's home—*our* home. In our bed. That pressure on my chest . . . it wasn't . . . it was just the heavy blankets that we always needed in his—*our*—huge, chilly bedroom, even though a fire burned in the fireplace.

Taking a deep breath, I stretched out my arm and rested my hand on his shoulder, reassuring myself that everything was okay. As long as Lucius was with me, I'd be okay.

Still, images from the nightmare came rushing back.

The stake, which I hadn't seen since the night Lucius pressed his fangs against my throat and recreated me as a vampire . . .

Why had I dreamed about it? And why had my birth mother—who would *never* harm me—been holding it?

I'd started dreaming about Mihaela back in Pennsylvania, and those dreams had become more frequent since I married Lucius and moved to Romania. It was like my mother, destroyed shortly after my birth, was trying to protect me as I tried hard to follow in her footsteps and become a ruler, relying on a journal she'd left for me for help. A posthumous wedding gift to guide me as I learned to be a princess.

My heart started beating faster again. Was I learning? I was trying . . .

Wriggling back down under the blankets, I moved toward Lucius in the massive bed—in which, as he'd once confessed, he'd probably been expected by the Vladescu Elders to take *my* life, conveniently removing his Dragomir bride from power and allowing the Vladescus to have unchallenged dominion over both our families. I kicked at the covers, sort of swimming through them, suddenly impatient to be right next to him.

Everything in his home—*our* home—seemed so big sometimes. Including the burdens.

Lucius slept on his side, facing away from me, and I pressed myself close to his back, feeling the coolness of his body. I shared that coolness, too, since he'd bitten me, sealing our fate and a decades-old pact that had decreed our marriage in the interest of stopping a war between our rival families. Pressing tighter against my husband—how weird that still sounded—I listened to his steady breathing, which always calmed me down when I got nervous. Lucius wasn't scared. He thrived on ruling the clans. That was what he'd been born and raised to do.

Or did he worry sometimes?

"Lucius?" I got up on one elbow and shook him gently, needing to see his dark eyes and hear his deep, reassuring voice. "Lucius?"

"Yes . . . yes?" he mumbled. He rolled onto his back and fumbled for me under the covers, which were expensive and stiff and made me miss the soft, worn-in flannel sheets on my bed in Pennsylvania. But how could a princess ask for *flannel?* "Yes, Jessica . . . ?"

Resting my hand on his chest, I felt it rise and fall so slowly that I wondered if he had already fallen back asleep.

3

But I couldn't help asking in a whisper, so the guards outside our door wouldn't hear, "What does it mean if a vampire dreams about a stake?"

Lucius didn't answer, and I realized he was definitely sleeping—probably exhausted from yet another day of struggling to unite our obstinate families—so I lay back down and nestled against him again. In response to the pressure of my body, he turned and pulled me close, so I could feel the entire length of his powerful warrior's body against mine, like a shield at my back.

High on top of that Romanian mountain, in the heart of a confusing castle that I supposedly governed but where I still got lost in the twisted corridors, the night got very still. Even the crackling fire seemed to get quieter. After a few minutes of forcing myself to forget about the nightmare, I started to drift off to sleep again, when suddenly Lucius muttered, barely whispering, his breath chilly against my neck, "Betrayal."

I stiffened in his arms. Was he answering my question or caught up in his own dreams? His own nightmares?

Even if it was the latter, that wasn't exactly comforting. Did my husband have disloyalty—treachery—on his mind? And Lucius, like all vampires, put great stock in dreams . . .

"Betrayal." I said the word out loud, trying to make sure it was even what I'd heard him say. "Betrayal."

At the sound of my voice, which was soft but audible enough to break the profound mountaintop silence, Lucius, seeming to get restless, wrapped his strong, scarred arm tighter around me, so I was trapped against his chest.

I took his hand and tugged to give myself some space to breathe. He didn't let go, though, and I tried to move him again. Against my fingertips, I could feel another deep scar— an X on his palm that marked him as mine, cut into his flesh at our marriage ceremony—and his wedding band on his left hand. His dominant hand. The one he'd used to wield the stake when he'd held me in a very different way, in that same castle, not too many months before.

Chapter 1
Antanasia

OF ALL THE grim chambers in the Vladescu castle—not counting the subterranean dungeons, of course—the one that served as a courtroom had to be the worst.

Like every other room aboveground, this one had a fire-place with a blazing fire, but the flames seemed more *hellish* than cheerful. They cast scary, shifting shadows on the gray rock walls and definitely didn't do much to warm up the stark décor, which consisted of a semicircle of benches for witnesses, a worn spot on the stone floor where the accused would stand, and a long table, where I sat next to Lucius in a hard, straight-backed chair. The Elders waited in similar seats on either side of us, all of the ten older vampires sitting remarkably still.

Shifting in my chair, I tried—and failed—to get more comfortable.

I should sue the people who designed the My Little Pony Crystal Rainbow Castle I played with in kindergarten. They led me to believe that castles were filled with rainbows and cupcakes and pastel-pink furniture. Not stone and fire and . . . blood.

Turning a little bit sideways, I tried to meet Lucius's eyes, but he was staring straight ahead, obviously preoccupied. He was also very still, except for his left hand, which absently rubbed his jaw right where he had a small scar. I knew that meant he was hiding tension, and the butterflies in my stomach got worse.

If Lucius is tense, how can I even imagine handling this?

My husband seemed to sense that I was getting very nervous, and he shifted his eyes just long enough to remind me, *"Don't freak out, Jess. We've talked about this. It's part of our duties."*

Well, Lucius had never used the phrase "freak out," but we had discussed how my new responsibilities included handing down justice, and sometimes sentences of—

"Let the accused come forward."

I jumped as Lucius's commanding baritone suddenly echoed off the walls, and turned with a sinking heart to see that we had been joined by a vampire who stood at the back of the room, hands shackled and head hanging low.

He's a killer, I reminded myself as *my* mouth got dry. *A bunch of witnesses saw him destroy* my *uncle Constantin Dragomir. And what I'm doing is just like serving on a jury. Regular humans do that all the time!*

I glanced to my left, seeking reassurance that I wouldn't be alone in deciding the fate of the prisoner who was shuffling toward that pale spot on the floor. But my uncle Dorin—the only Elder I considered an ally—wasn't there, and I ended up meeting the gaze of Claudiu Vladescu, who *smirked*. Maybe at the growing panic that must have been apparent on my face—or maybe at the prospect of hearing testimony about a murder.

My stomach got queasier. *Claudiu's just like his older brother, Vasile—another evil, vicious vampire, whom Lucius destroyed.*

Although I knew I was squirming way too much for a princess, I turned to watch Lucius again, just as he said, in a steady voice that I couldn't imagine summoning if I had to speak, "Tell your story to this panel, Dumitru Vladescu, and we will decide if you deserve mercy—or punishment."

I should have given my full attention to the vampire who was about to fight for his life, but I kept watching my husband, who had stood on that circle himself just months before and fortunately been found not guilty of Vasile's death. Luckily, the majority of the Elders—not counting Claudiu, of course—had believed that Vasile attacked first, giving Lucius no choice but to defend himself.

I never let myself think about what could have happened at that trial, and was glad I hadn't even known about it until long after the verdict had been handed down.

I continued studying Lucius. *How can he even bear to be in this room, let alone coolly direct everything? And if today's verdict is guilty, won't he have to . . . ?*

"Speak," Lucius urged his relative. "This is your chance to save your existence."

I heard both command and compassion in Lucius's order, but my cold blood suddenly felt like ice. *An existence might really end today. I'm not just part of a jury. I'm the judge, and Lucius might be . . .*

Fingers gripping my chair, I finally forced myself to face Dumitru Vladescu, who raised his head, so I could see his dark, terrified eyes, because if he was found guilty . . .

"No!"

I wasn't even sure I'd cried out loud, but the squeal of my chair as I jumped up probably drowned out my voice anyway. "Excuse me," I mumbled, bowing my head. "I . . . I need to leave. I don't feel well . . ."

I couldn't look at Lucius as I stumbled from his side. And I certainly didn't look at Claudiu or the other Elders, who would be all too aware of why the American girl raised by vegans was rushing out of the room, nearly tripping over her long formal dress.

"Excuse me." The Elders pulled in their chairs so I could pass behind them. "Sorry . . ."

I knew that I was—again—hurting Lucius's and my chance of winning a crucial vote of confidence later that year, when the most influential Vladescu and Dragomir clan members would convene at a big summer congress of vampires. A vote that could elevate Lucius and me to king and queen. Yet I couldn't stay there, even if leaving doomed us to failure.

I practically ran past the prisoner, not looking at him, either. But as I hurried toward the door, I did catch the eye of one vampire I hadn't noticed before, even though I should have expected her to attend the trial of her father's killer. My cousin Ylenia Dragomir, eighteen, like me, small and wearing black, sat alone in a corner, blending into the shadows as if she didn't want anyone to see her face while she heard the story of her dad's murder recounted in detail.

I wasn't sure what the verdict on the prisoner would be, but *I* had never felt so guilty as when I left that room, letting down not just my husband, but the first friend I'd made in Romania.

Chapter 2
Antanasia

"DON'T BE SO hard on yourself, Antanasia," my uncle Dorin urged. He hovered near my desk, twisting his hands nervously, sympathy in his eyes. "I . . . I didn't make a very strong effort to attend the trial, either. Sitting in judgment— it's not for everyone, you know?"

"Claudiu seemed okay with it," I noted miserably. "And Lucius was fine!"

At least, he'd acted fine, which was what really counted.

"Yes, well, Vladescus are legendary for their sang-froid," Dorin reminded me. "They all have ice in their veins. And a few, like Claudiu, salivate to mete out some punishment. We Dragomirs, on the other hand, tend to be a little . . ." He couldn't find the right word, but I could finish the sentence easily enough.

Soft. Meek. Cowardly?

But was it so bad to want to avoid ending lives?

I pushed myself upright in my huge office chair, which

had once belonged to my birth mom. The silk nightgown I'd changed into—in a desperate attempt to make everyone believe I really was ill—kept making my butt slip off the leather seat, and when I shoved back, my feet dangled, so I felt even more like a kid playing at being a princess. A *shamed* kid.

At least one Dragomir—Mihaela—never shied away from a trial.

Have I gone too far, with the pajamas?

"I guess there's nothing I can do now except try to redeem myself at tomorrow's meeting with the Elders," I said, looking glumly at a huge ledger that was open on my desk. "I can at least try to make a few intelligent points when we discuss this budget."

Yet I didn't have much hope for that, either, as I scanned columns of numbers that supposedly represented how much Lucius and I intended to spend to govern a shifting, borderless, crazy kingdom of vampires I hadn't even known existed until recently.

I slumped in my seat, thinking, *Sure, I'm a mathlete, but I'm also a* teenager *who just last year worked for three-dollar tips, not millions of euros in* taxes!

And who even knew vampires collected *taxes?*

"Dorin?" I closed the ledger with a thud, because my worried, distracted mind kept skipping ahead to an even bigger meeting that would take place later that year, making it impossible to focus on numbers. "What is the vampire congress really like, anyhow? I have trouble picturing this event where Lucius's and my fate will be decided."

"Oh, goodness . . ." Dorin stepped back and wrung his hands again, but this time he seemed happy and nostalgic about a week that *I* dreaded. "The congress is quite an event! The most prominent Vladescus and Dragomirs gather from all over the world, and while business is conducted, of course, it's also a chance for us to socialize. Parties every evening for a full week, with the best food and music. In the past, the estates have been decorated beautifully enough to rival your wedding!"

His eyes practically glowed, and I wished that I could get excited about the prospect of hundreds of my relatives wandering around the castle. "So it's basically an oversized undead family reunion?"

"Yes." Dorin nodded. "It has been held each year since the pact that decreed your marriage was signed, uniting our clans. And this year will be extra special, as we celebrate the lasting peace achieved at your wedding." He smiled even more warmly. "Your mother hosted the very first congress, shortly before her destruction. She would be so proud to see you take over that role."

I slipped on the seat again and pushed myself back up.

How would I feed and entertain eight hundred vampires when I couldn't even order dinner from the kitchen for Lucius and me? I would mess up the whole event, and my relatives would all laugh as they cast their "no" ballots in the vote of confidence on the last day. I was doomed to bomb at my own party, and ruin Lucius's future, too.

"It's going to be a disaster," I admitted out loud, for the first time.

"Antanasia!" I looked up to see Dorin pressing a finger to his lips, shushing me and nodding toward the door.

I knew immediately that I'd made yet another mistake.

11

Emilian, the young guard who was always posted just outside the room whenever Lucius couldn't be with me, was never supposed to hear me complain or show weakness. Servants— even loyal ones—were notorious gossips, according to my husband, who'd dealt with "underlings" his whole life, while I'd been mucking out stalls on a no-kill farm.

If Emilian told anyone I was predicting disaster at the congress, word would spread like wildfire that I couldn't even handle planning a party.

Dorin and I looked at each other, both of us probably thinking the same thing. That the only thing I did royally was *mess up.*

How is Lucius doing at the trial without my support?

And is my cousin Ylenia, whom I also abandoned, crying behind her thick glasses?

"Let's get back to the budget," I sighed, opening the ledger again and speaking more quietly. "I think I'm translating the Romanian wrong, because it seems to me that Lucius wants to spend sixty-five thousand euros on *rabbits* next year."

"I do have a taste for hare—but I could never consume more than fifty thousand euros' worth in one twelve-month span."

I froze at the unexpected sound of a deep masculine voice and sensed my uncle seizing up, too, as we both swiveled to see Lucius leaning against the door frame, arms crossed.

And although he'd just made a joke, his face looked troubled, maybe because I'd admitted my ignorance too loudly after all, or maybe because of what *he'd* just done at the trial . . .

"Lucius?"

Chapter 3
Antanasia

"I AM SURPRISED to see you here, Dorin," Lucius noted, then glanced over his shoulder to address Emilian. *"Ești demis."* My Romanian seemed to be getting worse, but even I knew that command. "You are dismissed." Not that I'd ever used it.

He pushed off from the door frame and entered the room, walking right up to my uncle without really greeting him—or me. "Your presence was needed at a trial, Dorin," he said, looming over the shorter vampire. "Did you forget the date?"

Lucius wasn't being rude—he was never rude, even with servants—but it was obvious that he was very displeased with my uncle, who licked his lips and stammered, "Yes, well . . . I—I was running late, and then I heard that Antanasia wasn't well . . ."

Lucius didn't say anything as Dorin trailed off. He didn't have to. It was obvious that the next time a vampire was on trial, Dorin's butt had better be in his seat.

I shot my uncle an apologetic glance as he moved toward the door, bowing slightly and telling us both, "I'll be going now." He looked to Lucius for permission. "If that's all right."

Lucius didn't try to stop him, and I wondered again, *Why can't my two closest allies be friends? Why can't Lucius ever forgive Dorin for his weakness, which in Lucius's eyes is worse than*

13

insubordination? "*Dangerous,*" he calls Dorin's instinct for self-preservation. "*Dangerous for everyone, most of all Dorin!*"

I wanted to understand that, but I didn't get it. Trying to survive seemed pretty reasonable to me. "I'll talk to you later," I told Dorin as he left us without even a good-bye.

Then, when the door closed behind my uncle and Lucius moved to me, still without a word, I braced myself for *our* confrontation. He had to know that I was faking.

But he didn't mention my pajamas, or the trial. He just took me in his arms and greeted me like he always did when we were alone: with a kiss.

Relieved yet somehow unnerved, I wrapped my arms around his neck, and the kiss became more intense.

I wanted to enjoy that rare private moment, but even as I felt the pressure of his fangs against my throat I found myself reaching for his hands, feeling for some small, sticky trace of the blood that I was afraid my husband, who was murmuring "I love you" against my ear again and again, had just shed, because I knew there was a chance that he hadn't been just jury and judge but executioner, too.

Chapter 4
Antanasia

"LUCIUS, WHAT happened this morning?" I asked softly.

He didn't answer. He'd grown very quiet again since drinking from me, and toyed distractedly with my engagement

14

ring, spinning it around my too-thin finger as he held me on the couch in my office.

"Lucius?" I lifted my head off his shoulder to see his face: his high cheekbones and straight, aristocratic nose and the strong jaw that made him look older than he was. Like most girls at Woodrow Wilson High School, including my best friend, Mindy Stankowicz, I'd been both drawn to and intimidated by his very mature good looks. And he seemed even more like a warrior prince since returning to Romania. "Lucius?"

"Yes?" He finally turned to look at me. "I am sorry . . . I was lost in thought."

"What happened today?" I repeated—although I was pretty sure I knew right then, just from the look in his eyes. The unhappiness that he was finally fully revealing.

"The verdict was guilty," he said. "There was no question. No doubt in the Elders' minds."

My heart sank. "And you? Did you have any doubt?"

"I cannot afford doubt," he said. "If I'd had even a sliver, I couldn't have carried out the sentence. My hand might have hesitated, and I would have caused the prisoner more agony. I want to be just, never cruel." His frown deepened. "And if the Elders had sensed hesitation on my part, I would have hurt myself—*us*—as well, by appearing weak."

"So you really did . . . ?" I couldn't even say it.

But Lucius could. "Yes, Antanasia. I destroyed him. The law is clear. Destruction is punishable by destruction. And destruction of an Elder must be answered by none other than the highest-ranking clan member." His eyes hardened a little.

"Besides, we both know that I am best suited to destroy with as little pain as possible. I have been trained since childhood to use a stake efficiently. Execution is not a chore to be passed off to a servant, like laundry."

"I'm so sorry . . ." *For poor, murdered Constantin Dragomir, and my orphaned cousin Ylenia, and the prisoner, too. And for Lucius, whom I shouldn't have left . . .*

"I am sorry, too, Jessica." His use of my old name told me that Lucius was also struggling inside. He had fought against using "Jessica" in Pennsylvania, insisting that I was "Antanasia." But lately he'd taken to calling me Jess in private. I thought he especially used the nickname when he missed just being an American teenager, like I did a lot of the time. Most days, I just wished we could go live in my adoptive parents' garage apartment, married but still sort of kids. But I couldn't even call Mom and Dad, who were on a research trip in a remote part of South America.

I knew they were traveling to avoid their new "empty nest," and I understood that, but I wished I could talk to them—even though I knew what my cultural anthropologist mother would say about the trial. *"You have to learn to live by the harsh norms of your new culture. Lucius warned you . . ."*

I remembered something from my birth mother's journal, too: *"As a princess you will be called upon to witness destruction."*

"I hate rule of law," I muttered.

For the first time that day, Lucius smiled. "Princess! We have agreed that rule of law is what is most needed in this kingdom, have we not?"

"Yes, but—"

"There are no buts!" He grew serious again. "Our clans have ignored our own laws for too long. Even in the last ten years, what you would call lynch mobs have been more common than trials, among vampires. And laws protect rulers, too." His smile returned. "See how much I learned in America, with its Constitution and orderly succession of leaders and endless licensing and regulation?"

"I know," I agreed. "Laws are good. But I just couldn't be there to enforce them today."

"Please, do not be so hard on yourself," he said. "You were raised among kittens by vegans." Then he made a rare admission: "It was difficult even for me, raised by killers on a diet of violence."

"But you did it."

"Yes, and I will do it again. And you will learn to stand at my side as you become accustomed to this culture, the way I became accustomed to yours."

My voice dropped to a whisper. "What if I can't?"

Lucius grinned. "I used to ask myself that same question when faced with your mother's lentil casseroles. 'What if I literally cannot lift the fork today?' And yet I did it, Jessica."

My eyes widened. "You can't compare today's trial to *lentil casserole*."

But Lucius arched an eyebrow and laughed. "Didn't you *taste* it?"

Then he rose and I saw him transform—like he often did—from spouse to ruler. Why couldn't I do that trick? "I am sorry, but I need to go now," he said, bending to give me a quick kiss. "I need to prepare for the meeting with the Elders tomorrow."

My heart sank again. "Where Claudiu will mention my freak-out . . ."

"Do not worry, Jessica," Lucius urged. "You are growing too thin, worrying so much. I promise you—I will handle Claudiu."

"Lucius . . ." I knew what the answer would be, but I couldn't help asking, for the hundredth time. "Are you *sure* we shouldn't postpone the vote of confidence? Maybe wait a year, so I have some time to impress the Elders?"

But he was already shaking his head. "The titles of king and queen are protective, like law," he reminded me. "They carry infinitely more force than prince and princess—and when you are as young as we are, trying to rule two nations of ruthless vampires, you need every advantage you can secure. The greater risk—to you, especially—would be to postpone the vote. I cannot leave you vulnerable when I know of a way to protect you."

I had to admit that I didn't want to be vulnerable. "Okay."

He kissed me again, then went to the door and, summoning Emilian back to his post, left me alone with a bunch of dusty Romanian books I couldn't read, papers I wasn't sure I should sign, and worries I didn't know how to handle. So I did the last thing I probably should have done, as a princess.

I grabbed my cell phone, went to hide in the closest bathroom, and dialed a familiar international number, desperate to hear an even more familiar voice.

Chapter 5
Mindy

"SURE, EVERY WOMAN should be financially independent, but there's nothing wrong with loving a guy who has a few dollars in the bank—or a Mercedes in the garage, for that matter."

"Yeah, totally," I said, way too loud.

Kinda embarrassed, I slid way down in my seat and looked around to see if anybody in class heard me talking to myself about the very interesting *Cosmo* article "Rich Man, Poor Man—Why Not Love a Guy with Money?" But lucky for me, everybody was busy listening to Dr. Wayne Prentiss talking on and on about the boring Italian art slides he was clicking through while he wandered around the back of the dark room, like he did every week.

I slid even lower, so I was practically lying down on the floor. Stupid community college "core curriculum requirements." I'd figured Foundations of Renaissance Art would be the easiest "humanity," but I hated the class, which turned out to be all about . . . Italy! And all the Italian paintings and naked marble guys made me think about . . . Italians. And I did *not* want to think about Italians. Not even Italian shoes. I hardly even ate *spaghetti* anymore.

I tried hard to shut out Dr. Prentiss's voice, but he kept blah-blah-blahing behind me, telling us all, "Contemporary artists still try—and inevitably fail—to imitate the way in which Michelangelo imbued in the male form a sense of grandeur."

There was a flash of light, and I looked up to see *another* slide of a naked Italian guy. A guy with a perfect body. I knew a body like that . . .

Stop remembering him!

I held the empty notebook I was using to hide my magazine up a little higher, to block out the screen, but when I turned the page to finish "Rich Man, Poor Man"—which I totally agreed with, after seeing my best friend get very happily married in a castle—I came face-to-face with an ad for Versace. And—big surprise!—another pretty-much-naked Italian guy.

They were, like, *everywhere,* with their rock-hard chests and their six-pack abs.

I didn't wanna do it, but I kept staring at that ad, and it was like I got hypnotized and fell back in time all the way to summer and Romania and that amazing wedding where Jess Packwood turned into Princess Antanasia Dragomir Vladescu—after turning into a vampire, of course. The wedding where I'd kinda changed, too, and not in a good way.

I could still see how it all started way too clear in my brain. It figured that I couldn't remember anything I studied in books, so I was bombing all my classes at Lebanon Valley, but I couldn't forget a single word of that conversation, no matter how hard I tried.

"You would like to take a walk, Mindy Sue? See the moonlight with me, yes?"

I am, like, nodding and shaking my head at the same time, so my brain is sloshing around in circles, 'cause I do not understand Raniero Vladescu Lovatu's crazy way of asking questions and telling you what to do at the same time. Is the right answer yes? Or no? Do I even know how I wanna answer? Do I wanna "see the moonlight" with the bloodsucking, *tattooed best man who is looking unbelievably hot in his tux, with his longish, wavy brown hair pulled back into a ponytail so you can actually see his very different, gray-green eyes?*

Raniero doesn't wait for an answer anyhow. He smiles—he's, like, always smiling—and takes my hand, and his skin is really cool, like Jess's is now. But Raniero's skin is dark from spending so much time at the beach, which has also given him this amazing surfer's body.

We start walking, leaving the reception, and I look over my shoulder and see Jess dancing with Lukey in the big clearing that he has paid, like, a million dollars to decorate just to make her happy for one night, and I'm pretty sure I am making a BIG mistake, but I go with Raniero, 'cause there's just something about him, that night . . .

My heart started racing right there in class, and I seriously wasn't sure if I was getting sick over that memory or excited, like I'd got that night, when I'd had my very first real kiss in the mountains Jess told me were Carpathi-something. A kiss that started pretty much the second me and Ronnie set foot on that dark, scary path through the woods and kept on going all the way back to the giant castle that was still lit up with a bazillion candles for the wedding. Everything had been, like, on fire that night. And Raniero had looked better than the Versace model in his tux—and out of his shirt.

Those muscles . . . That big mistake . . . That next morning . . . That whole summer!

"Oh, gosh!"

I yelped out loud 'cause I could hardly stand those memories, but also 'cause my magazine was all of a sudden being ripped out of my fingers, and I jumped straight up in my chair just in time to hear Dr. Prentiss tell the whole class, "It appears that Melinda has discovered a male form that interests her even more than Michelangelo's *David*!"

Then my face got beet red when my professor held up my *Cosmo* and spun around real slow to make sure every single person could see the almost-nude model—and, of course, laugh like crazy at me. It was a wonder some of them didn't pee their pants, they laughed so hard.

And before I could tell everybody that I wasn't drooling over that guy—I really wasn't—Dr. Prentiss slapped the magazine down on my desk and said just to me, "See me after class, Melinda."

"Yeah, I know the drill," I grumbled, sliding back down in my chair again.

All my professors at that stupid college were always asking to see me after class. And it was never to say, "Good job, Mindy!" They just didn't get that I'd never been so great at studying to begin with and now I couldn't seem to think at all.

I hung out as close to the floor as possible until my cheeks started cooling down; then I sat up again, crossed my arms on my desk, and buried my face, not caring that everybody would know I'd totally given up on even pretending to pay attention to Renaissance art and its "foundations."

STUPID ITALIANS!

And just when I thought I'd been humiliated as much as possible, my phone that I'd forgot to turn off started making noise, and by the time I got it to shut up—with the whole class laughing again at my Hello Kitty theme song ring tone and Dr. Prentiss sounding like it was the very last straw when he said, "Melinda, *please!*"—I saw I had *two* texts.

One from an Italian vampire who just would not give up, that said, *"Buon grno, Mindy Sue!"*

And one from a Romanian princess who musta been having a bad day, too, 'cause all it said was "☹."

Chapter 6
Mindy

"SPEAK UP, JESS," I told her. "It sounds like you're in a cave or something!"

A million miles away in Romania, Jess kept whispering. "I'm not in a cave. I'm in a bathroom. And I can't talk louder."

I held my pink Motorola flip away from my ear and gave it a shake, 'cause there was no way I'd heard *that* right. "You're, like, on the *toilet?* Because that is just gross."

"I'm not on the toilet," Princess Jess said, a little louder. "I'm just in the bathroom so my bodyguard can't hear everything I say."

I plopped down onto a bench outside Dr. Prentiss's office, which was in an ugly building full of cheap furniture. "You're a princess in a freakin' castle," I reminded her. "If you want privacy, go to a . . . tower or something. Don't hide on the toilet!"

There was a big, long silence, so I thought the connection got cut, like it did half the time I talked to Jess. That was the only problem with Jess's whole life. Her part of Romania was more stuck in the past than Amish country. They didn't even have malls where she lived. I shook my phone again. "Jess, are you there?"

"Yeah." She sounded super bummed. "I mean, yes."

"So what's wrong?" I asked. "What's with the frowny-face text?"

How come my very best—let's face it, my only—friend never seemed into being the only thing I'd ever wanted to be in my entire life, which was royalty?

Well, that and a hairstylist to the stars.

"I'm just having a rough day," she said. "There was this trial, and Lucius came back acting weird—kissing me like crazy without even talking about how everything had gone wrong—and the whole thing is going to mess up our chance at being king and queen—"

I didn't mean to laugh at her, but seriously, *that* was a rough day? She was hiding from her *servants* so she could complain about how the incredibly hot, rich *prince* she was married to wanted to *make out* in their castle? And jeez, she might not get to be *queen* and just get stuck at princess for the rest of her life!

Yeah, I wanted to, like, cry.

For me!

I'd had a guy who coulda been practically a prince—and a really rich one, at that—but gave it all up to . . . surf!

"Hey, Jess," I kinda cut her off. "This will make you feel better. I got a D on my Critical Thinking paper about recycling, 'cause my professor said I couldn't cite *Elle* as an academic source. Then my whole art class laughed at me, 'cause I got caught looking at a half-naked Italian guy, and now . . ."

I got this crazy feeling somebody was watching me, and I looked up and saw Dr. Prentiss standing in the door to his office. He had his arms crossed, and I couldn't tell if he was laughing at me or ready to kill me. Probably both. That seemed to be how everybody at community college looked at me.

He uncrossed his arms and crooked his finger, and I said, "Hey, Jess, I'm sorry, but I gotta go."

She gave a big sigh I could hear even from Romania and said, "I guess I gotta go, too. My friend Ylenia's supposed to come by any minute now."

I stood up and started following Dr. Prentiss's hideous tweed blazer into his office. "Okay, we'll talk later."

"Min!" I heard Jess try to stop me from hanging up. "You wouldn't want to come over here for a while, would you? I'll pay for everything—"

I didn't get a chance to answer, 'cause I was already clicking the phone shut. It was just too late to stop my hand. And what could I have said, anyway? *"Yeah, Jess, I'll ditch community college and just hang out in Romania"?*

But a few minutes later, when Dr. Prentiss swung his computer screen around so I could see all my grades in all my classes—the biggest bunch of 60s and 65s probably in the history of community colleges—I started thinking Romania might not be such a bad idea.

"You have got to focus," he kept saying, over and over.

"Yeah," I kinda agreed, looking past him to a big framed poster of that David Michelangelo statue and thinking, *Could I possibly get away from naked Italians in Romania?*

'Cause I knew that one half-naked Italian, at least, hated that place.

And when my professor said, "You understand that you're failing, don't you, Melinda?" I just nodded, hardly listening, 'cause the next-to-last thing Jess had said finally sank into my brain, and I felt like an even lonelier loser.

I could handle Jess having a husband who took her away from me. He was a guy, and he'd never take my place.

But did she really have a new *girlfriend?*

Chapter 7
Antanasia

I CLICKED SHUT my black luxury Vertu Signature cell phone—standard issue for Vladescu nobility—and sighed as I reached for the bathroom door.

I was pretty sure Mindy hadn't heard my desperate invitation before she hung up her own crystal-covered pink phone, which I could picture as clearly as my best friend's light brown eyes and wavy chestnut hair. Or maybe Min hadn't wanted to hear about spending winter break on a bleak mountaintop with vampires because she was caught up in the excitement of college, with new professors and "critical thinking" and . . .

half-naked Italians? Seriously, though, who would choose to spend the holidays in a place that held *executions?*

Yanking too hard, I opened the door—and jumped to find myself face-to-face with a girl who had a head full of almost-black curls, a mouth that was a little too broad to be classically pretty, and dark eyes that were half hidden behind thick glasses.

A girl who looked—discounting the glasses—a lot like *me.*

Chapter 8
Antanasia

"I BROUGHT YOU some soup," Ylenia Dragomir said, pulling a Thermos out of a huge tote that was slung over her shoulder. At least, the bag looked big on my cousin. In reality, it probably wasn't half the size of Mindy's favorite Louis Vuitton knockoff with the faux leopard trim. "I thought it might help you feel better."

"Thanks." I accepted the container, not sure if I should tell Ylenia that I wasn't really sick, because we were becoming friends. I knew what Lucius would advise: *"Trust no one . . ."*

"Have some," she suggested, before I could decide whether to admit the truth.

I twisted off the cap and sniffed, trying not to make a face at the strange odor. "This smells . . . great," I fibbed some more. "Delicious!"

"It's *ciorbă de pui*," Ylenia explained. "Sour chicken soup with lemon. It's very healthy!"

"Did you . . . make this?" I asked, stalling, leading us to the part of my office that was like a living room.

Ylenia followed me and perched on the edge of a chair while I sat down on the couch again. "Yes!" She smiled and shrugged. "Those of us who are still Dragomirs, not Vladescus, don't have a bunch of servants to prepare food. We learn to cook!"

She was laughing, but I felt bad. Should I ask Lucius about spending some of the money in that budget to fix up and staff my family's old castle, which was pathetically supported by tourists who paid to gawk?

Ylenia must've realized that her joke wasn't funny to me. "Hey, I was just kidding," she said. "I feel lucky to just have a place to live, now that my father is gone. I didn't have anywhere else to go, and it was nice of you and Dorin to give me a room."

Poor Ylenia. Her mother had abandoned the family when she was a little girl, and her father had shipped her off to boarding school for most of her childhood. Until he lost his meager fortune in a bad deal with Dumitru Vladescu, which had led to a fight to the death. She was not just parentless but poor and homeless, too, and I felt a twinge of guilt for thinking *my* existence was difficult. I had parents, and Lucius.

I set the Thermos and cap down on the mahogany coffee table. "So, do you want to talk about the trial? Although I understand if you don't."

"No, it's okay." My cousin leaned forward and poured a good dose of yellowish liquid into the cap, pushing it toward me. "The trial was difficult. Lucius dragged the whole story out of my father's killer, and it was hard to hear that. But now I feel like justice has been done."

I took a sip of the soup and forced myself not to make a face. "How did Lucius get him to talk?"

Ylenia smoothed an outdated long skirt over her knees. "He's Lucius. How could anyone not give up information under that stare? Your husband was intimidating as a child, and the older he gets, the more powerful he seems to become."

I took another drink, and suddenly the soup didn't seem as strange as most of what she'd just said.

I'm an outsider in my own marriage. Ylenia had crossed paths with Lucius before I even knew he *existed.* They'd been attending those summer congresses back when I'd been raising calves for 4-H and swimming in Conewago Lake while Mindy sat on the shore, not wanting to touch dirty water.

"Ylenia?" I suddenly needed to know if I was the bigger wimp, too, of the two Dragomir cousins. "Did you stay for . . . ?"

She clearly understood the question before I had to finish it, and she shook her head, so her curls, a frizzier version of mine, trembled. "No! I couldn't watch that, even to see my father's death avenged."

"I couldn't be there, either," I admitted then. "I just couldn't."

We sat quietly for about a full minute, me finishing the soup, because although I didn't love the taste, I actually felt hungry for what seemed like the first time in weeks, after having confessed that. I'd never had a close girlfriend, except for Mindy, and I needed one now that she was so far away. Dorin was great, but he was my uncle. And Lucius—while my eternal love—was also a guy. There were things he just couldn't understand or talk about like a girl could.

"I should get going now," Ylenia eventually said. "You look tired."

I was starting to get drowsy. We both stood up. "Yeah, I think I'm going to turn in."

"Sure." Ylenia screwed the cap back on the Thermos and handed it to me. "You can finish this later. Dorin says you hate trying to order food from the kitchen."

Lucius definitely would have frowned at that comment, but I didn't care right then. *I have a friend here, who understands what I'm facing.* "Thanks."

Then Ylenia led me to the door and used her fluent Romanian to direct Emilian to escort me to my room, because I was getting *beyond* tired. I was exhausted, and eager to get to the one place in that castle where I felt safest and most at home—at least, until later that night.

Chapter 9
Lucius

To: nightsurfer3@freeweb.net
From: LVVladescu@euronet.com
Raniero—

Instantaneous greetings from the heart of Romania, where the arrival of "broadband" is rendering it so much easier to keep in contact—and thus in control—of all my far-flung kin and kingdom. (I refer specifically to you, "nightsurfer3," as one cannot get "flung" much farther from the cold, wild heart of the Carpathians than onto the "mellow," sunny sands of Southern California, can one?)

Assuming that you've not yet been swept away by the "tasty waves" of which you speak so reverently—you don't actually taste that water, do you, Raniero?—I write, first, to inquire as to how you've fared since we last met, at my wedding. (I will restate that it was an honor to have you stand at my side—and the fact that you deigned to wear pants, *as opposed to "board shorts," was a source of great appreciation on my part. Appreciation—and no small measure of relief.)*

I will also admit: your failure to respond to my written invitation to serve as my best man did *give me pause. Yet I did not ask anyone else to stand with me in the event that you should fail to show up. Not only could I think of no one whom I respect enough to fill that most meaningful role, but I trusted you, Raniero, to do the right thing, just as I trusted you to stay your hand in that pivotal moment when you could have ended our training—not to mention my existence—in a pool of blood in the Vladescu dungeons.*

It is that unshakable faith I invest in you that also compels me to write today.

The next six months are crucial to my future as leader of the newly united clans. My goal is to press for a vote of confidence at the July convocation and coronation before the year is out.

You know me well enough to understand half of my motives. I have never been shy about seeking power, and I am confident that I have the vision and capacity to lead the clans out of the dark ages in which our families seem irrevocably trapped, socially, educationally, and technologically. (Honestly, Raniero, are we the only noble-born Vladescus who would know, for certain, that Bluetooth is not some dread, vampire-specific disorder involving lack of oxygen to the gums? I fear it is true.)

Beyond my personal ambitions, though, I wish to expedite this process for Antanasia's sake. She is striving, admirably, to transform from human teenager into vampire princess, yet the road is difficult for her. Even more difficult than I anticipated when I married her.

I was selfish, Raniero, in my desire to make her mine. And now, to protect her, I must put more weight upon her shoulders, pressing for early coronation so that I, especially, may rise to kingship. For as our ruthless but undeniably shrewd uncle Vasile always noted, "'Prince' is to 'KING' as 'cub' is to 'LION.' And one may kick a cub—but NO ONE baits a lion!"

So what do you say, brother? Will you temporarily—or permanently!—hang up your surfboard, shelve your Buddhist texts, and become once again the "wise warrior" that your very name, "Raniero," destines you to be? Will you assume your place at my right hand? There would be no dire consequences, as you fear. The past is past. *Do your "philosophies" not teach you that?*

I will add that it would ease my mind to know that someone else in Romania who doesn't suffer the contagion of cowardice was looking out for Antanasia. She forges alliances with vampires who seem harmless but whose very weaknesses pose threats she cannot recognize. She instinctively seeks out the soft kittens of her upbringing—and ones that are declawed, at that. (Actually, to equate Dorin Dragomir to a newborn cat is to insult the mettle of kittens everywhere. And of course, you recall Ylenia Dragomir's disposition . . .)

I look forward to your response, not demanding your presence here, which would be within my rights, but asking as a friend.

Lucius

P.S. Did you know that tradition holds that the "best man" is not a second for the groom but rather guardian of the bride? Believe me, brother, I would not leave that responsibility—even symbolically—to a vampire whose self-control I did not trust. Indeed, if I believed you posed the slightest risk to Antanasia, I would destroy even you, my closest friend, without mercy, before I let you come within one hundred miles of our home. Can you not have faith in yourself?

P.P.S. Bring Mindy if you like!

Chapter 10
Mindy

I WAS LYING in bed reading *Celebrity World* magazine to forget about how I'd pretty much flunked out of community college, when my phone rang. I almost didn't answer it, 'cause honestly, if Jess was gonna tell me she was bummed 'cause Lucius was buying her, like, a solid gold tiara instead of the platinum one she wanted, I was gonna scream so loud she'd hear me in Romania, even if the connection got cut off.

But when I flipped open the phone, I didn't recognize the number, so I answered. "Yeah?"

"*Buona sera*, Mindy Sue." There was a lot of static on the

line. Or maybe that was wind. Or *waves* in the background. *"Ciao!"*

I smacked *Celebrity World* against my head. "Oh, gosh, Raniero . . . What are you calling about?" I pulled the phone away and checked the number again. "And whose phone is that?"

I could, like, *hear* Raniero Vladescu Lovatu smiling in his peaceful beatnik way. "I am standing with my feet in the warm sand, watching the most beautiful sunset, with many colors, and I think of you, because you are very beautiful and colorful, yes?"

I totally ignored the compliment. And I tried, real hard, not to picture Raniero standing on the beach in his olive-drab surf trunks that kinda hung off his hips, maybe with some drops of water on his broad, muscular, tanned, naked chest. The arm that held the phone would be bent, so his bicep would be like a perfect, rock-hard . . . rock, and his teeth would be so white . . .

No, Mindy! Focus on the shack *in the background! The way those teeth* change!

"Seriously, Ronnie, did you get a new phone?" I asked, 'cause it wasn't like him to get a new anything. "What's with the weird number?"

"I do not know whose phone this is," he said. "I am walking past a beach towel, I see a phone, I think of you, and I call."

I thought I heard him wrong—he was always messing up English, so past and present especially were just a big jumble—and I sat up in bed. "What? That's, like, stealing!"

"Not stealing," he said, like I was crazy. "I am *borrowing*. Just as I allow others to borrow from me. There is too much worry about who owns what in this world. But if it makes you feel better, I will leave the mango I have just purchased for dinner on the towel."

I flopped down again. Of course he wouldn't buy a new phone. It was a miracle he spent, like, forty-five cents on a mango, even though his family had a gazillion dollars.

"Honest, Raniero, I don't care if you give your fruit away. I am having a really bad day, so why don't you just tell me what you want?"

"*I* want nothing." He burned up some stranger's minutes on more philosophy. I could picture him shrugging those broad, bare shoulders. "I just think of you, and call." I could also just see his gray-green eyes getting all sad when he gave me some pity. "I am sorry to hear that you are unhappy, though. There is something I can do to help, no?"

"No!" I sat up again and crossed my legs. "Not unless you can fix my brain before I flunk out of college in about two days."

He got real quiet. All I heard was that wind. Then he said, "I think your brain is *perfetto*, Mindy Sue. Just perfect. And I think you will be happy to leave college, because I do not believe it was ever your dream to attend."

"You don't know what my dreams are," I said, getting mad at him. Maybe my dream was to have a boyfriend who would at least get a job, if not use his trust fund. And one who would stand up for me when I needed it. And who would at least *offer* to bite me, even if I didn't *want* that, 'cause it meant commitment, to bloodsuckers. "You do not know my dreams at all!"

"Perhaps not." There was that shrug again. He was always shrugging those hot, buff shoulders. "But I think you wish to be a stylist of hair."

"Yeah, like, to the stars," I told him for the millionth time. "But that's a stupid fantasy that's not gonna happen. If I go to some lame beauty school here, I'll end up cutting hair at MasterCuts at the mall, working on screaming little kids, and I'll never even meet a decent guy with a future, like maybe I would've in college!"

Oh, gosh. All of that came out wrong. I didn't mean to hurt him, 'cause in a lot of ways *he* was a decent guy. He was sweet. Too sweet . . .

But like usual, Ronnie didn't care at all if I put him down or talked about other guys. "Do you wish to come here?" I heard him smiling again. "There is sunshine, and always room for you—although perhaps not for all of your shoes! And I am sure you can find a place to study beauty here, very near the stars you wish to meet."

What could I say to that?

Of course I'd love to go to the world-famous Ashton Academy of Aesthetics in Hollywood, where pretty much every stylist ever featured in *Celebrity Hairstyle* had studied, but I didn't have money to get to California, let alone pay tuition if I got into the school. I wouldn't even be able to buy a mango for lunch. And the minute I got there, he'd probably go to Tahiti, like he was always talking about.

No, if I was gonna travel anywhere, it was to visit Jess, 'cause she, thanks to *her* rich *husband,* could pay.

"Melinda, are you there?" Ronnie asked. "You are considering my offer, yes?"

I didn't answer him, 'cause I was "considering," all of a sudden, Romania, where I knew Raniero wouldn't go, 'cause for some reason he didn't like that country at all. *"It is too cold there for me,"* he'd told me. *"Much, much too icy and treacherous."*

There was more to it than ice and snow and bad roads, though. I'd almost flunked high school English, too, and I didn't get metaphors and stuff like Jess and Lukey did, but I'd got just from the look on his face that Raniero was talking about way more than the weather when he said that place was "icy" to him.

"Um, I'm actually thinking about going to visit Jess for a while," I finally said. "Winter break starts in a few days, and she offered to fly me there."

I heard wind and waves for about fifteen minutes—some poor sucker's minutes getting *totally* wasted—and then for the first time since I met Ronnie, he sounded super, super unhappy. "I wish that you would not."

"Well, I think I am." I pretty much made up my mind right then. I had to cut off this thing between us. This thing that kept me talking to and daydreaming about the world's most homeless, jobless, no-ambition, New Agey, long-haired *undead guy.* A bloodsucker whose very worst fault was the way he'd shrugged at *me* when I'd told him, *"I really don't think this is working out, Ronnie."*

I knew he didn't believe in fighting and had an arm full of peace tattoos to prove it. But couldn't he have at least fought for *me?* Offered to change, just a little?

"I gotta go," I told him.

The last thing I heard before I cut the connection was a vampire standing on a beach at sunset telling me, "I love you very much, Mindy Sue."

I jammed the phone under my pillow like I could snuff out those words, which didn't mean anything. Raniero loved everybody and everything. Even bugs, which he wouldn't kill if they crawled on you in that disgusting apartment in Lancaster where he'd crashed for a while.

If I'd really been special, he would've fought—and changed—for me.

STUPID, STUPID ITALIAN VAMPIRES!

Chapter 11

RANIERO

To: LVVladescu@euronet.com
From: nightsurfer3@freeweb.net
Lucius—

It is good to hear from you! But I think from your words that you secretly envy the cousin you are much too kind to call brother, who is just now waking up, at noon, thinking only of eating a fresh pineapple and not even needing to shower before going into the ocean for the day. A king-to-be has many burdens by comparison, yes?

I am sorry to hear of your worries. I beg of you—do not waste any of your regal energies fearing for Raniero, who does taste the waves of the Pacific, occasionalmente. What is a little water fouled by fishes to one who has dined on the dirt of the Vladescu dungeon floors, my poor, suffering head crushed to its present emptiness by the heel of your boot? (LOL!)

Like you, I joke—too much, I think, with a prince. You are kind to indulge my teasing and not remove what is left of my head for the sheer amusement of doing so. So I become serious now, yes?

Lucius . . . I do not understand this "faith" you have in me. It is misguided, no?

You sat at the table when the Elders decided my fortuna, *my fate. You know what I am. What I have done. You see the look in my eyes when I kneel above you, stake in hand!*

I wish to help you. I wish to repay what I owe you, and for you to become king, because while I do not share your desire for worldly power anymore, I believe that you do possess a very rare and unworldly power inside of your heart. Compassion. Yes? Something new for a vampire ruler, and very much needed!

It is unfortunate, though, that I am just learning to find such a quality within myself. I fear that the Raniero who was, just two years before, still exists inside of me—even peeks out at your wedding to catch a glimpse of his uncle Claudiu. Then, I am happy to say, I soothe him back to sleep by riding the steady waves, watching the restful sunset, and breathing deep, peaceful breaths.

Let us leave that unruly, angry vampiro *undisturbed again, yes?*

Certainly we should not allow him anywhere near to your wife! I see you look at Princess Antanasia when you speak your vows, and I do believe that you would destroy any who pose a threat to her. I prefer very much that this dead vampire not be me!

I am sorry, Lucius, that I cannot do more than stay far from

Romania. If, though, you *should ever wish to leave the pressure of your royal life behind, for even a few days, know that while my home is humble, the view is nice. And the door is never locked . . . because there is no door, really. Just a shower curtain with fishes on it. Push aside and come in!*

Pace, *Lucius . . .* Peace!

Raniero

I forget something and so "P.S." to you, too. I am afraid that per una volta—*for once—you are wrong, my future king. Mindy Sue is not with Raniero. (I think she is very surprised, when we return to America, to learn that I do not wear a tuxedo every day!) We are opposites who attract very much, though, and I wait patiently for her to realize that clothes are not so important. There is time, yes? Unless, of course, this very sweet girl comes to harm in your home, for I understand that she plans to travel there with-out myself.*

Who, I wonder, needs protection more, Lucius? A vampire princess brave enough to enter your castle, eyes open, or an inno-cent young woman who is blind to evil and wishes only to make the world beautiful, one hair at a time? (This is the very thing that I love most about her. That, and her ossessione *with shoes. How can this be, when I own but one pair? But it is true!) You spare my life twice, and I do not dare to ask you the favor of protecting one whom I very much love, but the question is some-thing to meditate upon, no?*

Chapter 12
Antanasia

"LUCIUS, WAKE UP!" I screamed. Tears were running down my face, and I shook his shoulder as hard as I could, even though I knew that might hurt him more. If it was still possible to hurt him, because he had to be . . . "Wake up! Please, wake up!"

The blood on him . . . On the sheets . . . The stake discarded between us . . .

I raised my hands to my face. *The blood on ME.*

I grabbed his shoulders again, shaking him so the blood got *everywhere.*

"Lucius, NO!"

Chapter 13
Antanasia

"JESSICA, DO NOT let memories of a nightmare unnerve you now," Lucius urged quietly. "You have nothing to fear from phantoms conjured by your subconscious. I am quite obviously alive and well." He smiled. "You will not rid yourself of me so easily!"

Yes, obviously he was fine. We stood alone in the anteroom where we always waited before meetings with the Elders, giving them a chance to gather before we made our

41

entrance, and Lucius was adjusting his tie, which covered his *unpunctured* chest. And yet . . .

"It was so vivid," I told him again. *More than just a nightmare. A vision. A* hallucination. *I felt the stake in my hand, and the sticky blood on my fingers, because I had been the one who'd wielded the weapon . . .*

Am I going crazy from the stress?

Lucius must have seen the unbearable loss, guilt, and confusion that I still couldn't shake hours after I'd been screaming in our bed, because he took my shoulders, steadying me, but venturing to joke. "I could have warned you about the dangers of eating sour chicken soup before bed. It is enough to induce unpleasant thoughts in broad daylight—much like your father's carob tofu ice cream substitute! If you want something edible, simply lift any phone, dial six, and say 'Häagen-Dazs.' The old woman who answers will understand, for it is a command *I* issue often."

I tried to smile, too, but I couldn't. The last thing I remembered—lucidly—was drinking that warm, strange soup and drifting off to sleep, then waking up to find Lucius with a gaping hole . . . I'd been *awake.*

"Jessica." Lucius grew serious and released my shoulders after giving them one more squeeze. "Try to put aside the dream, for we have reality to face—right now."

And suddenly, on some command I never saw issued, the door swung open and I faced my third formal meeting with the Elders—not counting a gathering at a Western Sizzlin' steak house in Pennsylvania, where I'd first met them all and where they'd beaten Lucius to within an inch of his life.

Chapter 14
Antanasia

AS I WALKED to my seat at the far end of the long table, I did my best, like always, to remember who was who among a bunch of vampires who looked way too similar, as if the passage of the hundreds of years that many of them had already lived through had worn them to gray uniformity, like rocks in a river.

Of course I recognized Dorin, who gave me a reassuring smile. And Horatiu Dragomir, whom I always knew because he'd lost a hand back in some war fought when catapults were cutting-edge technology. And there was an empty seat where my uncle Constantin would have sat . . .

Lucius, who had followed me, pulled out my chair, and as he helped me slide in, I recognized Flaviu Vladescu sitting next to Claudiu, and my skin crawled. Those two had been among the vampires who'd beaten Lucius on that awful night in Lebanon County, when the Elders had tried to force a suddenly rebellious prince to marry me and fulfill the pact.

My eyes darted to Lucius, who was calmly taking his own seat, and I couldn't understand how he could deal with Claudiu and Flaviu every day and never show that he despised them. Because he *had* to hate them. Had to long for revenge.

I stared at Lucius's strong hands, and I also couldn't understand how he'd allowed his uncles to beat him, because I had no doubt that Lucius could crush either one of his older relatives. But of course he'd been raised to accept punishment from the Elders and hadn't struck back against his uncle Vasile until directly challenged to fight.

Then I looked back at Claudiu, who had a weird smile on his thin lips, and who interrupted Lucius just as he began to call the meeting to order, by saying to *me,* just like I'd feared, "And how are you, Princess? We are all very concerned about your health, and hope for a full report on the illness that took you from the most important trial of this century!"

Before I could recover enough to answer—I was frozen in place—Lucius spoke for me, issuing a two-word command that would change everything.

"Silence, Claudiu."

Chapter 15
Antanasia

"LUCIUS, DO YOU honestly *silence* your uncle?" Claudiu asked, seeming genuinely surprised. "In that tone?"

I was shocked, too. Lucius was always in control in meetings, but I had never seen him address one of the Elders so sharply. But it had been clear that Claudiu was taunting me, and Prince Vladescu was letting everyone know *that* wasn't going to happen.

He's protecting me again. I should say something for myself...

But I didn't, and Lucius spoke again, less harshly but in a

44

way that still didn't leave room for debate. "You spoke without requesting recognition, Claudiu. And our custom—our law—demands that you seek acknowledgment from me or Antanasia."

"I merely inquire about your wife's health," Claudiu nevertheless protested. "You repeatedly ask me to accept a Dragomir as my *superior,* and yet when I make a friendly overture, you are displeased!"

"Displeased by your failure to abide by law," Lucius clarified. "I have made myself clear in this forum: we are now a culture that *abides by law.*"

"Law!" Claudiu snorted, abruptly dropping all pretense of concern for me—and daring to directly confront Lucius, too. "You speak too often of law, Lucius! In the past, Vasile allowed us to speak at will. He did not worry about *law.*"

"You speak too often, period," Lucius advised his uncle. He leaned back in his seat, as if still totally at ease. But I could see the tension building in his jaw. "And Vasile is no longer in charge here. So I suggest that you become accustomed to new leadership."

"For how long?" Claudiu muttered, shaking his head.

His voice was soft—but just loud enough to make sure everybody heard.

I sat shocked and silent. The other vampires got quiet, too, but when I searched their faces, I saw excitement, not concern. Only Dorin seemed worried, like me.

"What did you just say?" Lucius demanded, his voice dropping an octave. "Or do you wish to hide your words, like a coward?"

"Lucius . . ." I heard myself make a tentative attempt to interfere, but nobody even noticed me. Their eyes were all locked on Lucius and Claudiu, whose grayish cheeks got a little pink when he said, "Fine, Lucius. I will speak, for I have kept silent for too long."

Then he turned in his seat to point at me, and it seemed like the whole world stood still as Claudiu Vladescu voiced what every Vladescu—and maybe some of the Dragomirs—at that table probably believed was true. *I* believed it was true.

"She is not ready to rule, Lucius. She cannot even hand down justice!"

No . . .

I knew that Queen Mihaela Dragomir would have handed out some justice right then and there, but I stayed frozen, watching Lucius, whose eyes were getting completely black, just like on the night he'd taken me prisoner in the castle and nearly lost control.

Claudiu seemed oblivious, though. He was too busy voicing his own pent-up rage to recognize that the young vampire he'd long controlled was no longer under his thumb—and was getting angry, too.

"Lucius!" Claudiu's voice suddenly shook. "I have accepted Dragomirs at this table, as Elders, for nearly twenty years now. But I cannot—and WILL not—accept one as my sovereign. NEVER!" He turned slitted eyes on me. "Especially not a girl who *knows nothing of leadership.*"

There was complete silence in the room as his words died away.

And then Lucius rose, and I saw again the warrior prince

who'd stormed my ancestral castle vowing to vanquish the Dragomirs. Except this time, he was *protecting* a Dragomir—and that only made his power more threatening as he stalked toward his uncle, fangs bared.

Claudiu rose, too, and I saw that his whole body had started shaking. Maybe with rage—or maybe because he finally understood what he'd provoked in my husband.

I wanted to run between the two vampires and beg them to calm down, but I couldn't, in part because Lucius was almost strangely composed as he leaned close to Claudiu and warned, showing those teeth that could be so beautiful and so menacing, "The words you speak are treason. Remove yourself, and be grateful that I do not destroy you, before you can even face the trial which you are due under laws that I WILL ABIDE BY—even though I am strongly inclined to take your existence, and the sight of you *tests my resolve to stay my hand.*"

Claudiu hesitated for a moment.

"Leave *now,*" Lucius growled again.

"Fine. I will go," Claudiu finally agreed. But as he left the room, he still dared to turn around and snarl, "This is not over, Lucius."

The two vampires faced each other for a long moment.

And when Lucius finally spoke, of all the words he'd uttered during that meeting, none seemed more ominous, somehow, than the ones he said now, with his calm façade completely restored and his fangs gone: "Indeed it is not, Claudiu."

As his uncle slunk out the door, Lucius took his seat again and looked around the table, silently challenging any other vampire to defy him, and I got the sense that all the other Elders felt the same way I did.

What had just passed between Claudiu and Lucius . . . it wasn't just about Lucius protecting me or my right to rule. It was rooted far, far in the past, in both a feud between clans and a personal grudge between two powerful vampires: one who had tried to train a prince to do the bidding of the Elders, and that prince, who had grown too strong to be controlled.

And trial or no trial, it was *not* over.

Chapter 16
Lucius

To: nightsurfer3@freeweb.net
From: LVVladescu@euronet.com

Raniero—

Needless to say, I am disappointed by your decision to remain in California, especially as things grow more complicated in Romania.

I seem to have the inconvenience of a minor revolution on my hands. An uprising of one, which leaves me faced with the unhappy prospect of a trial for nothing less than treason. And we both know how that *must* end—for Claudiu.

Honestly, dealing with our Vladescu uncles is not unlike riding your beloved, battering waves. One struggles to handle Vasile until the huge, inevitable crash, only to turn around and discover that Claudiu is looming on the horizon, and after him, Flaviu.

I could use, if not a soldier, an experienced surfer here.

And while still not issuing a direct order, I reiterate that it is time for you to stop running from the past. You *are* a warrior, Raniero, and you know that someday you will have to engage the enemy that is yourself—and on this field, where your memories have such a stronghold. If, when that battle is concluded, you choose to return to your life on the beach, I will respect that decision. I will accept that you are the world's first Buddhist, vegan, pacific-as-your-ocean Vladescu vampire (the son-in-law who Ned Packwood no doubt secretly wishes had joined his little army of lambs, chicks, and calves, instead of me—as I do not hesitate to consume my fellow conscripts!). But until that confrontation occurs, are you not just hiding behind your tattoos and cowering in the waves?

And you are *not* one to cower, brother.

Lucius

P.S. Of course I will protect Melinda, should she arrive here. But would it not impress her more if you were to perform that task? Preferably while wearing *pants*?

Chapter 17
Mindy

"FLIGHT FOUR SEVENTY-THREE to Bucharest now boarding priority travelers."

I checked my ticket for the millionth time, 'cause I'd never traveled priority in my life. The four times I'd been on a plane, I'd had awful seats in coach with views of the wing.

But nope, there it was, my spot right up front, where Jess promised they'd give me a drink before we even took off. I'd be able to stretch out on a recliner, sipping fresh-squeezed orange juice while everybody else schlepped their bags back to the cheap seats.

Standing up, I grabbed the handle of my Gucci-look-alike carryon—the one I wouldn't want to get lost if my luggage went to Rome or something, 'cause you *could* mix up the two places—and headed toward the plane.

In a few hours, I'd be, like, a thousand miles away from Lebanon Valley Community College, which I'd ditched before finals even started. What was the point of trying for F-pluses?

And I'd be too far to hear my mom screaming again about how I wasted a few thousand of her dollars on tuition and should just forget the bum who reminded her way too much of my drifter dad—and who she woulda hated even more if she knew he was a vampire, for crying out loud.

I'd be in a castle full of servants, flopped down on a huge bed and eating half the Tastykakes I was taking Jess 'cause you couldn't get them in Europe for some reason.

And most of all, I'd be in a country that scared the shorts off my ex-boyfriend, even though he was undead, like half the people in Romania. I was pretty sure Ronnie wouldn't even call me over there, 'cause he'd texted me like twenty times begging me to stay home—and then just disappeared. Finally.

I gave the lady my ticket and dragged my suitcase down the tunnel toward the plane.

Yup, it was all first-class for me for the next couple weeks. First-class and deadbeat bloodsucker–free.

I bumped my carryon over the gap and saw those big leather seats waiting.

So how come I wasn't more excited?

Chapter 18
Antanasia

"IT WASN'T *that* terrible," Dorin insisted. But he was wringing his plump hands and hovering around my desk. "I've seen worse incidents at meetings of the Elders!"

I had my head buried in my hands, but I looked up to give him a skeptical glance. "Really? You've seen something worse than one of the most powerful vampires committing treason by directly telling a princess she's unfit to rule? Something worse than the way I didn't even defend myself?"

"You're being too hard on yourself." Ylenia chimed in from her perch on the couch. "You've only been meeting with the Elders for a few months. You can't fight them!"

I shot her a grateful glance. "You're right. I don't know how I could."

Then I turned back to Dorin, who was searching his memory for something worse than mutiny. "There was a time, years ago, when two Vladescus staked one another, right in the meeting hall." He waved his hands. "Not that I looked! Kept my head down on that one!"

I sighed. *Yes, of course he did. Because we're* Dragomirs.

"Lucius says there'll be another trial," I said glumly. "That treason is punishable by destruction." Like pretty much everything in the world of vampires.

"Where is the boy?" Dorin glanced around like Lucius might be hiding in a corner—as if that would ever happen. Then my uncle poured us all some of the tea Ylenia had called for. "What's he doing?"

"You know Lucius." I took a sip, wishing I could get tea whenever I wanted it. It reminded me of being home with my dad, who answered every crisis with chamomile. Unfortunately, I always forgot the Romanian word *"ceai,"* and the one time I'd tried to boil water myself, the old cook shooed me out of the kitchen, practically yelling at me. "He wanted some time to pace alone in his study and read his law books." I glanced at my own shelves, filled with my birth mom's books. "I should be reading the law, too."

"I can translate for you," Ylenia offered. "Just tell me what you need to know."

I tried to smile. "Thanks." But did I even know what I needed to know?

"Try not to worry, Antanasia," she added. "It sounds like Lucius handled everything."

"Yes, he was quite ferocious," Dorin confirmed, with a shudder. "If I were Claudiu, I'd be watching my back!"

"Yeah . . ." I corrected myself, trying to sound more "royal." "I mean, *yes,* of course Lucius took control." I slumped behind my oversized desk, which had also been brought from the Dragomir estate, back when I'd foolishly been excited about the idea of being a princess.

"We should go now," Dorin noted, and I glanced at my clock, surprised to see that it was almost midnight. "Antanasia will have a busy day tomorrow." He looked at Ylenia. "And we have a long drive home."

I set down my teacup, realizing I'd been rude to keep them so late. "Why don't you stay here tonight?" I offered. "There are dozens of bedrooms." Maybe hundreds? "And that drive down the mountain is so dangerous in winter."

Dorin and Ylenia exchanged glances, and both seemed relieved. "If you're sure," Dorin said. He blanched a little. "If Lucius would not mind . . ."

"Yes, it's fine," I promised them. I might not be able to fight my enemies, but I could at least protect my friends from a drop off a cliff. "Please, stay." I addressed Dorin. "You know where the guest rooms are."

"Yes, thank you, Antanasia," he agreed. "I'm very familiar with the castle!"

"Thanks so much," Ylenia added.

"No problem." I stood up and felt almost lightheaded, probably because I hadn't eaten anything since that morning. And I had a sudden urge to see Lucius. It seemed I was always nervous in that castle, but right then, it was gelling into a powerful uneasiness, almost like a . . . premonition.

But I don't believe in premonitions. Do I?

All at once, I wasn't sure.

"Ylenia? Would you please tell Emilian that I want to go to Lucius's office?"

"Are you certain you shouldn't go straight to bed?" she suggested. "You seem pretty exhausted."

"No, I really want to see Lucius." *I* need *to see him.*

Okay," she agreed, but with a strange look on her face. "If you're sure." She went with me to the door and directed Emilian, *"Prendere Princess Vladescu Antanasia al principe della biblioteca."*

I left my relatives with a quick exchange of good-nights, and as Emilian and I made our way through the dark hallways, my concerns seemed to grow with each step I took. But when I got to Lucius's study and opened the door, my husband wasn't pacing, like I'd expected. A fire burned in the fireplace, his laptop was open on his desk, and his basketball trophy glittered on his bookshelf.

But Lucius was nowhere to be found.

Chapter 19
Antanasia

I COULDN'T DECIPHER my mother's Romanian law books, but I could read the journal she'd left for me, and even though I was incredibly groggy, I took out the little book, hoping to find something that would ease the strange fear that was starting to *suffocate* me.

Where is Lucius?

Stretching out on the bed with my head toward the fire, I lay down, reading sideways, because I felt like I couldn't even sit up. And my curious mixture of worry and overwhelming fatigue made the words blur on the pages.

"Trust no one. . . ." "Blood is both life and an inevitable part

of death, for vampires . . ." The strange word *"blestemată,"* written next to an even stranger symbol drawn in the margins . . .

Where have I seen that before? And why did Mihaela write that in Romanian?

And then it happened, just as I completely lost focus and my eyelids began to flutter closed.

I saw the stake again. Lying right in front of my face on the bed.

Recoiling, I squeezed my eyes shut.

NO. IT ISN'T THERE! I'm NOT going crazy!

I felt my chest rising and falling hard, but I refused to open my eyes. Refused to let them trick me again. But of course, I had to look . . .

And when I did, the stake was gone. And somehow, because I was so incredibly tired, I closed my eyes again and fell into a sleep that must have been very, very deep, because when I woke up, my head was on my pillow. And Lucius was next to me, sound asleep, both of us on top of the covers. He wore jeans and a T-shirt, like he'd been exhausted, too, and hadn't even bothered to get undressed before coming to bed.

I checked his face by the firelight and he looked fine, but I wrapped my arm around him anyway, reassuring myself that there was no blood on his chest, like the last time that stake had appeared so vividly before my eyes. But even feeling him breathing wasn't enough for me to shake the lingering sensation that something was wrong. "Lucius . . ."

I was just about to wake him up when there was a knock on our door, and his eyes opened right away, like he hadn't been sleeping after all. He was usually quick to wake at any strange noise, but that night I actually jerked back at how fast he'd reacted. "Lucius?"

The knock sounded again, and he stood up, telling me calmly but firmly, "Stay here."

I sat up, confused. "Are you expecting someone?"

"No. I'm not."

That worried me more. And as he went to the door, he looked over his shoulder and compounded my fears. "Do not move unless I tell you to. But if I tell you to leave the room, you know where to go. And quickly."

It wasn't until he opened the door that I realized Lucius was dressed and alert because he thought somebody might be coming for us. Or for *me*.

Claudiu. Maybe with other Vladescus he's rallied. They're going to finish the plot that Lucius wouldn't carry out. They're going to destroy me, because they can't live under Dragomir rule. That's what he's ready for.

I barely had time to be *terrified*, though, before I heard Emilian's familiar voice and took a deep, calming breath.

". . . *este mort*," I heard Emilian say.

"*Unde? Cum?*" Lucius replied.

I caught the words "where" and "how"—but nothing else.

A moment later, Lucius closed the door and came back to bed. But he didn't go to his side. He sat down next to me and took my hand, saying, "You need to get dressed, Antanasia."

I searched his face, but it was almost like there was so much going on in his head that I couldn't keep up, and my fear came creeping back. He'd used my formal name, too. "Why should I get dressed?"

Lucius's eyes were impossible to read, but his mouth drew down into one of the most severe frowns I'd ever seen as he informed me, "Claudiu is destroyed. We need to go. Now."

Chapter 20
Antanasia

I CLUTCHED LUCIUS'S hand as we made our way through the halls, heading toward the foyer, where Claudiu's body waited. Even in a crisis we didn't rush, because royalty never hurried, and when we passed by one of the thick leaded windows, I had a second to notice that it was already dawn.

I stole a look at Lucius's face. *How late was he out? Where was he? And how did I not even feel him shift me on the bed and put my head on my pillow?*

I wanted to ask all of those questions, but he looked very preoccupied—and of course Emilian and the guard whom Lucius seldom bothered to use were both close on our heels, so I stayed quiet.

It was Lucius who spoke first, when we came to another corner. He looked back at the guards, ordering, *"Rămâneți acolo."*

They stopped in their tracks, and he led us a few more steps forward, then bent to speak to me in private. "I need to release your hand now. You will look stronger standing on your own."

I nodded. "I understand."

Lucius's dark eyes met mine, like he was trying to shore me up. "And there may be much blood. Be prepared for that."

I nodded again. "I know." My birth mother's journal warned me. *"Blood is . . . an inevitable part of death, for vampires."* "I'll be okay."

I promised him, but when we stepped around the corner into the huge foyer where Lucius had once named me the first prisoner in a war he'd declared on my family, I did press my hand against my mouth and nose, not at the sight of the body, but at the *smell.*

Chapter 21
Antanasia

SEVERAL OF THE Elders had already gathered, and at first I couldn't even see Claudiu, because I was short and the older vampires, who formed a circle that followed the curve of the walls, were almost uniformly tall, with the exception of Dorin, whom I spotted looking nervous and even paler than usual, with his black coat buttoned to his throat.

Ylenia was there, too, bundled up like Dorin, and at first I couldn't figure out why they were in the estate at dawn. Our castle was so big, like a self-contained city, that the Vladescu Elders roamed at will and often stayed for weeks at a time. But my Dragomir relatives almost never slept there.

Then I vaguely remembered inviting them both to stay the night. I had been so wiped out that I barely recalled making the offer.

Forcing myself to pull my hand away from my face, I gave my uncle and my cousin a small nod as the Elders parted to make way for Lucius—and me, although I barely squeezed through before they closed ranks again.

"What has happened here?" Lucius demanded, heading directly to the center of the floor and kneeling down. Not sure about my role, I stopped short and struggled even harder not to gag as the familiar—and this time repugnant—smell got even stronger.

Blood.

Ever since becoming a full vampire, I—like every member of the undead—had developed a keen nose for blood. The scent of it was as distinctive, to vampires, as fingerprints or DNA. And Claudiu's blood stank like . . . Claudiu.

While Lucius's blood smelled sweet and intoxicating, Claudiu's smelled like decay to me. Like he'd already been rotting before he was even destroyed. The scent nearly took over the room.

Still, I mastered my gag reflex long enough to finally look down at Lucius's uncle, and although I wanted to be strong right then, I was as much the product of a kindhearted vegan family as I was a vampire princess—probably still more vegan than vampire—and I covered my mouth again when I saw the body that lay in my husband's shadow.

Then I looked from the corpse to Lucius, who was kneeling next to his uncle, and that urge to get sick intensified when I remembered how Lucius had very publicly threatened Claudiu's life, not a day before.

Chapter 22
Antanasia

"SOMEONE SPEAK," Lucius commanded, looking from one Elder to the next. "How did this happen?"

No one volunteered an answer, and Lucius let the silence linger, continuing to scrutinize each face even as he slipped his hand under Claudiu's lifeless head, cradling it in a gesture that I didn't quite understand.

Did Lucius respect—even love—his uncle, in a way?

But Claudiu beat him when he was younger, and defied him . . .

I didn't want to, but I couldn't keep myself from looking at Claudiu's corpse again. It almost looked like he was sleeping, until Lucius gently rolled him onto his back and I could see where the stake had entered.

I found myself counting. *One, two, three wounds. There's a lot of fresh blood on the floor, the body . . .*

With his free hand, Lucius closed Claudiu's eyes, which had been open and terrifyingly vacant, but the gesture did little to make the whole scene less awful.

I covered my mouth with my hand again, frustrated that I could drink blood, that it had been part of my wedding, even, but that I could barely handle the sight of it right then.

Don't get sick. You pressed your hands over a wound like that once, back in Jake Zinn's barn, in hopes of saving Lucius. You can do this. You've seen plenty of dead animals on the farm.

"Who found him?" Lucius finally demanded, when no one answered his first question. He remained kneeling, seeming not to notice the blood pooling around him, staining his pants. "Someone can at least answer that."

"It was me, Lucius. I found him." I turned to see my uncle Dorin stepping forward, all the pink in his cheeks drained away, and the right hand he was raising shook. "Ylenia and I were leaving at dawn, and we found him here."

Lucius watched my uncle for a long moment, his expression even more grim.

No, a part of me protested. *You can't be angry with Dorin just for being in the wrong place at the wrong time! That's not fair!*

But I didn't speak up, because although I wanted to protect my uncle, I knew it was even more important not to show any division between me and Lucius. He always said presenting a united front was crucial.

Or was I afraid to speak because I might say the wrong thing?

And how could we all be so calm? There was a body there. It wasn't some TV crime scene. It was *real.*

I kept my hand pressed to my mouth. *This is my world.*

Lucius slipped his hand from beneath Claudiu and gently rested his uncle's head on the floor again, rising, and although the wound had been to Claudiu's chest, my husband's fingers were stained with blood, just like they must have been after the execution he'd performed less than two days before.

"Someone send for servants to clean and prepare the body," he ordered the Elders in general. "I will stay here until they arrive, and we will reconvene late this afternoon in the meeting hall." He looked pointedly at Dorin, who flinched. "I expect everyone here to be in attendance. Every Elder."

Dorin nodded. "Yes, of course."

I tried to shoot Dorin a sympathetic glance, but his head was already bowed, his eyes hidden.

There didn't seem to be more to say, so, as if following Dorin's lead, we all bowed our heads, offering Claudiu a spontaneous moment of silent respect. As we stood quietly, Flaviu stepped forward and laid his coat over the body, then took his place among the others again.

I thought I should probably close my eyes, but I didn't. I watched Lucius through lowered lashes as he looked down on his uncle, his expression unreadable again.

"Excuse me?"

Everyone turned toward the small, tentative voice to see Ylenia still standing against the wall.

What?

"Umm . . . I don't want to interrupt, but the *stake* hasn't been found, has it?" she asked.

We all stared at her, and she got red and adjusted her eyeglasses, and I got the clear sense that she wished she hadn't spoken up, while I sort of wished I *had* said something. Anything. I was a princess and should have stepped up next to Lucius.

Then all of us turned to face the gigantic door that led outside as it squeaked open on its old hinges and somebody else joined us, exclaiming as she stepped into the circle of vampires, clearly not understanding what was hidden under the coat at her feet, "Holy Toledo! Did I come at, like, a bad time?"

Chapter 23
RANIERO

To: LVVladescu@euronet.com
From: nightsurfer3@freeweb.net
Lucius, my friend—

Early this day at one o'clock p.m. yours truly is about to order the delizioso *bean burrito at Terrible Taco, a most famous eatery that is parked very conveniently near to my own shack of domicile, when there is a taptaptap upon Raniero's bare arm.*

"Si?" I look down, expecting to find a turista *in search of surfing lessons (I have a small word-of-mouth business in surfing education, did you know? Sadly, I never remember to ask for payment—which I think helps commerce. It is a vicious cycle, no?).*

But it is not a turista. *It is a* vampiro, *who looks closely at the arm which I despise and says, "You are Vladescu Lovatu, no?" (I am as famous as Terrible Taco! LOL, but with sad face.)*

My new friend—who wears many piercings to tell the world that he fears nothing, not even Raniero!—does not wait for my denial of identity. He is too busy offering me congratulations on my many achievements in the fields of death, dismemberment, etc.

You can imagine that this is not the kind of praise I wish for, so I thank him for his kind words and reach for my food.

Tuttavia, *before I can walk away, my misguided young fanatic says to me,* "You heard about Claudiu, right, dude?"

I stop and nearly drop a very good burrito to hear his next words, which I quote to you: "That dude is toast, man."

Lucius . . . is this story true? Is Claudiu destroyed? If so, when? Because we have been in correspondence this very morning, several times, and you mention nothing.

I do not believe in worry, but I admit that this news shakes my peace, just a little.

I very much look forward to the messaggio *in which you laugh at me and advise,* "Do not listen to young vampires who can barely speak for the silver posts that hinder their foolish tongues!" *I anticipate, too, the lengthy* paragrafo *in which you express unhappiness with bean burritos, shacks of any kind, and places in which people say "dude" and are not ashamed. If you like, I will lecture myself, and spare you the trouble, LOL!*

Though per favore, *. . . answer* presto, *Lucius, if it is no difficulty.*

And if you do not mind telling me . . . is Melinda Sue there, in the middle of this possible-if-unlikely death and destruction?

Raniero

Chapter 24
Mindy

ME AND JESS huddled on the big bed in my guest room, totally giving up on unpacking my suitcases. We'd tried to pretend like we were both okay, but Jess's hand started shaking when she tried to unzip the bag with all my shoes, so we just sat down next to the black dress I brought along in case something fancy happened.

I gave that dress a real sad look. Too bad the something fancy was gonna be a funeral.

"I'm really sorry this happened now," Jess said. She bit her fingernail, which was a habit I knew she was trying to break. I didn't remind her, though. She had enough on her mind without worrying about her manicure.

One of the old vampires had actually been killed. When I walked in the door, I'd thought there was, like, a dead dog on the floor, and I was totally confused about why Lucius was covered with blood. When I finally caught on to what was happening . . . that was like the first time I kinda understood why Jess might think being a princess wasn't everything it was cracked up to be in storybooks.

"Are you okay?" I asked her. Her eyes had big black circles under them, and she was way too thin. I was glad I brought the Tastykakes.

"I should be asking you that." She gave me a real worried look. "And I understand if you want to turn right around and go home."

She said that, but I knew my best friend, and she wanted me to stay. "No way, Jess," I told her. "I'm not leaving you now!"

Jess looked way relieved. "I honestly believe you're safe here." But she still gave me one more chance to back out. "But I really do understand if you want to leave."

Gosh, I kinda did want that. Then I thought about spending break with my mom bugging me every day to get a job at McDonald's or KFC, 'cause she was gonna start charging me *rent,* and all of a sudden the alternative didn't look so bad. It wasn't like any of those old vampires—and let's face it, one of 'em was guilty of murder—would bother me. "Jess?" I said. "I gotta tell you something."

"Yeah?" She got mad at herself and tried again, 'cause she was working to make her speech more royal. "Yes?"

"I kinda flunked outta school," I confessed. "I don't really have anyplace else to go right now, 'cause my mom is *pissed.* If I go home, I gotta pay just to live in my stupid bedroom."

Jess blinked about ten times, like she was almost as surprised by my news as by a dead vampire in her house. "Wow . . . I'm so sorry. I guess you've had a rough fall, too. I'm sorry if I was too busy complaining about my life to really listen to your problems."

I shrugged. "It's okay. I didn't really get what was up with you, either. I thought you were being kinda whiny. Until today."

"Yeah. Yes." Jess got almost scared and whispered, "I'm really worried about Lucius."

It was my turn to blink. "Why?" I couldn't imagine anybody I'd worry about less.

But Jess got even quieter, even though the only vampire within a mile was her personal bodyguard, Emilio. "Lucius had a fight with Claudiu yesterday, in front of the Elders. A *bad* fight."

I was no mathlete, but I could at least put two and two

together. "Oh, wow. Sorry, Jess." Then I had to ask, "You don't think he coulda . . ."

"No." She shook her head. "There's no way." But her eyes got, like, desperate. "You believe that, right?"

I took a sec to think. I'd seen Lukey bang Frank Dormand up against a locker, and I knew he was no saint. But I'd also seen him at their wedding, and there was no way he would mess up what he had with Jess by killing another vampire. Plus, if Lucius was gonna kill somebody, he wouldn't hide it. He'd do it in plain sight, then stand there and tell you why. And you'd probably end up saying, "Sure, Lucius. I get it!"

Last but not least, Jess needed me to believe her. I made up my mind, right then and there. "I believe you, Jess. Lukey's totally innocent."

I was glad I could say that and mean it, 'cause it seemed to mean a lot to her. She even tried to smile. "I'm sure it's going to be okay, right?"

"Oh, yeah, definitely." I tried to smile, too. But I wasn't sure about *that* at all.

Then we both got real quiet and just sat there being bummed about our lives.

After a minute, 'cause we could never shut up for long, Jess looked at me like I was some math problem she wanted to solve. Like the world's sorriest algebra equation. "What happened at Lebanon Valley, anyhow? You were never in Honors Club in high school, but you never flunked anything, either."

I got red and almost wished we were talking about dead vampires again. "I don't know. I just couldn't think there."

I wanted to tell Jess about Raniero. I really did. But there was no way I could tell a princess who was married to the guy who'd just dominated at a murder scene that I had spent even a month with the only vampire who woulda *cried* at the sight of blood, and maybe run away, 'cause he hated violence. Violence was the *only* thing he hated.

I would never have a real prince—*not* being royal was, sadly, the only thing Ronnie ever put his foot down about—but I wanted more than a poor, lazy, New Age peacenik who wouldn't stand up for me. Even if he was the world's best kisser, with eyes that drove me crazy.

Jess knew me well enough to read my mind, though. She bent her head, trying to see my face. "Min . . . whatever happened with you and Raniero? At my wedding?"

I knew I'd have to tell her soon—shoulda told her months ago—but I was still glad when somebody knocked on the door. Until that person popped her head in. A head covered with curls that were like Jess's, only frizzier, like they needed a date with a product with silicone. And she wore a purple shirt that was Jess's signature color. This new girl's mouth was like Jess's, too—which wasn't really her fault.

Still, I couldn't help thinking, *This chick's a Jess knockoff. And I know knockoffs!*

I crossed my arms over my Anna Sui–look-alike shirt and watched Elaine or Elainey, whatever her name was, stutter and stammer and apologize her way into my room like she was sorry she existed—but wasn't gonna let *that* stop her from trying to cozy up to a princess.

So . . . *this* was Jess's new friend.

Chapter 25
Antanasia

"YLENIA, THIS IS my best friend, Mindy."

My cousin took a few hesitant steps into the room and smiled shyly. "Hi. Nice to meet you. I've heard a lot about you."

Mindy nodded—but didn't smile. "Yeah. I've heard stuff about you, too."

I looked at Min, surprised, by the cold greeting.

Then I turned back to Ylenia. "I guess you and Dorin came back for the meeting, huh?"

"Well, I won't be attending, of course." She glanced at Mindy, the even bigger outsider, to clarify. "Since I'm not an Elder. But yes, Dorin needs to go. Obviously."

"So you really found the body?" Mindy asked. She was cocking her head like tiny Ylenia might have staked a six-foot-tall vampire. "That musta been awful."

Ylenia shuddered, a trait that seemed common to all Dragomirs in the same way a cynically arched eyebrow marked Vladescu males. "Yes. It was terrible. But Dorin actually saw Claudiu first, and he tried to turn me around, before I could see too much." Her voice got a little thick with emotion. "I guess he knew it would upset me to see the body, given what happened to my father so recently."

"Ylenia's father was just destroyed," I explained, for Mindy's benefit. "That was the trial I was telling you about."

"I'm sorry about your dad," Mindy told my cousin. "My dad's gone, too. It sucks."

Ylenia blinked some more. "Your father . . . died?"

"No, he just left," Mindy said flatly. "But he's, like, a jobless loser anyhow, so it's no big deal, I guess."

Mindy had spent so much time at my parents' farm that I sometimes forgot about her shiftless dad, who hardly ever even called her from wherever he happened to be crashing at any given time.

"My mother left like that." Ylenia trumped Mindy in terms of family dysfunction. "I haven't seen her in years."

"Sorry," Min said. "That sucks for you, too."

Ylenia shrugged. "It's okay. I got to attend a good boarding school in England because of it. At least until the money ran out." She managed to smile at me. "And now I'm fortunate to live in Antanasia's family home, since she lives here."

Mindy didn't seem to have anything else to say, and although the awkward dynamic between them was making a bad day even worse, I had to ask Ylenia, "Do you want to hang out with us? Or with Mindy, because I have to go get ready for the meeting soon."

My semipermanent sense of foreboding deepened again at the thought of that gathering. *Lucius threatened Claudiu. Everyone saw them fight. Heard them both declare, "This is not over."*

"Actually, I wanted to talk to you about that," Ylenia said. "I know that I have no say in what happens at councils, but I thought I might just suggest"—she held up her hands—"not that I have any right to suggest *anything* to a princess . . ."

"Ylenia, we're friends," I reminded her. "And I could use a suggestion right now."

"Well, I imagine that Lucius has thought of this, but in case he hasn't—maybe *you* should ask all of the Elders to produce their stakes."

"What?" Mindy blurted the question before I could.

"That's how my father's killer was ultimately convicted," Ylenia explained to both of us, since of course I'd missed the trial. She looked at Mindy, though, assuming I would understand what she said next. "Every male vampire has a stake that is given to him by his father, at the achievement of manhood."

I remembered, then, something else from my mother's journal. "*A stake, like blood, is distinctive to its bearer . . .*" And I knew that Lucius had only one stake.

I turned to Mindy, too, putting it in terms she'd understand. "Ylenia's right. A stake is like a . . . a bar mitzvah gift."

Mindy frowned. "That's a pretty twisted present."

"Perhaps," Ylenia agreed. "But most male vampires, in particular the nobles, will use *only* that stake when a weapon is needed. It becomes like an extension of one's arm." She paused. "And a stake is never 'misplaced.'"

I nodded, understanding. "So you're saying if one of the Elders destroyed Claudiu, his blood would be on their weapon."

Ylenia nodded too. "Yes. The scent of my father's blood was on his killer's stake. It was unmistakable."

"This is getting a little weird," Mindy interrupted. "No offense."

"It is weird," I admitted. And yet simply requiring everyone to produce a stake might be an effective way of finding the killer. Or at least of helping vindicate Lucius, whose stake would be clean.

"I'm sure Lucius has thought of this," Ylenia added again. "But on the off chance that he's distracted—and grieving—I thought I'd offer the suggestion to you."

I wasn't sure if Lucius was grieving, but he was definitely distracted. "Thanks."

"I just want to help," Ylenia said. Then she looked at the door. "I'll get going now."

"Thanks," I repeated. "Let's hang out later. The three of us."

Ylenia brightened. "That'd be nice."

When she was gone, I started helping Mindy unpack again. I felt a little better, but she had gotten very quiet. She started moving her shoes from her suitcase to the floor of the wide, double-doored closet, which looked like it might not be big enough to hold them all.

I didn't say anything, either. I was preoccupied as I hung up a dress that looked perfect for a party we probably wouldn't have.

How worried am I about Lucius?

Where was he last night?

All of a sudden, Mindy interrupted my thoughts with a question I'd never thought to ask before. But when I heard it voiced, it really intrigued me.

"That Ylenia girl . . ." She said it almost offhandedly. "She's, like, a real vampire, right? Like, her teeth grow and she drinks blood? Just like you started doing after Lukey bit you."

I turned to look at her. "Yeah, I think so."

"Hmm . . ." Mindy knelt down to arrange her shoes more neatly. "I wonder who the heck bit *her?*"

Chapter 26
Lucius

To: *nightsurfer3@freeweb.net*
From: *LVVladescu@euronet.web*
Raniero—

I will forego expressing my dismay to learn that another young vampire defects to the beach. (Is this to be a trend? I know that we do not disintegrate in sunlight, but should there not be limits on exposure for beings who rule the dark side of the universe? Can one induce awe while reeking of coconut-scented lotions?) And I will also postpone the lecture about burritos—which is, as you predict, inevitable—to inform you that the news is true. Claudiu is destroyed.

I imagine this intelligence inspires in you the same conflicting emotions that I experience at losing an uncle who was without scruple and who tormented us both, often with a sneer of pleasure upon his lips—and yet who was so fiercely, proudly a Vladescu. Or perhaps you see nothing but his viciousness at this point in your own existence.

As for who committed the act . . . that is yet undetermined, and a topic which I would much prefer to discuss face-to-face.

I imagine that you have little to pack, even for an extended stay, which should make your journey much easier on your muscles, if not your mind.

L

P.S. Melinda has arrived—and in quite dramatic fashion, as is her endearing way. Rest assured that of course I will protect her—although I reiterate that the job would be better done by a trouser-clad second-to-the-throne.

P.P.S. You will note that I chose not to even address your use of the word "dude," a course which I will continue to follow. It pains me enough to write the term once, here, without ever bringing it up again.

Chapter 27
Antanasia

LUCIUS PACED IN his study, hands locked behind his back and head bowed, no doubt mulling over everything we'd—*he'd*—just read aloud from all the old books that outlined who did what when a vampire got destroyed, because there were no official police for the undead.

Sitting on the leather couch, I followed his progress back and forth, counting every time he stepped on a dark mark on the Turkish carpet. A bloodstain, which no amount of scrubbing seemed capable of removing. It was as if Lucius's uncle Vasile—whom Lucius had destroyed on that spot—refused to leave us.

And then, just as he stepped right on that stain for the

fifty-fourth time, Lucius turned to me, arched one of his dark eyebrows, and jolted me by suggesting the very question I couldn't quite figure out how to ask without making it seem like I doubted his innocence. Which I *didn't*.

"Do you not wish to ask where I was last night, Jessica?"

Chapter 28
Antanasia

"NO, LUCIUS," I promised him. "I don't need to ask."

He smiled and came over to sit next to me. I moved to make room for him, but he grabbed my hand, trapping me at his side. "That is interesting, because I've seen the question in your eyes for at least an hour."

I flushed. "Lucius, no!"

"It is all right," he reassured me. "Like the others, you saw me threaten Claudiu. And unlike the others, who will be suspicious based only upon that, you came to this office late and found me gone."

I felt my eyes get wide. "How did you know that?"

Lucius smiled again. "I do not track you in secret, Jessica. When I came to bed and dismissed him, Emilian merely mentioned that you had sought me here and found me missing." He grew serious. "And you did not even feel me shift you in the bed, so I imagine you have no idea when I joined you."

"Yeah . . . Yes, I slept hard last night." After seeing another *stake* on the bed. That awful feeling of premonition came creeping back, and I tried hard to dismiss it.

But it didn't help when Lucius added, "The fact that I have destroyed before . . ." His gaze flicked to the stain on the carpet. "Including another of my uncles, an act for which I was tried . . . I am certain that none of those things helps to quell anyone's suspicions about my actions last night."

"So where were you?" I asked. "Not because I don't trust you. But if the Elders are going to ask questions, I should know."

Lucius squeezed my hand. "Are you *certain* that you trust me?" His eyes clouded. "Because I did warn you, in this very room, that I would always be a vampire prince, and always treacherous. I am certain that is the exact word I used, for I remember that night more vividly than any other, as it was the worst—and best—of my existence so far."

I stared into Lucius's incredibly dark eyes, where I'd seen even darker aspects of his heart reflected. I knew that he was capable of things that made me shiver both in good and bad ways. He was definitely capable of destroying another vampire, and wouldn't hesitate to do it . . .

He didn't even blink, allowing me to search his soul.

But Lucius would only destroy another vampire if doing so was unavoidable, just, and legal according to the code that he hopes to better establish in our kingdom.

"I trust you, Lucius," I told him. "No matter where you were last night, I know you didn't destroy Claudiu."

There were a lot more things we should have talked about before going to meet with the Elders, but I forgot them all—

including Ylenia's suggestion about calling for a show of stakes—when Lucius leaned forward and kissed me, saying, "Thank you for your faith, Jessica. I fear it may be the only trust I possess now, and I will need it in the days to come."

"Mindy believes in you, too," I told him. It sounded silly when I said it, because really, what did her support mean? She wasn't even a vampire, let alone an Elder.

But Lucius had always liked Min, and he seemed grateful. "She has a good heart." He smiled wryly. "Perhaps she can speak on my behalf, if I ever need what you Americans call a character witness. I'm sure she would assure the Elders that I 'rock'—although they'd have no idea what that meant."

"Oh, Lucius . . ." I was laughing, but also gripped with fear at the reminder of a possible trial, and I leaned closer and kissed *him*.

We stopped talking then, but it was like we were still speaking as we continued to kiss, tenderly but deeply. Every few seconds, we would pull back to see each other's eyes, and I got so wrapped up in his arms, and so lost in the feel of his lips against mine and our silent but intense communication, that it was days before I realized he never did tell me where he'd been that night.

And by then it was too late to ask him *anything*.

Chapter 29
Antanasia

"AND SO IT is agreed that we will inter Claudiu five days from today?" Lucius asked the Elders. He closed the leather-bound planner that he used in meetings because the laptop he'd tried to bring once had unnerved some of the older vampires who'd been around for papyrus and inkwells. "We are in accord on this?"

"Yes, yes." The murmur of assent went around the table, and gray heads nodded.

I let out my breath, and it felt like I'd been holding it for hours. I hadn't even realized how tense I was until the meeting started to look like it was wrapping up without incident. Maybe without Claudiu, the Elders were less likely to make trouble.

I looked at Lucius.

Or were they terrified that what had happened to Claudiu would happen to them if they dissented? There was definitely a quiet sense of distrust in that room.

"I thank all of you for coming on such short notice," Lucius added. "Antanasia and I will keep you informed as we determine the next steps in the inquiry into this crime."

My breathing got steadier, and I managed a shaky smile at Dorin, who seemed to share my relief, no doubt because Lucius hadn't put him on the spot. Or maybe he was just happy that nobody else had gotten *murdered*. The whole agenda had revolved around reassuring the Elders that we would conduct a thorough investigation and deciding when to bury Claudiu, because we had to leave time for word about his destruction to spread all the way through the global rumor mill, since there was no newspaper, let alone CNN or a website, for the undead.

Lucius sat back and began to say, "We are adjourned."

But of course my relief had been premature.

"What, exactly, will this 'inquiry' entail?" Flaviu Vladescu asked. "And who, precisely, will conduct it?"

Oh, no.

I shifted to look at Flaviu and my heart sank. He had always been overshadowed by his older brother, Claudiu, but it was clear that now it was Flaviu's turn to step up, just like Claudiu had risen in power after Vasile's death. Already the bony, beak-nosed vampire sat a little straighter, and he drummed his thin, knobby fingers on the table like his brother used to do. And Vasile before him.

I had a flash of suspicion. *Is there a chance* Flaviu *had something to do with Claudiu's destruction?* I looked at the younger vampire savoring his new status while trying to appear griefstricken, and it seemed possible.

"As you undoubtedly know, our laws regarding punishment are extensive," Lucius reminded his uncle. "But investigation has been virtually ignored. Suspicion alone has been enough to unleash mobs to dispense 'justice.'" He looked at me. "Antanasia and I wish to establish a more modern, empirical protocol. We ask only for time to discuss what should occur next so we can put this to your vote."

Although I hated drawing attention to myself, I nodded to support that plan. We definitely agreed that vampire justice placed too much emphasis on getting revenge and moving suspects to trial—and the stake—as quickly as possible. And the closest thing to police were vampires who sounded more like bounty hunters, chosen for their especially ruthless natures.

"Rest assured that Claudiu's destruction will not go unanswered," Lucius added.

But Flaviu didn't seem reassured. He seemed angry, and looked around the table for support. "Are none of you brave enough to speak what we are all thinking? Which is that the one who *claims* to believe in 'law' was the last seen quarreling—"

I felt my fear bubbling up inside me and struggled to keep it under control. *This is how it started yesterday.*

"Be careful if you are about to make accusations," Lucius interrupted, with a sharp, warning look at his uncle. "This is not the time or the place. I promise you, we will determine who committed this act."

"How?" Flaviu pressed for details. "What does this 'empirical' process entail?"

Although Lucius was opening his mouth to answer, we didn't have a process yet, and I imagined the whole situation sliding out of control, just like it had with Claudiu. That was probably why, although I'd hardly spoken a word during any of my meetings with the Elders, I blurted out, "The first thing we intend to do is call upon each Elder to produce his stake."

Flaviu seemed shocked to hear me pipe up, but he whipped around and asked, very quickly, "When, Antanasia?"

I hadn't considered that, but I had to say something. And it was probably the sooner the better. "Tomorrow. We'll meet here at the same time."

There was dead silence at the table. I thought they were all stunned that I'd finally announced *anything*.

Then, all of a sudden, instead of dismissing me—or laughing even, like I half expected—I heard murmurs of approval and saw heads nodding.

In spite of the awful circumstances, I felt a rush of relief that bordered on pride.

I'd finally done something right, as a princess, and I looked at Lucius for his endorsement. But when I met his eyes, I realized that he didn't think my suggestion was so great. And although he publicly supported me, saying, "We shall do this as Antanasia decrees, and meet tomorrow at dusk," I knew from the way he rubbed his jaw before adding, again, "Meeting adjourned," that I'd *really* messed up this time.

I just couldn't figure out how, because it seemed like my—well, Ylenia's—plan to determine who had destroyed Claudiu was pretty foolproof.

Chapter 30
Lucius

To: nightsurfer3@freeweb.net
From: LVVladescu@euronet.web
R—

My apologies for my brusque tone and even more terse command: If you have not already departed for Romania, as I suspect, because you ARE a noble Vladescu, your presence at the estate is required now.

L

P.S. There is no need to pack any of your few belongings. My tailor is preparing a suit for you to wear to the interment, where you may be called upon to serve as my surrogate—the funereal equivalent of a best man—as there is a strong possibility that attendance on my part will be impossible.

Chapter 31
Mindy

"THANKS FOR BRINGING these," Jess said, real quiet. Her head was hanging down, and she picked at the icing on her favorite butterscotch krimpets. "I get really hungry here sometimes."

I reached across the big mattress where we were sitting cross-legged, like we used to sit on Jess's bed back in Pennsylvania, and grabbed another pack of chocolate juniors. "How can you get hungry here? Don't the servants get you anything you want?"

Jess looked up and her eyes were red and tired. "I don't know how to talk to the cook. So sometimes if Lucius isn't around, I just don't eat. It's easier."

I looked at her like she was crazy. "Jess, you gotta eat!" She was down to like a size six. Maybe four—which was *way* too skinny for her.

"I know." But she still picked at the icing.

I watched her for a sec, then asked, "You're not still upset about that meeting, are you?"

"You didn't see Lucius's face when I called for a show of stakes," she said again. "And then, when everyone was gone, he acted all distant and said, 'We need to talk later.'" She looked up at me with miserable eyes. "It's never good when a guy says, 'We need to talk.'"

Yeah, that was true—when girls said it, too. I'd said that every time I broke up with Raniero. But Jess and Lukey weren't gonna *break up*.

She pushed away the krimpets and gave a big sigh. "I don't know what I did wrong."

You listened to that cousin of yours. That's what you did wrong. I wanted to say that, but I didn't. I just watched my best friend, who I'd known since we were little kids, thinking that even though we'd never been popular, she'd always had a lot of confidence. It was weird how being a princess and having a husband that most girls would *kill for* was sucking all that away.

Seriously, where was the girl who had put on a hot black

dress and marched into the winter formal and stole Lucius Vladescu away from the world's most evil cheerleader?

"I'm failing at this." She dug her hands into her curls. "The whole thing. It's so frustrating."

"Jess, unlike yours truly, you've never even failed a quiz," I reminded her. "You're gonna be an awesome princess. You just need a little time."

"I don't have any time," she said. "That's the problem."

I reached out and shook her too-bony knee. "Jess . . ."

"I'm sorry to dump all this on you, Mindy," she added. "But I'm really struggling." Then she got this weird expression on her face and asked, much softer, "Would you believe me if I told you that I've started *seeing* things sometimes?"

I stopped licking chocolate off my fingers. "What?"

"I think I'm *hallucinating*. From the stress."

I dropped my Tastykake and got crumbs on the velvet blanket. "Um . . . what are you seeing?"

Jess watched me, like she wanted to see my reaction when she said, "A stake. I see a *stake*. And I swear it's REAL. I didn't think much about it, at first, but . . ."

Wow. I was not a psychiatrist, but I did believe in visions and dreams. "Whaddya think it means?"

"Nothing, except that I'm exhausted." She tried to laugh it off. "But Lucius says—at least, I think he said—that dreaming of a stake means . . . *betrayal*."

"Betrayal . . ." I didn't know Jess's vampire circle too well, but I understood people—undead or not—and right away a bunch of faces came to mind. But I didn't get a chance to name names, 'cause somebody knocked on the door, and

Lukey came in without even bothering to check if we were decent. He probably had other stuff on his mind.

"I apologize for interrupting your reunion, Melinda Sue." He came over to the bed and held out his hand. "But it is getting very late, and I need my wife." He arched an eyebrow at Jess, just like Raniero used to do to me. It was, like, their Vladescu thing. The one way Lucius and Ronnie were actually alike. "If you are ready?"

Jess untwisted her legs and shot me a look like, *Here we go!* But she told Lukey, "Yeah . . . yes, I'm ready."

Then he helped her off the bed, and when she stood up, he closed his eyes and bent down and kissed the top of her head, and it was like the sweetest thing I'd ever seen. I mean, it had been intense when they got married. There were sparks flying everywhere. But when he did that . . . it was the most romantic thing ever. Then he opened his eyes and told me, just like Jess had, "I feel certain that you are completely safe, Melinda. Whatever is happening here, it has nothing to do with you. But I will leave Antanasia's guard, Emilian, at your door." He looked down at Jess. "Because you will be safe with me."

I almost sighed. *He is* so *protective. I so want a guy like that!*

Jess looked up at Lukey and nodded. "Okay." Then she told me, "Good night, Min. Thanks again for coming—and staying." She gave me a private look. "And please don't worry about that stuff I mentioned. I'm just tired and saying stupid things."

"Sure, Jess," I told her. But I wouldn't forget any of what she said. In fact, I was gonna look up "stakes" at DreamSymbol .com as soon as I found a computer. "Night, you guys."

"Sleep well," Lucius said. "And tell Emilian if you need anything."

"Definitely," I promised him. I mean, *I* always wanted a servant, even if Jess didn't.

Then I picked up my cupcakes and licked the plastic wrapper and watched Prince Lucius and Princess Jess go out the door, and I knew without even a teeny bit of doubt that I'd been right to tell Jess that Lukey was innocent. 'Cause, just from the way he kissed her head and held her hand, I knew for sure that Lucius would never risk ruining what they had together.

But *somebody* was causing trouble for both of them, and it was starting to piss me off.

Chapter 32
Antanasia

"LUCIUS, YOU WANTED to talk?" I prompted him as we made our way—so far in silence—through the dark castle, hand in hand. *He's too quiet . . .*

"Soon," he said softly. He still sounded preoccupied, and I got more worried.

This is going to be a bad conversation. And why did I tell Mindy that I was hallucinating? I don't want even my best friend to know that.

We kept walking through the corridors, which were lit only by moonbeams coming through the occasional window, and as usual I let Lucius lead. I assumed we were going toward our bedroom, though, and hardly paid attention to the route.

But after about five minutes of turning blind corners and stumbling down the tiny, seemingly pointless steps that were everywhere in our house, I realized we weren't headed to our room, which shouldn't have been more than two minutes' walk from Mindy's. And even though I didn't think there was any reason to whisper, I asked quietly, "Where are we going?"

He didn't answer but squeezed my hand. His fingers felt tense around mine.

"Lucius?" I ventured again, after about three more minutes of twisting and turning, during which I got the sense we were descending, although those little steps were so random that it was hard to tell for sure.

I didn't want to be scared—I was with my husband, who would protect me with his very existence—but it seemed to be getting darker in the halls, and mustier, too, like this was an area where few vampires ever ventured. "Where are . . . ?"

Before I could finish, though, he stopped us both, and I could just barely make out, in front of my nose, a very narrow door. It looked almost like a black slit in the stone. Like the lid of a coffin, nailed to the wall. The faintest light seeped out at our feet, as if Lucius had been there earlier and illuminated whatever waited inside.

Something about that pale glow was ominous, like the hellish flames in the courtroom, and I actually tried to disengage our fingers and take a step backward.

He held on to me, though, and said, "I have something

I need to show you, Antanasia." He paused, then added with what seemed like reluctance, "Something I should have shown you long ago, perhaps before you even married me."

Then, before I could say anything more, he reached out, opened the door, and ushered me through the tall, thin portal with a reassuring hand at the base of my spine, which didn't stop me from gasping and stepping back as I cried softly, "Lucius . . . what *is* this place?"

Chapter 33
Antanasia

AS AN AMERICAN who couldn't even name her great-grandparents with any certainty, I still found it hard to grasp just how far back Lucius's vampire lineage dated. Even though I'd signed, at my wedding, the thick genealogy that he so prized, adding my name to a roster of undead that dated back thousands of years, I never really got the idea of a family that measured time in millennia and that included living members who might have rubbed elbows with Aristotle, or Henry VIII, or Hannibal as he crossed the Alps.

No, the vampiric concepts of history, legacy, and birthright didn't really hit home until I saw that heritage measured out in *stakes*.

"Lucius, this is . . ." *Amazing? Unbelievable? Disgusting?*

"Yes, the *camera de miză*—the room of stakes—is all of those things," he agreed, no doubt reading my mind, like I sometimes thought he could do. "It is all of those things and much more, to me."

The room was small, just big enough for two or three occupants and a table at its center, but what that chamber lacked in size, it made up for in weaponry. Almost every spare inch of wall held a bracket that in turn held a stake, point down, so the entire room looked like the upper jaw of a great white shark. Maybe scarier. I sort of felt like I was being eaten alive as I ventured a step forward, unnerved but curious, too.

I'm in a museum of destruction.

"Each of these stakes belonged to a Vladescu male who has been destroyed," Lucius explained, stepping up behind me and resting a hand on my shoulder. "At one time, each weapon was a prized possession." He reached past me and pointed to a tiny slip of yellowed paper under one of the stakes. "See—the name of the owner, and the date of his destruction."

The room was lit by only two candles, and I leaned closer, trying to read, but the name was inked in some long-lost precursor of Cyrillic, and I couldn't even come close to deciphering it. I recognized the number, though: A.D. 53.

I also recognized the distinctive stain that ran halfway up the weapon, which told me that whoever had owned that stake had used it—probably more than once.

Mesmerized, I stepped out from under Lucius's hand and began to look more closely at each artifact, following the dates as they slowly climbed—*358, 765, 822 . . .*

Although wielded in different eras, the weapons themselves showed no evolution. Each was nothing more than a crude, sharp piece of wood. It was like the design was so effective that there was no reason to update it. I flinched, staring at a row of stained points.

Any of those would get the job done.

Then I stopped and peered more closely, comparing a group from the Middle Ages. Yet there were small distinctions. Designs carved in what served as the hilt. Inlaid initials. Grooves worn by ancient fingers, back in even more violent times, when vampires would have kept their stakes with them constantly.

Lucius stood still and silent, allowing me to explore, and I moved clockwise, not sure how I felt to be in the middle of so much history—and so much old blood.

And then, when I was about at the end of that bizarre collection, just after I read, with a sharp intake of breath, *Valeriu Vladescu,* next to a date close to Lucius's first birthday, my eye was caught by another familiar name, next to the only stake *encased in glass.*

What?

I turned to Lucius, baffled. "Why is *Raniero's* stake here? He's alive. He was your *best man.*"

Lucius stepped toward me. "That is a story for another time. A long story, which I will relate when we have a few hours to spare on some equally long winter's night."

I cast another glance at the name *Raniero Vladescu Lovatu*— and at the *pacifist's* stake, which was *covered* with blood—and opened my mouth to insist that I get that story now.

But when I turned back to Lucius, he was reaching for my hand again, and the expression on his face made me decide to wait. And even though I'd guessed by then what he really wanted to show me in that room, my heart pounded harder as he led me to the table, which held a shiny black container that looked like a little coffin inside the coffin we'd stepped into.

I knew what was under the lid of that box before he opened it, and I looked up at my husband. "So this is where you always keep it?"

He nodded, his glossy hair gleaming in the candlelight. "Yes, Antanasia. It is *usually* here."

His using my "official" name even though we were alone struck me as odd—as did his emphasis on "usually"—and I cocked my head, getting even edgier. "Why, Lucius?"

Why are you showing me this now? What does it have to do with whatever mistake I made at the meeting?

"It is unusual for a female vampire to use a stake," he continued, answering my half-finished question in his usual roundabout way. "If you could read Cyrillic, you would know that there are no feminine names upon these walls." He rested his hand on the box. "But these are new times, and you are *my equal,* Antanasia. You may be called upon to act as such, in a way that your predecessors—with the exception of your birth mother—would never have dreamed of doing. Mihaela was the first to rule as a true queen, and you have her strength inside you."

I shook my head and backed away again, not liking where the conversation was headed. "No, Lucius. I really couldn't dream of doing anything with a stake, no matter what my mother did."

But Lucius was nodding, contradicting me. "Yes,

Antanasia. If something should happen to me, you need to know where this is—and get used to the feel of it in your hand. If you ever need it, you will not want to flinch or hesitate." He paused, then added, "And there is another reason you need to see this now."

Then, when I was still processing what he was trying to say—*Why am I suddenly going from princess who can't even attend a trial to lessons in stake wielding?*—he lifted the lid of the box, and my nose wrinkled under assault from a very powerful—and recognizable—odor, which caused me to gag for more than one reason.

It was the smell of decay. Of rot.

Of *Claudiu's* blood.

Chapter 34
Antanasia

"LUCIUS, YOU'RE SURE you have no idea how Claudiu's blood got on your stake?" I asked for at least the tenth time. I felt like those jagged shark teeth were closing in on me, pricking at my skin. "You're *sure* you don't know who did this?"

Of course we had discussed the possible suspects, chief among them Flaviu and other disgruntled Elders, which included most of those old vampires. But I couldn't seem to stop asking that same question over and over.

Am I afraid he's hiding more *stuff from me? Not telling me everything?*

"I promise you, Jessica," Lucius said again. "I came here shortly before the meeting to plan Claudiu's burial and made the discovery. I know nothing more than you do."

But he *had* known more than me, at the meeting, and I stared at him, feeling not just scared that someone was obviously trying to frame him, but a little . . . betrayed. "Why didn't you tell me about this? And why did you come here in the first place?"

Lucius raked his hand through his hair, like he felt guilty. "I believed that you had enough to worry about, with the threat of chaos at the meeting. If I had told you that *my* weapon was tainted with Claudiu's blood—"

I flushed. "You thought I'd freak out—and maybe do something stupid."

"Please, do not make it sound as if I didn't trust you," he said. "I only wanted to spare you knowledge—and pressure— that I didn't think you needed at that moment."

"Because you *couldn't* trust me with the truth." My indignation faded and my cheeks got exceptionally warm for a vampire as I thought about how I'd so willingly followed Ylenia's advice without even talking to Lucius. "And I did something stupid anyway, by insisting that everybody produce their stakes."

"No." Lucius shook his head. "You thought the idea was a good one—that it would vindicate me. This problem is my fault for withholding information from you. If I had told you about the stake right away, you would have known that I wished for time to investigate." His eyes projected misery. "The mistake was mine."

Lucius and I stared at each other, and although he was

accepting blame for the crisis, he had also admitted that we really *weren't* equals yet. *Will we ever be? Did I force him to keep a secret?* I thought of the stake I'd seen in our bed, which had seemed as tangible as any of those around us. *And he doesn't even know how I'm really cracking up . . .*

"Why did you even come here after Claudiu's death?" I asked again. My voice sounded tight in my throat. "What were you checking? Or *getting?*"

"One of the Elders was destroyed in our home." Lucius crossed his arms over his chest, like he was challenging me to dispute his logic. "I thought it best to arm myself, the better to protect you, until I could teach you to protect yourself."

Again, I need protection.

I studied his face by the light of the small candles. His strong jaw, with the scar I couldn't see in that dim room. His high cheekbones, shadowed by the firelight and stubble, like he needed to shave. And his eyes, which were so sweet and tender . . . and so well trained to conceal things. "Were you going to tell me that you were carrying around the stake . . ."

. . . that you nearly used to destroy me? That I hadn't seen since that night?

"Yes," Lucius promised. "I would have told you."

We faced each other for a long time, in a very strange silence. Like we were trying, with our eyes, to smooth over a fissure that had opened up at our feet. It was like the stake—that awful stake, which was still visible in the open box—had been plunged down and created a chasm in the floor between us.

Would it always be between us?

"Why didn't you ever show me this room?" I finally asked. "Why did you hide this from me, too?"

"Look around you," Lucius said, without taking his eyes off mine or uncrossing his arms. "You are already plunged into a world of violence. You *married* violence. I did not wish to shock you with an unnecessarily graphic lesson in just how brutal your new family is, and the extent to which we Vladescus have enshrined aggression. Not yet."

Oh, the million thoughts and emotions that ran through me when I heard Lucius's pained explanation of why he'd kept me out of that chamber. Family was incredibly important to him. And yet he had also come to learn in America that violence was not the only way to maintain order. He was struggling, too, to understand a new way of life, and I felt bad for him. I was ashamed, too, that he'd once again judged me too weak to handle my new life—even if I was too weak.

Yes, we had a lot of challenges ahead of us.

I stared at the stake, which presented the greatest problem.

How would we explain it to the Elders? Why had I jumped on Ylenia's idea, which seemed so horrible now, because the older vampires would smell the blood, too, and believe that Lucius was responsible?

"Jessica?" I looked up to see Lucius reaching for my hands and felt his fingers wrap around mine. Felt the X that marked his left palm and that helped to connect us again, as it had at our wedding, when we'd both cut our hands and commingled our blood. "I had other reasons for not wishing to show you this room," he confessed. "Selfish reasons." His eyes clouded with apology. "Do you think that I am eager to remind you of what I once nearly did to *you?* Do you think that I was in any great hurry to revisit that night, in the shadow of all my ancestors' darkest moments?"

"Lucius . . ." I held his hands tighter and struggled for words, because I thought about that night a lot, too. I could still feel the way the point of his stake had pressed up under my breastbone—and how his fangs had pierced my skin in a very different way, just minutes later. "Don't forget that that night was also one of the best of my life. You said it was *the* best for you."

"And the worst," he reminded me.

"It was both," I insisted. "Both."

It was the first time I'd ever thought of the two events that had taken place that evening—the terrible way Lucius had threatened to destroy me, and the beautiful moment when he'd first made me his for eternity—as one seamless whole, instead of two jarringly separate occurrences. For the first time, I saw them as indivisible, like the yin-yang symbol that Raniero wore on his arm. "Maybe it all just had to happen the way it did, for us to be together," I told him. "Maybe the stake is a *good* part of our story."

Lucius smiled grimly. "You will forgive me if I have difficulty, right now, seeing a bloodstained weapon that I almost used upon you—and that has been turned against *me,* now— as any kind of harbinger of happy endings."

Then he released my hands and blew out the candles, and I heard the snap of the lid of the box and the scrape of wood against stone as he lifted his stake off the table to carry it back to our bedroom. And even though he'd initially wanted to retrieve it to protect me, I knew I wouldn't sleep any easier with that thing in the room.

It *wasn't* a harbinger of anything good. It might even be the instrument of *Lucius's* destruction. His own weapon, used against him.

My throat tightened, and I almost couldn't breathe as I suddenly remembered our law as outlined by Lucius. *"Destruction must be answered with destruction,"* and *"The destruction of an Elder must be answered by the highest-ranking member of the clan . . ."* Which meant, if Lucius ever really was found guilty for Claudiu's destruction, *I* would be expected . . .

STOP, JESSICA! It will NEVER come to that. Lucius won't let it happen!

Yet I felt very sick as I followed him to the door, knowing that I'd been fooling myself, moments ago, about the stake. That I'd started fooling myself months earlier, when I'd promised Lucius that I was ready to be a vampire, and his for eternity.

Chapter 35
Mindy

I HONESTLY DIDN'T feel scared about being in Jess's castle—until about midnight, when I was totally alone in my bed, and completely out of Tastykakes, and the fire was getting less bright, and I started wondering if the cute little vampire named Emilio was really still right outside my room, 'cause I did not hear him making a sound.

Tossing off the covers, I tiptoed to the door, undid the lock, and opened the door up, just a crack.

Emilio snapped to attention. "You wish . . . something?"

"Uh, no." I shut the door, happy that he was still there. Even if he was a vampire himself. I flipped the lock. "Thanks anyhow," I called.

Then, just to be on the safe side, I went to the other side of the room to check if the windows were locked, too, even though my room was on, like, the fifth floor, looking out over the front of the castle, so I had a great view of the big valley that looked like it was gonna swallow up the whole place. I knew vampires didn't really fly like bats like in the movies—they *surfed*—but I wasn't taking any chances.

When I got to the first window and looked outside, I saw it was snowing. Big fat flakes were falling past the window and all the way to the ground. I leaned my head against the glass, looking down at the little circle of light that marked the front door—right outside of where Claude had been "destroyed," which was the word vampires always used. Not killed, "destroyed."

Then I thought I saw something move just outside that light, and I blinked twice.

It was dark down there, but was that somebody *walking* in the snow?

Was that . . . ?

No way!

I blinked again, and the person—or vampire—was gone, and I moved real quick to check all the locks, twice, then jumped back in bed and pulled the covers up to my chin, thinking that maybe something in that place really did make you hallucinate, 'cause I was starting to see things, too.

Chapter 36
Antanasia

I RESTED MY head against Lucius's chest, trying to enjoy the slow, rocking rhythm of the horse as it picked its way through the deep snow that had fallen overnight. But the still-unanswered questions that had kept me awake all night kept ruining what should have been a peaceful dawn ride deep into the silent Carphathian forest.

How did Claudiu's blood get on Lucius's stake? How will we explain it? Because we can't . . .

"Lucius?" I started to fret again and heard echoes of Dorin in my voice. "What *will* we tell the Elders?"

"Try not to worry now, Jessica." He wrapped his arm tighter around my waist.

Of course I was a good enough rider to have my own horse, but Lucius had wanted to ride together that morning, not even bothering to saddle one of the few gentle mares in a stable that he preferred to stock with slightly wild rides. "We will tell them what little we know," he said. "Just as we've discussed." He nuzzled the back of my neck, whispering, "And so for now, because we cannot do more, let us just enjoy being together, all right?"

"I'll try." But I didn't understand how he could enjoy any-

99

thing right then, and I wriggled inside my down jacket, because I felt very cold. Not temperature cold or vampire cool, but *scared* cold.

Maybe we can just keep riding into another country. Moldova is close, and nobody would look for us there.

We rode quietly for about twenty minutes, until I started to hope that maybe we really were headed for the border, when suddenly the mare stepped out from under a thick canopy of trees into a gloomy gray clearing and I realized where we were. And just like I'd done the night before, when Lucius had shown me the room full of stakes, I pressed myself back— this time to steady myself against Lucius's body, because this spot . . .

Finally seeing it made me recoil in a different way.

Chapter 37
Antanasia

THE BLACK IRON gates to the cemetery where both our families were buried stood in stark relief against the snow, and I hung back, even when Lucius undid the latch and held out his hand, saying, "Please, Jessica. There's nothing to fear in here."

Oh, but there is . . .

What could I do, though, except take a reluctant step forward and join the prince who was beckoning me? And as soon as I passed through the gate, I saw that death mirrored life in the realm of vampires. I didn't even have to ask which of the two biggest mausoleums—obviously the tombs of the royals—belonged to the Vladescus and which belonged to the Dragomirs.

The Vladescus—the kings and queens, at least—rested in a soaring, spiky black stone-and-marble structure that echoed the Gothic castle I could see looming over us in the distance.

And my parents . . . I knew without asking that their bodies were inside the shorter, more subdued white marble crypt I saw on the opposite side of the burial ground.

I stopped in my tracks, and Lucius stopped, too.

"Even in death, we have always been separate," he said with quiet reverence. "As vampires, we are segregated from humans, and forced to bury our corpses in this hidden place high in the mountains. But within this graveyard, we have divided ourselves, too. Your family is far from mine, as if we can *never* share the earth." He looked down at me. "That seemed natural to me, once—before I fell in love with you."

I never got tired of hearing Lucius remind me that his love for me had wiped away hatred for my family that was probably embedded in his genes. But I didn't want to face this. Not now.

"I don't want to go any farther," I told him, not moving when he started to advance again.

He stopped, and I looked up at his face, and I thought he was going to protest and push me to walk closer to both families' tombs. He'd been pushing me toward those crypts—toward confronting the loss of my parents and our own possible futures—since the night back in Pennsylvania when he'd shown me his prized genealogy. And he'd stood at my back, one hand resting on my shoulder, as I'd signed my name at our wedding, taking another step closer to this spot.

But right then, I dug in my heels. "No closer," I insisted. "Not today."

I'm already facing too much. I can't face, head-on, my parents' destructions. Or what might happen to us, too, because although we have a chance for immortality, we may also end up here.

Lucius seemed ready to protest for one more second; then he nodded. "Of course. In your own time."

Maybe never. Maybe, like the trial I couldn't attend and the justice I couldn't hand out . . . maybe never.

"Why are we here?" I asked him, searching his face. I might have been avoiding looking at my family's mausoleum. "Why today?"

Lucius's eyes didn't offer much comfort. They were as grave as . . . the graves we stood among, and he took my hands in his, so I thought about my wedding again. We stood like a bride and groom. But I didn't want to think about that in a cemetery, either.

"You know, Antanasia," he said, "that what we face, in the coming hours—and perhaps weeks—may be very bad indeed." He pressed my palms together and his gaze flicked past me to the crypts that he wasn't afraid to look at. "And until we discover who did destroy Claudiu, you will need to be as steady and strong as these stones around us, *daughter of the formidable Mihaela Dragomir.*"

I knew Lucius loved symbolism and similes, but I hated

them right then. They *sucked*. And I felt almost ashamed to be compared to my powerful mother, because it was starting to be obvious that I *wasn't* like her.

"Can't we take some time?" I suggested. "Postpone the meeting, at least? It wouldn't be like running away."

Lucius shook his head, though. "No, Jessica. We are trying to create a new order among vampires. We have agreed that we need rule of law. How would it look if I try to evade the very structure we are establishing?"

I hated, too, that I'd agreed—in theory—that our clans needed updating.

"A ruler who defies his own laws is not a prince but a despot," Lucius added. "And we do not want to be despots, correct?"

"I'm not sure, right now." Tears started pricking my eyes.

Why did Lucius Vladescu have to choose *now* to embrace democratic rule of law? Back in Pennsylvania, he'd talked incessantly about royalty and autocracy and how "peasants" needed a "firm hand." But my family had changed him. We'd taught a prince to fold his own laundry and changed everything.

Lucius smiled, like he knew what I was thinking. Then he drew me close and urged, "Cry now, Jessica, so it doesn't happen when I am led away, for there is no bail in our world. Of course I will be detained when the crime is destruction and the evidence so damning. That is our law, too."

"Of course," I agreed, like he was making perfect sense. But in my head I kept hearing his words. *Led away . . . He's going to be led away from me . . .*

I was terrified for him. Would he stand, again, on that worn circle in the courtroom? Would it get that far? And a smaller part of me was scared for myself. Afraid to be alone, trying to rule without him. "What if we can't figure out who really did it?" I asked, barely able to get the words out.

Lucius cupped my chin. "We will find the truth. The truth is always revealed in the end."

My family had given him a television, too . . .

"We aren't on *Law & Order*," I reminded him. "And I don't even know how to start searching for the truth, especially if you're not free to help me."

Lucius smiled again. "Your intelligence was one of the first things that I loved about you, Jessica. That and your skill at mucking out stalls," he teased. His eyes clouded a little. "And as we both know, I have—for better or worse—vast experience in the area of diabolical plotting. I have complete faith that, together, we will determine who destroyed Claudiu. I may actually be well served by incarceration, for I will have nothing but time to think and unravel the scheme."

"So much for the vote of confidence and our coronation, too," I managed to say, wiping at a tear that fell. "I guess that's *really* done for!"

Lucius slid his hands up to hold my arms and stopped smiling. "Let us worry about proving my innocence first and coronation later. But I have not given up hope—for either."

My chin started quivering, and I couldn't control my crying. "Oh, Lucius . . ." I buried my hands under his coat and started to sob in earnest, and when I ran out of tears, he took my arms again and for the first time since our marriage pushed me away, just a little, like he was already forcing me to stand on my own two feet, even though I was nowhere close to ready.

"Antanasia," he said softly but firmly. "I know that it is difficult for you to face this place today. And I don't pretend to be wiser than you. But I know something of suffering, and I learned a long time ago—both by experiencing violence and by *anticipating* it—that fear is the worst kind of grave, because it buries one alive. I beg you, as your husband, don't place yourself in a tomb prematurely, for as all here would attest if they could, the time for that comes soon enough."

I was too upset for wisdom right then, and his words didn't sink in. "Let's go now," I said, still not looking at the white crypt that rose above the whiter snow. Or the black one, for that matter. "I'd really like to leave."

"Of course." He glanced at the sky. "It looks as if another storm is about to break loose, doesn't it?"

"Yes, it does," I agreed, without bothering to look at the clouds, either. I didn't have to. There was always some kind of storm brewing in those mountains.

We rode back in silence as the wind picked up and got home just as it started to snow even harder than usual, which was saying something in the Carpathians. Even the wildest of Lucius's horses seemed to huddle in their stalls, like they knew it was going to be bad.

"Lucius. Princess."

The low voice came from the shadows in the gloomy barn, startling me and the mare that Lucius was leading to her stall. She shied and nearly knocked me over as both Lucius and I turned to find a vampire *I* hadn't anticipated seeing—maybe ever again—and who must have arrived in the dead of night.

Lucius, though . . . he hardly seemed surprised at all.

Chapter 38
Antanasia

"RANIERO." LUCIUS DROPPED the lead and extended his hand to the cousin he called brother. "It is good to see you—although I did not expect to find you *here*."

The hippie-throwback surfer I hadn't seen since our wedding came closer, pulling his hands out of his pockets to accept Lucius's handshake. "I sleep in the stables last night," he said in his thick Italian accent, mixing up tenses like he always did. "I arrive very late and did not wish to trouble you." He looked at me. "I heard you come for the horse this morning, but was too lazy to get out from under my blanket and say hello."

"I believe that you were lazy." Lucius grinned. "But I also think that you slept here because you prefer not to enter the castle. You wish to avoid that fate for as long as possible."

Raniero smiled, but it wasn't exactly the placid, carefree expression he'd worn almost continually at our wedding. "I do not care much for opulence anymore."

"No, you seem to have shed that, along with your taste for pants."

Raniero's smile got a little warmer at that joke, although his body must have been freezing, because he was indeed wearing a pair of faded olive shorts and a brown T-shirt that advertised something called Terrible Taco. A Godzilla-like cartoon taco tromped across his chest, crushing a cityscape, lettuce flying everywhere.

Vampires were cool by nature, but we weren't polar bears and needed more than a T-shirt in a blizzard. I looked at his bare arms. Those tattoos wouldn't keep him warm, either.

What is it about those tattoos? And why didn't he want to come inside?

I suddenly remembered something I hadn't thought about since being distracted by Claudiu's blood on Lucius's stake. *And why is Raniero's weapon retired—and covered with gore?*

"Um, I don't mean to be rude," I said, interrupting what was obviously a conversation that only the two men fully understood. "But why, exactly, is Raniero here *at all?*" I asked Lucius.

He reached to take the mare's lead again. "I'm sorry that I failed to tell you that he would be joining us. I was somewhat worried that he might defy my order to come, which would have placed me in the difficult position—"

"—of needing to destroy me for insubordination," Raniero finished the sentence. "And so I perform the favor of answering Prince Lucius's summons." He turned to me, and I honestly couldn't tell if he was joking when he added, "I much prefer not to force my best friends to kill me so directly. It is my wish to do no harm!"

I was getting more confused. "So why . . . ?"

Lucius slapped the mare's rump, sending her into her stall. "Antanasia, we both know that the law is clear. I will be detained. And although you are growing into your role"— *Yeah, right*—"you will need protection," he said. "More than Emilian can offer." His gaze flicked to Raniero, who was slouching, hands in his pockets again. "I trust Raniero to watch over you."

I was terrified at the thought that Lucius might actually be jailed. But as I looked at Raniero, I almost laughed. *He* was going to guard me? Because he was less terrible than the taco on his shirt.

Then I thought of the retired stake, and my eyes tried to trace his strange tattoos in the gloom. There was something there . . . and maybe some method to Lucius's madness.

"Antanasia, do you mind if I speak to Raniero as we walk?" Lucius looked between the two of us. "There will be much opportunity for you to get to know one another, but this may be the only chance I have to bring him up to speed, to use the American expression. And at breakfast, we can all discuss what will most likely happen next."

My heart almost broke at the mere mention of what would happen next, but I tried to be as stoic as Lucius. "Sure. You two talk."

Then Lucius clapped one hand on Raniero's shoulder and began to guide him toward the castle he didn't want to enter, for some reason, both vampires conversing in a mix of what sounded like Romanian, Italian, and English, with maybe a little German thrown in for good measure.

I followed in the tracks they left in the snow, my eyes traveling again and again from Lucius's straight back, long dark coat, and neat black hair to Raniero's slumped shoulders, completely inappropriate shorts, and messy, wavy, sun-kissed mane. The contrast was great, yet their heads were bent together, and they communicated easily in that mishmash of languages—and there was no doubt that they were equals physically. Raniero was just a shade shorter, maybe because of the way he carried himself, but he shared Lucius's lean, muscular build.

Still, I couldn't imagine Raniero protecting me like Lucius did.

I pulled my coat tighter against the increasing storm.

I couldn't imagine Lucius not being there to protect me in the first place. I couldn't rule without him. I would be destroyed, if not literally, at least figuratively, as a princess.

When we got close enough to the castle to see it clearly through the snow, I saw movement in one of the windows and looked up to see Mindy watching the three of us, and the expression her face . . .

It was like *one* of us was already a ghost.

Chapter 39
Antanasia

I SAT THROUGH most of breakfast in silence while Lucius and Raniero continued to confer in their jumble of languages.

The servants came and went and set down the inky, sweet

coffee that Lucius preferred and poured tea for me and Raniero. Out of habit I took a piece of the bread that was served almost every day, in the Romanian tradition. But I didn't really eat anything. It was like I'd gotten numb out there in the snow. Numb and hypnotized.

Over and over again, I found myself studying that swirling mess of tattoos that reminded me of a game I used to play as a kid: *Find the hidden objects in this picture.*

Raniero rested his hand on the table, not eating, either, and thanks to years of living with a hippie-throwback father, I was able to pick out *"aum,"* written in Devanagari, and the Chinese characters for "peace," and the open hand of the Jains, who vowed, like Raniero, to do no harm.

"Antanasia?"

Lucius's voice brought me back to reality, and I realized that both vampires had been watching me intently as I stared at Raniero's arm. "Yes?"

"Raniero—as always—has offered a very good suggestion," Lucius said.

I looked at the guy in the taco shirt and didn't think I'd ask him for something as simple as directions if I saw him on the street. Unless I wanted to find a beach with public access or a good burrito.

Then I looked more closely at his face. Or was there a new spark in his eyes?

Who is he?

"What's the suggestion?"

"You are interested in establishing rule of law, yes?" Raniero asked me. "And you also wish to establish that you are in power—have authority, yes?"

I nodded warily. "Yes . . ."

"Then I think it is best if *you* are the one to order that Lucius be detained, and then to oversee the procedure by which he is taken away."

I dropped the bread I'd been shredding and stared at both of them in disbelief. And I'd thought *my* cousin's plan, about the show of stakes, was bad. But I could tell by the look on Lucius's face that this was exactly how it was going to happen. Still, I had to protest. "You're joking, right? I can't order you taken away!"

But Lucius shook his head. "Raniero is correct, Antanasia. The Elders will perceive you as powerful—and understand how serious we are about adherence to law—if you enforce my detention. There will be a vote, of course, but you must be the one who controls what follows."

I shook *my* head. "But—"

"You need to prove yourself as a sovereign *today*," Lucius insisted. "As your American countrymen would say, 'The training wheels are coming off.' And now."

I suddenly had a very vivid memory of crashing my bike when my dad first let me ride without those two little wheels for support. I'd slammed right into a tree next to our house. "I don't know, Lucius . . ."

"There really is no choice," he said. "Whether you like it or not, you are coming into power this afternoon." His eyes softened, like he could tell that I couldn't imagine speaking words that would take him from me, even if he was going no farther than the catacombs beneath our castle. *Especially* if he was going there.

"It is only symbolic, Antanasia," he said encouragingly.

He was definitely reading my mind. "You can do this. It will feel wrong to you, but it is *for* us, really. For your protection and our future."

I didn't think I could do what he was asking. But there was nothing I could say—especially since Raniero was watching us—except "Okay. I'll issue the command."

Then I sank down in my seat, not unlike Raniero.

My first real act as a princess is going to be ordering my husband bound and taken away.

And even though I had a lot to worry about, I noticed that Mindy—who was definitely awake and loved a good Romanian bread breakfast even more than I used to, when I still ate—hadn't joined us at the table.

Chapter 40
Antanasia

LUCIUS AND I stood in the anteroom where we always waited before councils with the Elders, and I was keenly aware that these would be our last private moments until . . . *when?*

"Do not look so worried," he whispered. And although we usually used that space to prepare to look and act like leaders—at least, to the extent that I ever managed that—Lucius took me in his arms. "We will not be separated for long," he promised. "And remember, too, that you now think in terms of eternity, and a few weeks are nothing."

I rested against him, wanting to draw on his strength. The

time—would it really be weeks?—*would* pass slowly. And yet weeks also seemed like nothing when I tried to imagine how we'd figure out who destroyed Claudiu before a trial became inevitable. "I hate this."

He moved to tilt my chin up with his crooked index finger. "You *are* a princess now," he reminded me, sounding at once tender and a little tough. "There is no more time for tears."

"I know." I nodded. "I promise I won't cry again." *Not until I'm alone in bed tonight.*

"Rely upon Raniero," he urged. "I know that he does not look like much of a savior, but his appearance can be deceiving. He is a vampire of many talents, *most* of which you may find useful in coming weeks. Discounting, of course, his ability to 'get amped' about 'carving' a wave." He'd started smiling but quickly got serious. "And with the exception of you, he is the only vampire whom I trust. The only one."

"I wish there was time for you to tell me about him."

"I am afraid we do not have that luxury." Lucius glanced toward the doors that would open any second now, then met my eyes again. "And I think it best if Raniero determines what he wishes to reveal about himself. For he has a strong inclination toward privacy." He pulled me closer. "Just trust *my* faith in him, Antanasia, and let him help you."

I felt my throat getting tight, because I knew we were running out of time. "I love you," I said. "I love you so much."

"I love you, too, Jessica." Lucius's arms got even tighter around me. "I love you for eternity—and we will weather this small and temporary storm."

I nodded like I actually believed that, and he bent down

and brushed his lips against mine, then pulled away, so I was standing next to him but completely alone. Straightening his shoulders and tugging on his cuffs, he transformed from husband into ruler who would probably soon be prisoner, and his voice was even firmer when he told me, "It is time for you to *truly* assume your role as princess. And I have complete faith that you will succeed beyond anyone's expectations—especially your own."

Then, on that silent cue I would need to learn if I ever had the guts to assemble the Elders without Lucius, the doors swung open.

Chapter 41
Antanasia

THE ELDERS WERE already gathered at the table, and before each I saw a box similar to the one that waited at Lucius's seat. Even my uncle Dorin had a small pine container, although I couldn't even imagine him using a stake to make kebabs.

As I pulled my chair closer to the table, I looked at my husband, who was already calling the meeting to order. "I wish to waste no time," he said. "I see that you have all brought your weapons—let us proceed."

My throat seemed to pinch shut so I could hardly breathe.

I want to waste time. I want to run away with you and live like Raniero, in a shack on the beach.

But that wasn't going to happen. Lucius was already nodding to his left, to Flaviu, who wordlessly opened the box before him and produced his stake, slapping it down on the table with an assurance that proclaimed innocence. A moment later, Horatiu Dragomir followed suit. Then it was Dorin's turn, and I saw his hands shake, even though his stake was completely clean. Not a drop of blood on it, because he was a runner, not a fighter.

Like me? Because I'm not sure anymore . . .

On it went around the table, boxes opening, pale hands reaching in, stakes clacking against wood. It was like watching a very grim wave that skipped over me before going down the other side to reach Lucius.

NO! I wanted to scream when it was his turn. *We need more time!*

But all I could do was watch in horror as the vampire I loved essentially damned himself.

For the moment Lucius opened the box before him and slammed his own stake down with as much assurance any of the other Elders, every vampire in that room gasped, and the air was filled with Romanian voices that sounded shocked and outraged and . . . accusing.

Chapter 42
Antanasia

"EXPLAIN THIS, LUCIUS!" Flaviu demanded, rising. "That is clearly Claudiu's blood!"

Yes, it definitely was. I fought hard against the urge to cover my nose again. The blood was dried, but still fresh enough that the smell permeated the room.

"Indeed, it is Claudiu's blood," Lucius agreed calmly. "That is obvious."

"Then how did it get there?" Flaviu cried. He remained standing and his eyes glittered, like he could barely conceal his glee over his rise in power—and Lucius's abrupt, apparent *fall.* "Are you *confessing,* Lucius?"

"Now, now, Flaviu." Dorin made a rare interjection. "I'm sure that Prince Lucius has a good explanation for this." My uncle gave Lucius a shaky, hopeful smile. "You do, don't you, Lucius?"

But Lucius shook his head. "No, I do not know how Claudiu's blood got there, but I will find the explanation." Then he locked eyes with each of the Elders, adding, "And justice *will* be served. Not only for Claudiu's destruction, but for this obvious attempt to destroy *me.*"

Flaviu dropped into his seat, like he was exasperated. "But this exercise was meant to determine who destroyed my brother!" He pointed at me and I cringed. "Your own wife suggested it!"

I felt my face reddening.

"Yes, and if Antanasia and I had wanted to hide anything, we would not have pursued this course of action," Lucius reminded everyone. "And yet we did call for a show of weapons—"

My cheeks got even warmer. *At least,* I *did.*

"—and I have come before you and willingly produced my own stake," he added. "Because I am innocent and will be proven so."

"And in the meantime?" Flaviu asked with a sneer. "We do what?" He addressed Lucius. "With all due respect, it is difficult to justify letting you loose in this estate!" He appealed to the others. "The evidence would seem to warrant a vote on Prince Lucius's detention, do you not agree?"

There was a long, tense silence, during which I looked around the table. *They all think he's guilty. Except maybe Dorin.*

But even my uncle wouldn't meet my eyes again. He fidgeted with the box that held his stake, closing it with fumbling fingers.

And when I finally turned to Lucius again, I realized that my moment had arrived. He was willing me with his eyes to speak—and reassuring me that I could do what we'd discussed. Still, my voice quavered as I said, too quietly, "Flaviu is right about the evidence."

I had never done more than hold the office of 4-H treasurer, and the words felt strange on my lips when I added, "We will vote now."

I knew the Elders were shocked to hear me take charge—and to realize that Lucius really was going to abide by law. Yet for all his insistence that what we were doing was right, I couldn't look at my husband as I said, "Those who believe that Lucius Vladescu should be detained until either vindicated or tried, raise your left hand and say 'Aye.' Those who believe that he should walk free, raise your right and speak in the negative."

With the exception of Flaviu's, which shot up, left hands rose tentatively, because everybody knew that if he was eventually absolved, Prince Lucius would remember how this vote went down. But the evidence against him was so damning that one by one the Elders said, "Aye."

Even Dorin seemed to have no choice, although he started to raise his right hand. But it was only because he was a rare right-handed vampire and often got confused when voting. Then he caught himself and lifted his left, which trembled like a leaf.

"It is unanimous," I said miserably, when every hand was up. "Lucius Vladescu will be incarcerated."

I thought it was again testament to his courage that Lucius didn't look upset or scared. He mainly looked proud—of me. Even though I couldn't stop feeling like a traitor, especially as I rose and ordered guards, using the words he'd helped me memorize: *"Intrați, gardieni."*

I was relieved that they actually came on my command, and yet close to throwing up as Lucius stood, turned, and offered his hands, held out behind his back. I thought I heard the guard mumble an apology as he bound Lucius's wrists with an iron chain.

And when the ancient padlock was slipped in place, the Elders—including Flaviu—sat very still.

I realized then that Raniero's strategy had been right. We had rocked their world. A prince was obeying the law when it didn't suit his aims. It had probably never happened in the whole brutal history of vampiredom.

Lucius and I locked eyes, and although I wanted to use my new power to set him free, I forced myself to say, *"Luați-l."*
Take him away.

He gave me another nod, reassuring me that I'd done everything right. Then, head held high, he turned to the Elders and said, "Do not forget this. We are *all* governed by law now, and I submit, willingly, to prove that we enter a new era." His eyes narrowed in a way that made it hard to believe he was really a prisoner, though. "And remember, too, when I am vindicated, that the punishment for whoever *did* destroy Claudiu will be swift and harsh—also in accordance with our laws." A hint of his old autocratic self emerged. "I promise you that when I sit as *judge, I* will not forget this moment, either."

He looked at me one more time just before the guard opened the door, allowing Lucius to walk through first, untouched. Prince Vladescu might have submitted to being bound to make a point, but there was no way he would have stood for being dragged away—or even gently led.

I stood there in helpless silence.

Even after his footsteps died away, I kept standing, because my knees were shaking so badly that I was afraid I'd fall down if I tried to sit. But before I could say "Meeting adjourned," Flaviu interrupted, raising his nondominant right hand, which signaled a request to speak.

No! Panic gripped me. *We didn't plan on this. I'm alone!*

But even I understood that I had to recognize the vampire who was probably bent upon bringing my whole world crashing down, maybe even at the expense of his brother's existence.

I knew that his stake was clean. But I also knew that Flaviu Vladescu was just plain nasty, and capable of doing things I couldn't even contemplate, for reasons I couldn't imagine.

Yet what could I do except allow him to do even more damage?

Chapter 43
Mindy

I SAT IN my room flipping through *Catwalk* magazine, but I might as well have been reading about art in college, 'cause I couldn't focus on anything. I could hardly even think about Jess's problems, 'cause someplace in that castle there was a guy in shorts . . .

I looked over at the door for the millionth time. *Not that I want him to come for me! I do NOT!*

And it was just me being a total klutz—I *wasn't* in some big rush—when somebody *finally* knocked and I fell out of bed and kinda crawled—'cause my feet were totally tangled in the two-million-thread-count sheets—to answer it. "Coming!" I yelled. I kicked free of the stupid sheets and got up on my feet. "I'll be right there!"

I took a sec to fix my hair—not that it *mattered* how I looked—and hauled open the door and . . .

STUPID VAMPIRES!

Chapter 44
Mindy

GOSH, HE WAS a mess.

A hot, *HOT* mess.

When I opened the door, Raniero was slouching against the wall with his hands in the pockets of the worst of his four pairs of shorts, and he had on the absolute worst of his five T-shirts—the one with the scary taco on it—and his hair was an even bigger disaster than the last time I'd seen him, in the summer. It was like he hadn't even thought about cutting those long brown waves with the highlights from the sun. And his goatee needed shaping up, too, even more than usual.

He pulled his hands out of his pockets and crossed his arms. His muscles were still nice, though. I finally really looked at his face. And so was his nose, which had a little bump in it, like he'd been slammed down by the surf one too many times. And his lips that were all rough from the sun. And those gray-green eyes that were, like, boring into mine . . .

"Hey," I finally said, 'cause he didn't say a word. He just stared at me with those eyes. Those amazing, sexy, *unemployed-drifter* eyes. I knew what he was, so why was I having trouble talking? I crossed my arms, like him. "What, um . . . what are you doing here?"

Raniero still didn't say anything. And when he finally talked, it was, like, the first time I ever heard him sound close to mad. "I tell you many times not to come here. That it is dangerous. And yet you come."

I kinda looked away, not sure how I felt about the way he was talking to me. I mean, I always wanted him to be more, like, forceful, but . . . "Jess needed me," I said. I looked at him again. "So why are *you* here?"

For me? Did you follow me?

Not that I want that!

"Lucius summoned me, and to defy a Vladescu prince is punishable by destruction," he said. "And so I obey."

"Oh." A few days ago, I woulda laughed at that. But all of a sudden I wasn't so sure it was a joke. "So you *had* to come 'cause you didn't wanna get in trouble?"

Ronnie kept slouching against the door, but his eyes turned a weird color. A dark color I'd never seen before. "Do you truly believe that I am afraid to lose my life, Mindy Sue?" he asked. "I come—against my better judgment—only so I do not cause difficulty for Lucius. I do not wish to force him to choose between enforcing laws that are important to him and destroying one whom he considers a brother. It is not kind to give one's friends such difficult choices. *Specialmente* when they already face hardship."

I hugged myself tighter. So he'd come for Lucius—and to save his own butt. "Yeah, I get it."

Ronnie took a step closer, and I was surprised at how he filled the whole doorway. He seemed bigger than he used to be. And not as happy.

"And of course, I come for you, Mindy Sue."

Of all the stupid things, the stupidest was how much I wanted to hug him right then. I wanted to jump on that stupid Italian vampire I'd missed so much and tell him how glad

I was to see him. I wanted to kiss him again. And touch his messy hair, and feel his mouth against mine.

But I was really glad I didn't do any of that when he said the exact kind of protective thing I'd always wanted to hear— "I come here because I am worried about you. I cannot sleep in peace knowing that you are in this dangerous place"— followed by the *worst* thing he'd ever said. "And I also wish to tell you that you are right. We are not a good couple, yes? I will watch over you as a friend, and will not talk to you of love again. It is better that way, as you have said for many weeks now."

It was like a big balloon popped in my heart. "Oh, sure."

We stared at each other for a couple more minutes, and even though I'd broke up with him a million times—once in person and 999,999 more times over the phone—it never really felt like the end until right then, when he said, "It is good that we make this clear now. And both agree."

"Yeah, definitely."

Then he reached out and shut the door with his inky hand, and I stood there like an idiot, not sure what had just happened. All I knew was that Raniero had finally agreed to break up with me—right when he'd almost started acting like I'd always wanted him to act.

Cool, and tough, and strong.

That was what every girl wanted, right?

Chapter 45
Antanasia

"FLAVIU IS RECOGNIZED," I managed to say, although I barely heard my own words. It almost felt like my ears were ringing, I was so frightened.

He saw—and probably smelled—my fear, just like we'd all smelled the blood on Lucius's stake. I looked at Lucius's chair, but of course it was empty. Then I looked at Dorin, who was no help, and I had no choice but to turn back to Flaviu, who said, "We have not established the *conditions* of confinement. There are laws that govern detention, too."

He seemed outraged by this oversight, but I saw a different gleam in his eyes. The look of a wolf going in for the kill.

I didn't know what to say, so I let him keep talking, although I knew it was a mistake.

"The killer of *Constantin Dragomir* was held in solitary confinement with a restricted diet of bread and water," he continued, appealing to each of the Elders. "We determined that this was the law in a capital crime involving an Elder." His voice seemed to catch. "And this Elder was my brother— and one whom Lucius publicly threatened."

Solitary confinement? Restricted diet?

My head started spinning. Lucius hadn't prepared me for this. I didn't even know if Flaviu was telling the truth, because I'd never read all those law books. Had Lucius made a mistake? Had he underestimated Flaviu, who was demanding, "Well, Princess? What do you say?"

"But . . . Lucius isn't even formally accused," I stammered, because I couldn't allow him to be detained that way. I wouldn't be able to see him. And without blood, he would . . . "I don't think . . ."

Yet I wasn't sure what I thought, and I appealed to Dorin. "Was that really what happened with Constantin's killer?"

Dorin had appeared conflicted before, but his cheeks got even whiter as he confirmed, "Yes, Antanasia. That was determined to be the law."

"It is true," one of the others—Horatiu?—agreed.

I took a second to try to think, but I couldn't. I just couldn't.

"Well, Princess?" Flaviu again pressed for my decree. "Is the destruction of a *Vladescu* to be treated as the destruction of a *Dragomir,* now that *you* are in charge?"

There was nothing I could do. I was the world's most powerless princess. Not only had Flaviu quickly turned our own rule of law against us, but he'd brought into play thousands of years of Vladescu-Dragomir hatred. I couldn't play favorites. Not if I was going to create the truly united kingdom Lucius envisioned.

And so, even though I knew I was potentially dooming the vampire I loved, I found myself saying, "If this is the law, then Lucius will be detained in solitary confinement, with only bread and water. Just like Constantin Dragomir's killer."

I was so flustered that I never even considered whether I could have put *that* to a vote. Could have maybe convinced a few of the Elders to support Lucius's right to at least have the blood that he would need, and spare him from a fate that some said was worse than destruction.

I'd just allowed Flaviu to pressure—to *trick*—me into

making a decision that I could never undo. *I'll have even less time to find the real killer, because Lucius will need blood. I might have to call for his trial before we have evidence to exonerate him. And I won't be able to visit him and get his help.*

Frustrated, I finally said, "Meeting adjourned." And although I was supposed to leave first, I couldn't get my legs to work, so I broke protocol by telling them, "You are dismissed."

It was the most commanding thing I'd ever said to the Elders, but I was sure they all knew I'd only spoken that way because I needed to be alone so I could bury my face and cry.

Dorin made a weak attempt to stay, giving my shoulder a pat. "Antanasia . . . I am sorry."

But I shrugged off his touch. "Please. Just go."

I was still sitting with my head in my arms maybe an hour later, when I felt a much stronger hand squeeze my shoulder. The grip was so powerful and comforting that I didn't even jump, even though I hadn't heard anyone come into the room, because for a split second I thought that Lucius had somehow come back. That the whole detention thing had been a joke or mistake.

But when I turned my face to see my shoulder, I found not Lucius's gleaming wedding ring, but a swirl of ink. And just as the vampire who held me said quietly, "Antanasia . . . we should talk, yes?" I finally found the hidden symbol I'd subconsciously noticed, concealed among all his swirling tattoos. The same Cyrillic "b" I'd seen in my mother's journal, drawn next to the Romanian word *"blestemată."*

A word, and a symbol, reserved for vampires who were *damned.*

126

Chapter 46
Antanasia

LUCIUS'S STUDY WAS close to the meeting hall, and so I took Raniero there to talk.

I sat down in Lucius's chair, and when I pulled it in, I bumped the desk and his laptop's blank screen came to life, revealing that he had never logged out of his e-mail. There was a string of messages there . . . which were none of my business, even if we were married. "Do you want something?" I offered Raniero. "Are you hungry?"

"No, *grazie,*" he said, to my relief. I couldn't face failing at one more thing that day, even if it was only ordering tea. "You are very tired," he observed. "Perhaps you do not wish to talk tonight."

"I'm tired, but I'll never sleep. We might as well talk."

"It went badly today." It was a statement, not a question.

"Yeah . . . yes, it went badly," I said. "I . . ."

But Raniero held up a hand. "You do not need to tell me what happened. I listened to everything from the anteroom."

I felt my cheeks redden, but Raniero shook his head. "Do not feel bad. You did very well handling Flaviu for one who was not raised among vampires. He is very slippery, yes?"

"Yes," I agreed. "And I lost total control, and now Lucius won't have any blood."

"*Si,* that is their time-honored way of compelling the accused to confess," Raniero explained. "It is what many would call torture, but what vampires call very reasonable action."

He gave me a reassuring look. "But Lucius is strong, as you know. You must not worry. And I think there is no way that you could have avoided this for him. He wishes, above all, to follow the law. He would approve of your action."

I didn't know Raniero well, and had reasons to both trust and distrust him. But he'd been a vampire longer than I had, so I asked him, with a cold knot in my stomach, "How long can he go without drinking blood? What really happens, because I've only heard stories . . . ?"

"I wish to be honest with you," he said. "Although Lucius is strong, he will begin to grow very tired within a few days, because he is accustomed to drinking often. And before even a week passes, it is possible that he will begin to slip into what the Romanians call *luat* and the English speakers call limbo."

His answer stunned me. I'd thought Lucius would have much longer. Weeks or *months,* even. And my stomach got icier when I asked, "What, really, does that mean? *Luat?* Is it like a coma?"

"No, not a coma. Something different." Raniero met my eyes with a steady gaze. "Those vampires who come back say that it is a realm of terrible dreams, between existence and eternal darkness. There are undead who linger there forever, unable to return even after being provided blood again. And those who do come back are almost always altered. Mad, often, or on the brink of insanity." His eyes seemed to get even darker, but he continued to give me the information unvarnished. "It is the rare vampire who returns whole, unchanged."

I didn't say anything. The fire crackled in the grate, but it didn't seem to warm the room.

"You must be careful to drink enough, too, Antanasia, while apart from Lucius," Raniero reminded me. "I know that you will not wish to, but you must. Your body does not yet need the amount that Lucius's will demand, but you are a vampire now, and require blood."

I was sitting with a vampire who was *marked* as untrustworthy, but I found myself confiding, "I only ever drank once before Lucius." I remembered standing in my parents' garage and pouring blood down my throat. I'd been angry at Lucius for telling me what I now knew was true—that I wasn't ready to be a princess—and I'd picked up a cup that he'd always carried and I'd drunk it all, telling him that I *was* a vampire. "Since then, it's only been with him."

That was part of being married. Sharing only each other's blood.

"It is not wrong to drink to survive," Raniero promised. "If you are separated for more than a few days, you must drink from the blood available here, in the cellars, and not feel guilty. It does Lucius no good for you to be weak. And he would not want you to risk yourself."

I nodded. "Okay." But I would feel guilty.

"You did not doom your husband," Raniero also assured me again. "It is a cruel culture that does this—and there is a good chance that he will be freed before you need even worry, yes?"

My voice was strangled. "And if he's not?"

"Lucius is strong," Raniero repeated. "I doubt that he is afraid of specters in dreams." The mysterious vampire smiled, but it was another grim smile, very different from his happy grin at our wedding. "If he does not fear Raniero Vladescu

Lovatu when that terrible vampire holds a stake to his chest, he will not fear demons in his own imaginings."

I recalled, then, how Lucius had recently urged *me* not to fear my dreams.

"You have the power to call for his trial," Raniero noted.

"No!" I shook my head, appalled by the suggestion. "All of the evidence points to Lucius's guilt right now. They'd convict him in minutes!" *And he'd be destroyed immediately.* I couldn't even bear the thought, the responsibility, the *loss*. "I would be killing him!" I looked at Raniero like I was begging for his approval, because a part of me knew what Lucius, a fearless risk taker, might say. "Lucius *is* strong," I added, maybe trying to convince myself. "He'll fight off this limbo. I *can't* call for a trial until we have evidence to save him."

Raniero shrugged, like the decision wasn't monumental. Like life-or-death choices were nothing. He seemed to be like Lucius in that way, too. "Perhaps you are right."

I could tell, though, that he wasn't convinced. That he was thinking about what Lucius would probably do.

We got quiet then, just sizing each other up, until the fire popped loudly in the grate and I said, "I think it's time you tell me who you really are, Raniero."

He arched one eyebrow, a Vladescu mannerism. "Lucius tells you . . . ?"

"Almost nothing."

"And you wish to know . . . ?"

"Everything. Tell me everything."

Raniero nodded, and although he sat more stiffly than the surfer I knew him as, who seemed to be slipping away, somehow, I recognized the philosopher in him when he said, "Then we should begin at the beginning, yes?"

And the story he told me . . . It was more complicated and awful than I'd ever imagined, even when he'd mentioned, almost offhandedly, holding a stake to my husband's heart.

Chapter 47
Antanasia

"I AM BORN in a villa outside of Tropea, *Italia*, in sight of the Tyrrhenian Sea, to one of the world's most wealthy families of vampires," Raniero began. "I am much loved by my parents. Doted on especially by my mother, who is the sister of Valeriu Vladescu, Lucius's father."

I already knew the family connection. Although they called each other brother, Lucius and Raniero were cousins. I didn't know much else, though. "How did your mom end up in Italy?"

"My mother is not like most Vladescus," he explained. "She wishes for a more peaceful life than can be found in Romania. She is like me, and does not like *violenza*. And so at a young age, she moved to Calabria, where there are many vampires—but much sun and laughter, too. A different culture, yes? It was there that she met my father, Alrigo Lovatu, and they married."

I already had a million questions but let him talk.

"Soon after, they have a son, whom they name Raniero,

and for many years we are very happy and want for nothing. Least of all love." He looked at me again. "We are unusual for *vampiri*. We love much, as you and Lucius do."

"So what happened?"

He shifted on the couch and pressed his palms against the leather, like he was bracing himself for bad news, and I tensed, too. "When I am only eight years old, the Elders arrive on our doorstep and tell my family that it is time."

"Time for . . . ?" My heart ached for him, because I already guessed the answer.

"Me to leave my family and travel to Romania, where I will be trained as lieutenant—possible successor—to a vampire prince who was born in the same year as myself. A prince who shows much promise and is being schooled to lead the clans." He shot me a meaningful look. "And prepared to marry a princess."

"And your parents let you go?" I asked, incredulous. My birth parents had given me up, too—but to a kind family, to save me.

And the pain I saw in Raniero's eyes . . . It was a shocking contrast to the mellow, blissed-out expression he'd worn the first time I'd met him.

"My mother fought very hard," he said. "I remember her weeping, for she knew Romania. Knew the Elders. But in the end, my father agreed that it is our duty to serve the vampire world." A flash of anger crossed his face. "Perhaps my father is also ambitious and wishes to be close to the most powerful vampires on earth? For although the Lovatus are wealthier than the Vladescus, our name is not as feared and famous. Until *I* am *given away*."

132

I sucked in a surprised breath. The Lovatus were *richer* than the Vladescus? I couldn't imagine that. But of course, that wasn't the point of the story. "What happened when you got to Romania?"

"My new *uncles* begin my training." Raniero didn't try to hide the bitterness in his voice. "I am forced to fight Lucius, and beaten when I fail to live up to expectations for a warrior—even one who is a child." His gaze flicked to me again. "But you know this story."

"Yes," I said softly. "Lucius told me that he was beaten often."

Raniero nodded. "*Si.* But Lucius was raised with this from birth, and never knew soft touches. And he is stoic by nature. To be knocked down—flogged and scarred—only makes him rise stronger and more resolved to fight harder."

I was proud of my husband, yet I wanted to cry for him like I had the first time he'd admitted to being thrashed—and like I wanted to cry for Raniero now. "And you?"

He clutched the arm of the couch so his knuckles whitened. "I grow physically strong but *angry.*"

Another endless Carpathian winter storm was raging, and the wind rushed down the chimney so the fire flared, causing me to jump. Or maybe it was the look on Raniero's face.

He didn't speak for a minute, and I let him stare off into the distance. His chest rose and fell, and I thought he might even be practicing some meditative technique, trying to calm himself down. When he finally met my eyes again, he did seem less agitated—although I knew that the worst of the story was yet to come. I'd seen his stake . . .

"Raniero?" I finally prompted him, although warily.

"How did you get that tattoo on your hand? The one that is *not* a symbol for peace?"

Chapter 48
Antanasia

RANIERO LOOKED AT his hand like he'd never seen it before—or maybe *hated* it. He turned his fingers back and forth, studying them like they were his mortal enemies. Then he raised his eyes again, and I saw that he wasn't angry anymore. Just tormented—and confused.

"I do not know, entirely, what happened," he said. "There is a point where it all seemed to become madness. When the pressure became so much that it became pain."

My chest tightened. I knew what that was like. I was cracking under the pressure, too. Had dreamed so vividly that I'd *sworn* I hurt Lucius . . .

"I began to feel less able to control myself." Raniero smiled the bitterest smile I'd ever seen. "And yet, I was becoming exactly what they wish. The greatest warrior. So cunning and vicious that when I am fifteen, the Elders decide that Lucius and I have trained enough and I am useful in another way. Given a new purpose."

"A . . . purpose?"

"*Si.*" Raniero mastered his emotions and gave me a steady gaze. "I am dispatched to travel the world, finding and bringing wayward vampires to justice."

I recoiled a little, then felt bad. But I knew what he was talking about. Lucius had described those vampires to me when he'd explained how "justice" worked.

"I was sent as what you would call a bounty hunter," Raniero clarified, using the very term that had crossed my mind when Lucius had read the law books to me. "And ordered to destroy those who will not come willingly to trial."

I barely heard my next question, I was so reluctant to ask it. "How often did that happen?"

Raniero's eyes were remorseful. "You are beginning to know our race." He paused. "There are some who would say that I was not a bounty hunter but an assassin. When Lucius speaks of ending the lynch mob as the primary form of vampire justice, he speaks of me and others like me. I was that mob, but I worked so efficiently that I needed no assistance. I was a 'mob' of one."

The wind roared around the castle, and I stared at Raniero, not sure if I was horrified or relieved to know the truth about him. Probably a little of both. The vampire who now wouldn't kill a bug had taken many lives.

I knew the story wasn't quite finished, though. "Why did they take your stake away?"

He raked his hand through his hair, a gesture that also reminded me of Lucius. *Is Lucius cold in this awful storm? Does he have a fire? Or is he so deep in the castle that he doesn't even know the whole place is practically shaking in the gale?*

"It is confusing even to me, even now," Raniero said. "In the summer of my sixteenth year, I returned to Romania for the congress of vampires . . ."

I flinched at his mention of the meeting at which Lucius's and my fitness to rule would be voted on—if we got that far.

"... and of course I am unhappy to see those who have made me into something I do not wish to be. Who twist me until I do not know who or what I am." He seemed even more confused as he relived the memory. "And one evening, everything goes wrong."

"Wrong?"

"*Si.*" He answered me but was lost in thought. "One moment I am angry—but in control. And the next I begin to do things which I do not understand. Very *wrong* things . . ." He shook his head, seeming baffled. "*Finalmente,* not even knowing what I do, I *destroy* a vampire without reason." He shrugged, like the act had meant nothing—at the time. "I simply see him, take out my stake, and destroy for the thrill of doing so." He knitted his brows and frowned more deeply. "It is as if I watch the whole thing. Dream it—but it is real. An *allucinazione* that I wake to find has truly happened."

My own fingers tightened around the arms of Lucius's chair. I struggled with Romanian, but I recognized the Italian word he'd just used. *Hallucination.* I shivered like the windows rattling in the wind. Could the pressure of this place *really* drive you mad?

"I have never experienced anything like this," he said. "I was a killer before, but never without order from the Elders."

"And to destroy without provocation is the highest crime, isn't it?"

"*Si,*" Raniero confirmed. "I am fortunate that those who witnessed my act did not destroy me that night."

"So why are you still . . . ?" *Alive.*

"Lucius dispels the crowd, for though he is young, vampires already listen to his command. And at my trial, he pleads for my life and has enough power to win my reprieve from destruction." He held up his hand. "I am instead marked as *blestemată.* A vampire who will be destroyed without even promise of a trial should I commit another act of violence." He dropped his hand. "Of course, no vampire marked as such has lived long, for violence begets violence in our world, but I am grateful to Lucius for his mercy. I did not deserve it— especially from him."

I was a little confused by Lucius's compassion, too. "Yes, because you fought each other until you *bled.* How did you end up 'brothers'?"

Raniero finally smiled again, more genuinely. "You do not understand. We are forced to fight. But the Elders know that in truth, this will forge a bond between us. When we are not battling, we laugh, with bleeding mouths, about our sad fate." His smile grew warmer. "And we are rebellious together, too—especially when we are very young. We are not easily controlled, and like to make trouble for our uncles."

I managed my first small smile of the day. I could picture Lucius as a mischievous child. I was glad that he'd had a friend.

My smile quickly died. And what if Lucius *hadn't* known friendship? Would he have become like his uncles? Would my husband be missing that light in his eyes, and his willingness to sacrifice for others? Would he be cold and unable to love even *me?*

I realized then that Raniero's childhood had been stolen and spent on *my* behalf, too. And suddenly, as I grasped the bond that existed between these two very different vampires, I also understood the sacrifice that Raniero was making to come back to Romania. "You feel like you're risking everything to come here, don't you? That you might lose control again, or get sucked into the violence that's already started. That's why you live like you do, surfing and meditating on the beach."

"I follow a new path, yes." He shrugged. "But to come here is what I owe Lucius, who does not believe that I will ever lose control again. He believes that I can help you both without becoming that vampire who destroys wantonly—or destroys at all."

I studied Raniero's troubled eyes. "You don't have faith in yourself, when you're here with terrible reminders of your childhood, do you?"

He didn't say anything for a second. "I think the question, Princess, is whether *you* have trust in me. For you hold the throne now. You can dismiss me or enlist my aid as Lucius wishes, for I will admit that I understand how to find, and punish, the worst of our race."

I nodded, clearly understanding my choice. Did I trust Raniero not to snap? I'd already seen him get agitated that very night. What if his bloodlust came back and he walked up to me—or Mindy or someone else?

As the wind roared around us, an awful thought struck me. *And if he does lose control and do something terrible, I will be responsible for destroying my first vampire—or vampires. His act—and its consequences—will be on* my *hands, because I self-*

ishly wanted him to save Lucius instead of turning him loose to "follow his path."

"I have a lot to think about." I stood, so he did, too. "I need time, but I don't have that, do I? I didn't realize how quickly Luicus would get weak."

Raniero nodded. "Yes, you have choices to make, and quickly." He moved toward the door. "I will await your decision about me."

"Raniero?" I stopped him as he reached for the knob. "Mindy . . ."

"Do not worry," he reassured me. "We are very fond of each other." He smiled sadly. "Although she does not always think so!" He paused and grew wistful. "But we agree there is no future."

I noticed how he didn't say "for us." It was like he was resigned to having no future if he got caught up in a world he'd abandoned. "Okay. I just want her to be safe, you know?"

"I wish that also. She is the one person or vampire whom I cannot imagine hurting, even if I should lose all trace of sanity."

For some reason, I believed that. "Does she know about your past?"

"Very little," he admitted. "I have tried to convince myself that the old Raniero does not exist, and she does not need to know of him." Of all the things he'd told me that night, that confession seemed to make him the *most* miserable. "Of course, I was fooling myself—and worse yet, her."

"I've fooled myself, too," I told him. "And Lucius, by pretending I could handle this life. Don't feel so bad."

"I wish that you will not tell Mindy my story," he added. "There is no reason, now."

"If you're sure there's nothing between you. Because if there was, I'd have to tell her."

I could tell it pained him to say, "I am certain. There is nothing."

Then, as Raniero twisted the doorknob, he turned back one more time. "I forget to tell you the story of how I nearly destroy Lucius—at the urging of Claudiu."

I froze in place. "Yeah . . . why did that happen?"

Raniero opened the door and shrugged again. "Claudiu merely toyed with the idea of having me rise to the throne. For as the only other son of a full-blooded Vladescu—sister to Lucius's father—I am next in line to rule. But that is a story for another day, yes?"

Next in line? And Claudiu . . . ?

I was too surprised to talk, and Raniero left me with my jaw hanging open and a lot to think about, from trials to succession to the chilling revelation that I wasn't the only one to hallucinate in that castle . . . and the awful consequences suffered by the *first* vampire to see things.

Chapter 49
Lucius

RANIERO—

Of the various luxuries that I will no doubt come to miss (freedom, light . . . sustenance) as a prisoner in my own home, technology is already proving to be high on the list of things that I crave the most. (I purposely omit the companionship of my wife from this roster; words such as "crave" or even "long for" are inadequate to explain how I already feel to be forcibly separated from Antanasia. Perhaps there is no descriptor in even my substantial vocabulary?)

Weighing only those losses which I can express, I would have to say that e-mail, the Internet, and the various "apps" on my cell phone constitute my most irksome deprivations.

Time and again I find myself reaching for my Vertu Signature with the intention of trading a stock, checking the state of global affairs—and, I will admit, playing the occasional game of virtual polo. Then I catch myself, recalling that there are no "bars" behind subterranean bars, and I must resort to the only diversion available, which consists of kicking at a persistently aggressive rat who apparently believes he has squatter's rights to this dismal corner of the world. (The fight for supremacy goes on even here. Perhaps it is waged more fervently when the stakes are the only crust of bread!)

Most distressingly, I am reduced to surreptitiously "passing you a note," as if we were both at Woodrow Wilson High School. (And trust me, Raniero, you are fortunate to have missed that experience. You may have suffered the occasional concussion-inducing blow at the Vladescu estate, but at least you never endured a year of "Health Concepts" with substitute phys ed instructor "Vic" Baker. Imagine, an entire mandatory course dedicated to encouraging mature individuals to brush their teeth—while basic economics was an "elective"! When the American financial system collapses once and for all, at least the denizens will have gleaming teeth to gnash over their self-induced fate!)

And yet I will grudgingly admit that high school does hold a certain charm, in comparison to my present accommodation.

Raniero—the situation is a bad one. I've no idea how Claudiu's blood came to stain my weapon, but the unfolding plot, as I begin to piece it together, shows promise of being compelling, to say the least.

To orchestrate my destruction by employing my own insistence upon rule of law against me . . . It has a certain elegance that I would appreciate more if I hadn't just kicked a rat.

But as I reflect, sometimes "bouncing ideas" off my companion as he bounces off my foot, I also wonder at the perpetrator's wisdom in choosing me as first target of the scheme.

You and I were both schooled as hunters, Raniero, and the first lesson the predator learns is to take down the weakest prey first. Then, fed on that victim, one has strength to pursue more powerful quarry.

I do not wish to paint Antanasia as weak—although she increasingly perceives herself as such—but we both know that I am a more formidable mark, and will play this game as ruthlessly as any opponent. (At the risk of expressing hubris, more ruthlessly—and more adeptly.)

So the question becomes: Is the vampire who attempts to undermine me incredibly brave and powerful himself, or merely unwise? Or is the plot so twisted that I am missing something entirely? An end I have not yet imagined?

These are the questions we need to answer—and expeditiously, brother.

I also need you to "spread the word," quietly, that if any harm should come to Antanasia during my imprisonment, I will not only tear down these walls stone by stone, but—once freed—shatter the rule of law and destroy, with great satisfaction, anyone who arouses in me even the slightest suspicion. Indeed, if so much as one hair on my wife's head is disturbed while I cannot protect her, this kingdom will see retribution that will go down in the history books—to be read by the very few who remain standing.

Lucius

P.S. You will note that I choose to correspond with you and not Antanasia. While I am not allowed visitors, there is at present no rule governing whether I may communicate in written form. I know that you, as one skilled in subterfuge, will have no trouble exchanging letters without drawing attention to this "gray area." Further, should I begin to seem weak or even incoherent, I would only worry Antanasia and distract her from duties that she must shoulder bravely now. It is better for her not to witness as I—let us be blunt—inevitably falter, should my incarceration continue. In short, your complete discretion regarding our communication is requested.

P.P.S. If your response could include a brief update on standings within the NBA, that would be much appreciated, too.

Chapter 50
Mindy

SOMEBODY SHOOK ME awake in what seemed like the middle of the night, and I about screamed till I saw Jess sitting on my bed. Actually, I almost screamed then anyway, 'cause she really looked like heck. Like she hadn't slept all night—which I'd hardly done either, 'cause there is nothing like a blizzard on a Romanian mountain, even when you're in a stone castle.

Then I remembered everything that was going on and I felt bad for even thinking about how Jess's hair was in knots.

"What happened?" I asked, scooching up in bed. I picked up my Hello Kitty watch and saw that it was actually seven a.m., Romanian time. "How'd the meeting go?"

"It was awful," she said. "They led Lucius away, and he's being held in solitary confinement." She got a weird look on her face. "And without blood, which I didn't expect."

"Oh, gosh, Jess. I'm so sorry. Even though I don't know what that last part means."

"He . . . we . . . can't last long without blood," she told me. "We—vampires—go into something worse than a coma."

Wow, her life seemed to get more and more terrible, and I didn't even know what to say. I just made some room for her on the bed, and she climbed in like we were kids at a sleepover again.

She changed the subject anyhow. "I didn't really come here to talk about Lucius. I mainly wanted to ask you about Raniero. About what happened between you guys—and what you think of him. Really."

I guessed there was no more hiding that mess. That hot, *hot* mess. "I shoulda told you months ago," I said. "But I was embarrassed that I left your reception to make out with him." I got kinda red. "That wasn't cool."

"It's okay," she promised. It was good to see her smile, even just a teeny bit. "I know what it's like to be swept off your feet by a vampire in a tuxedo."

144

"Yeah, except Ronnie didn't always wear the tux." I picked at the folk design on my blanket. "I also shoulda told you that he kinda drifted back to Pennsylvania with me for a while." I looked over to see if she was shocked—which she was. "He crashed with a bunch of stoners who had a band in Lancaster, and we hung out—and made out—a lot."

I got sad, wonderful chills just thinking about that. It had been so disgusting and so good.

Jess's eyes were huge. "You didn't . . . He didn't ever *bite* you, right?"

"No, I'm no vampire." That came out wrong, and I gave her the world's sorriest look. "I didn't mean that like it sounded." If anything, I was mad that he never even *offered.*

But Jess was used to me sticking my foot in my mouth. "No offense taken."

"Anyhoo . . ." I shrugged. "It didn't work out."

"What happened, exactly?"

"Jeez, what *didn't* happen?" I started listing it all on my fingers. "He didn't get a job. He didn't cut his hair. And he never had any money, even though his parents are super rich."

"Yeah, I've heard that." Then she, like, put me under a *microscope.* "Did he ever seem . . . dangerous? Like, violent?"

I had a half-broken heart, but I still had to laugh. For a second. In a sad way. "Jess, the worst thing he *didn't* do was stand up for me when one of his stupid roommates accused me of stealing pizza outta the fridge, even though *I* bought it. Me and the stoner got in this big fight, and he *shoved* me, and I was like, 'Ronnie, did you see that?' And all my boyfriend did was say, in his crazy accent, 'I am sorry, Mindy Sue, but I can do nothing.' Then he walked away—and I left, too. And that was that!" I sighed. "He's a drifter just like my dad, anyway. It was never gonna work."

"Raniero really just walked away, after *you* got shoved?"

"Yup." I was so embarrassed to say that to a girl who was married to Lucius Vladescu, flattener of Frank Dormands. And I didn't get why Jess said, "Good for Raniero." She looked at me again, real close. "And you're sure he *never* seemed the least bit violent?"

"Jess, he never even offered to *bite me.*" I grabbed one of the million pillows on the bed and slammed it against my stomach. "That was *really* the worst part, to tell you the truth." I gave a big Raniero-style shrug. "I guess he just didn't wanna commit."

I wasn't sure what I said, but it was like Jess made up her mind about something, and she said, "I'm really sorry it didn't work out for you guys, but thanks for telling me everything. I need to know who's living in my castle now that Lucius isn't here to guide me."

"Oh, I *know* Raniero, Jess, and trust me—he is the world's nicest guy. A bum with no ambition, but nice."

I wanted to sit there and talk, maybe call for breakfast in bed, but all of a sudden there was a knock on the door, and the next thing I knew, somehow Jess's new friend Ylenia was there with us—at freakin' seven fifteen a.m.—and saying, in her way that was sorry but not sorry at all, "I don't mean to interrupt, but I tracked you down, Antanasia. I was afraid you forgot that we need to plan a funeral today. We were supposed to meet in Lucius's office at seven."

"Oh, gosh, I did forget." Even though she still seemed

tired, Jess hurried out of bed like *Ylenia* was the boss. "Sorry, Min," she said. "We'll talk more later. Maybe have lunch, okay?"

"Yeah, sure." But I was sizing up Jess's cousin, who looked like *she'd* slept okay.

"Hey, Jess," I said, before she and her new pal could get out the door. "If you're gonna use Lucius's office, can I use yours?"

She looked surprised but said, "Sure, I guess so."

I watched Ylenia, who was ordering Emilian around in Romanian like she was his boss, too. "Thanks. I just wanna Google some stuff."

Or some*body*.

I just hoped I could figure out how to spell that girl's name right.

Chapter 5-1
Antanasia

MY UNCLE DORIN was waiting for us outside Lucius's office, and he hung his head as Ylenia and I approached. "I'm so sorry about Lucius. I feel as if I played a role . . ."

It was irrational to be angry with him for just telling the truth—he'd had no choice, and I'd put him on the spot—but I couldn't help feeling a little upset about the way his words had helped land Lucius in such a terrible position. But of course I said, "It's okay." I unlocked the door and changed the subject. "I know Lucius has the right book here. We just have to find it."

"Yes, yes," Dorin said. "I'll start looking."

We were supposed to be searching Lucius's overstuffed bookshelves for something called *Carte de Ritual: Nașterea, Moartea, și Căsătorie,* but I went to the desk, sat down, and shook the mouse on Lucius's laptop so his e-mail came up again. There were at least six messages dated from the morning of Claudiu's death between my husband and somebody with the screen name nightsurfer3, who had to be Raniero. I couldn't imagine any other "nightsurfers" he'd know.

"I found it already." I looked up to see Ylenia tugging on a book that was almost as big as she was. I half expected her to topple backward when it tumbled into her arms, but she seemed to catch it easily and handed it to Dorin, who thudded it down on the desk, nearly smashing the laptop.

I pushed the computer aside as my uncle said, "The burial service is actually very simple, even for an Elder. Vampires are big on ceremony, but we don't overdo the whole mourning thing." He sighed. "And let's face it, for a lot of us, there's not much good to say, really. Eulogies tend to be short—and awkward."

I asked both Ylenia and Dorin, who were crowding me a little, "I suppose I'm in charge of the eulogy?"

My cousin nodded, and her curls shook. "Yes, the reigning sovereign *must* deliver the eulogy for an Elder. Lucius delivered my father's."

"Not that I don't believe Ylenia . . ." I swiveled my chair toward Dorin. "But are you *sure* I have to give the speech? There's no way out of it?"

I felt bad that Claudiu was gone, but it didn't change the fact that he'd hated me. What would I say? *"I appreciated the way he hadn't destroyed me . . . yet. He seemed content with just undermining me and Lucius."*

Talk about short and awkward.

"Well, we can check." Dorin flipped open the *Carte de Ritual.* "I suppose it's possible."

I'd seen the *Book of Ritual: Birth, Death, and Marriage* before my wedding. I hadn't understood any of the Romanian then and didn't grasp much more now. "You'll have to read it for me," I reminded them both.

"Yes, happy to do so," Dorin agreed. He ran one finger down what was apparently the proper page, translating snippets. "Let's see . . . burial rite for Elder . . . ebony coffin . . . orderly viewing of body . . . tolling bells . . ." Then he paused and knitted his brows, reading more closely—to my disappointment. "Yes, I'm afraid that the highest-ranking clan member *must* address the gathering before interment. And since Lucius will not be attending, for obvious reasons . . ."

He trailed off, and he and Ylenia shared uncomfortable glances.

My gaze darted between them. "You *both* believe he's innocent."

"Yes, yes!" Dorin nodded—too quickly. Then he added, more sincerely, "Lucius is not rash. He doesn't act in anger, and he is too ambitious to risk his—your—future on a momentary, if understandable, impulse to destroy someone who challenged his authority as Claudiu did. Lucius would follow the proper channels if he wanted to punish an insubordinate!"

It wasn't exactly the world's most complimentary defense of character—my husband wouldn't kill someone because it would wreck his career—but I knew that Dorin could only view Lucius as a ruler who was often dismissive of him.

Why can't they be friends? Lucius could use another ally, too.

"I am sure that Lucius is innocent," Ylenia said, more convincingly.

I gave her a grateful look. "Thanks." Then I turned helplessly to the book spread out before me. "Now if one of you would please keep reading . . ."

Ylenia and Dorin shared a glance again, and my uncle placed his hand on my shoulder. "Why don't you go rest for a while?" he suggested.

"You've had a difficult few days," Ylenia added. "Dorin and I can translate everything you need to know and write up a summary, in English. Maybe we'll even come up with suggestions for the eulogy."

"Yes," Dorin agreed. "We can take care of everything— and tell Flaviu anything he should know, too."

I knew I should stay with them, but I *was* exhausted. And to be honest, I didn't want to think about that eulogy . . . or deal with Flaviu. "Thanks. That'd be great."

I stood up to go, but Dorin kept his hand on my shoulder. "Do you want me to order dinner, Antanasia? I know the cook doesn't speak English."

I flushed, wishing I hadn't confided that once, hoping to surprise Lucius, I'd ended up requesting a Romanian dish appropriately called *saramură de crap*.

Lucius had laughed when he'd seen it on his plate. *"Really,*

Antanasia?" he'd teased. *"Carp in brine? You make me long for lentils! For Vladescus do* not *eat bottom feeders!"*

Just the thought of Lucius—especially Lucius laughing—ruined any appetite I might have had. "I don't really want dinner. I'm just going to lie down."

Then I left my relatives alone to do *my* work, while Emilian escorted me back to my room, walking ahead of me, although I knew the route by then. The castle, blanketed in heavy snow—and without Lucius around—seemed extra quiet, and when Emilian rounded a corner, I was suddenly keenly aware that by having him lead me places instead of following me, I'd left my back exposed. It was a creepy, vulnerable sensation, and when I looked over my shoulder a few times, I could have sworn I saw a figure following me in the shadows.

Or maybe I was just hallucinating again.

Chapter 52
Mindy

SOMEHOW, WITHOUT LUKEY on the case, I ended up without a bodyguard, and it took me forever to find Jess's office. I musta tried fifty doors and said, "Princess? Office?" to twenty girls who I figured were maids, the way they were all dusting and scurrying around.

After what seemed like an hour, I finally opened a door and saw a gigantic desk with a very sweet picture of Ned and Dara Packwood smiling at me from a gold frame. Jess's

Romanian-English dictionary was there, too, and I thought she should carry around *that* in her pocket.

Sitting down on the big chair, I turned on her MacBook, and it only took me three tries to figure out her computer password, which was, duh, *Lucius1!*

I mean, her *husband's name* and a *number?* The only part that threw me was the exclamation point, which wasn't like Jess at all. "Still not very tricky, Mrs. Vladescu," I said out loud.

A few seconds later, I could get into every one of the million programs on her pimped-out Mac, and on the Internet, where it did take me a while to spell "Ylenia Dragomir" right.

But I finally got it, and at first I thought I had to be wrong. There were hardly any results, and the only stuff I did find was about her time at boarding school. The Lanier Academy had all their old yearbooks online, and there were pictures of Yleni every year she was there. It looked to me like she tried every clique in the book—and never fit in. There she was hanging at the edge of Science All-Stars, and then at the bottom of a pile of cheerleaders, and in her junior year—I guessed before "the money ran out"—it looked like she totally gave up and just hung with the outcasts and stoners, 'cause she was only in one picture and it was a random shot of kids on the bleachers, looking bummed. The loser gallery. You could just tell half of 'em lit up the minute the photographer walked away. They all looked like Raniero's old roommates to me.

It musta sucked for her, but it wasn't what I'd hoped to find—like a picture of her *stabbing* somebody.

"Come on, Min," I told myself. "Do some research for once in your life!" And maybe I really shoulda tried harder in school, 'cause it didn't take long at all to track down a newspaper called *Splash Romania!,* which looked like the *Enquirer* for this neck of the woods, and where I found another, very different picture that I locked away in my head, knowing I'd never forget *that.*

It wasn't the way Ylenia looked, exactly. It was mainly who she was with that made me suck in my breath like I'd just got kicked.

When that photo was burned into my brain, I surfed over to Amazon, where I knew two bookworms like Jess and Lukey would have one-click shopping, and I used their credit card to buy Jess a gift that was gonna go a long way toward making her a *real* Romanian princess.

And it wasn't a new gown or tiara or scepter, like I woulda thought a few weeks ago.

What I bought her for $69.95—plus $38.00 more for the fastest international shipping—was *power.*

Chapter 53
RANIERO

LUCIUS—

I am sorry to learn that you suffer even a little from deprivation in your captivity. If I could take your place, I would do so. I would like very much to meditate with only a rat for companionship! Does it help to think upon the words of the venerable Cheng Yen? "Happiness does not come from having much, but from being attached to little."

I repeat this wisdom often in my humble shack, reminding myself that I am very happy with almost nothing. Better, for one such as me, sand running through otherwise empty fingers than blood on hands full of money, yes?

Then again, who is Raniero Lovatu to tell a prince to set aside worldly desires? Especially when I sleep so comfortably in a soft bed at your expense? (LOL!)

Of course, I am sure that you wish not for the wisdom of Chinese philosophers, but for news of your wife, whom I do watch over as I would my own life—if I prized that still.

Sleep in peace tonight, Lucius. Antanasia does not cry, even before friends, and this tells much about her, I think. She is stronger than perhaps even you believe, my brother.

You advise me, many times, on the subject of clothing, and so I will dare to offer you words for consideration, too.

I do not wish this experience upon either of you, but do you wonder if your wife will not grow to fill her role as principessa *more quickly when not shadowed by the huge oak that is Lucius Vladescu? All things become stronger in sunlight and wind, yes?*

It is something to muse upon in your hours of quiet companionship with your rat friend, no? (Do you also think of trying to coexist and not KICK, Lucius?)

Know also that I investigate, as you urge. Of course Raniero will find the true killer. (I imagine that as a collector of American sayings, you are thinking now, It takes one to know one. *And feeling reassurance! LOL, very sadly.)*

I even believe that I answer one of your questions already. There is good reason your foe chooses you as his first prey. He fears the retribution you write of, should something befall your wife first. (I am fearful, just reading your last messaggio!*) And so we solve one part of the puzzle, and quickly.*

The bigger riddle is, to what end is this plot?

And why do we "dance around" discussion of the fact that I am the most likely suspect, as your lawful successor in line for the throne?

R

Chapter 54
Antanasia

THE MORNING OF Claudiu Vladescu's funeral—and the fifth day of Lucius's incarceration—dawned in a way that reminded me of the deceased himself. The day was gray and cold and damp, with an almost moldy smell in the air, like the few people brave enough to live in the scattering of houses in the valley shadowed by our castle were burning rotten wood in their stoves.

Shoving open the heavy window, I leaned out and saw smoke curling from chimneys that were hidden by the trees, and my constant companion, fear, gripped me even harder than usual.

Lucky humans, who will do regular human things today.

Will I be able to remember the words I've memorized?

"Jess, are you ready?" I turned to find Mindy letting herself into the dressing room. "It's almost time, right?"

"Yeah . . . Yes." I reached out and hauled the window shut before we both froze. Then I turned around and smoothed my black dress, which was long, plain, and made of heavy wool, because I'd have to walk to the burial site after my eulogy. "What do you think?"

Min cocked her head. "I guess that's how you're supposed to look." Her gaze traveled to my curls. "But let's do something with your hair."

I noticed, then, that she was dragging a small wheeled carryon that I recognized from my wedding: Mindy Stankowicz's traveling salon, which was probably better equipped than most actual beauty shops. I also realized she was dressed in black, too, somehow having managed to conjure from her other suitcases an outfit suitable for a funeral. "Mindy, you don't have to come."

She came over and grabbed my shoulders, shoving me toward the chair in front of my vanity. "Of course I'm gonna support you, Jess. You woulda tutored me through Renaissance Art and Critical Thinking if you weren't so busy ruling a sort-of country, right?"

"Of course." As she grabbed my chin to steady my head, I added, "Thanks."

But Mindy was already working in her quick, efficient way. "I'm gonna give you a total Princess Grace. Pulled back very tight and serious."

"I trust you."

I thought of Raniero and the decision I hadn't made yet. *Do I trust him?* "Min?"

She yanked my curls into submission. "Yeah?"

"You said Raniero didn't even offer to make you a vampire . . ."

Her hands stopped. "Yeah?"

"Would you have really . . . done it? Become one for *him?* Like I did for Lucius?"

Her fingers dug harder into my hair. "I don't know. I really don't." She shrugged and started working again. "Not that it matters now. He's over the whole thing."

I could barely move, she had my head trapped so tightly, but I managed to see her face, and I realized with a jolt . . . *She loves him.*

Mindy Stankowicz clearly didn't want to, but she loved a guy she thought was an aimless hippie just like her loser dad but who was actually the world's greatest vampire assassin and second in line for my husband's throne—a fact that had kept me awake for the last several nights.

Does Raniero secretly want to be king? Is the vow-of-poverty peacenik thing all a ruse? Do the proclamations of brotherhood hide a treacherous heart? He's damned, for crying out loud, and has killed without provocation. . . .

I needed to decide what, exactly, I believed about Mindy's ex. And in the meantime, I had to convince her to keep him that way. *Ex.* "Well, it really is a good thing you two broke up, right?"

"Yeah. Definitely." She didn't sound sure, though.

All at once, her hands moved even more swiftly, and a few seconds later she turned me fully to the mirror, and I saw that my hair looked suitably severe for a funeral. But my face was haggard, and my eyes were exhausted and haunted and . . . lonely. I needed Lucius. Needed *blood* but couldn't bring myself to drink it.

How weak is Lucius now? Raniero predicted that he would begin slipping toward luat *before a week passed, and it's been five days since he drank.*

Lucius was definitely strong, but I knew my husband, and he had a huge appetite for . . . me. I reached up and touched my throat where his teeth sank in. It always seemed like he held back, never taking as much as he really wanted. And in Pennsylvania, he'd rarely been without a huge cup, even in school. Might his body—and mind—already be shutting down?

Mindy must've thought I was frowning at my appearance, because she said, "You look great. Seriously."

"My *hair* looks great, thanks to you. But *I* look scared and tired. And this day is so important." I turned to face her. "It's not just about burying Claudiu. I need to prove to everybody that I'm ready to lead, because a lot of the nobles who will eventually vote on my fitness to be queen will be there. I need to do this right for Lucius."

I couldn't even let myself consider that we might not get to that vote.

"Hey, Jess!" Min grabbed my shoulders and shook them. "You're the girl who led the Woodrow Wilson math geeks to regional semifinals—and remember the year that cow you raised, Stinky, went all the way to the state farm show?"

"His name was Sammie," I corrected her. "You just called him Stinky."

All at once the total absurdity of our conversation—not to mention how pathetic my "accomplishments" were— seemed to strike us both, and all my stress came bursting out in a wave of hysterical laughter that swept up Mindy, too.

We both cracked up until I cried. Then I cried until I *really* cried, and Min hugged me, promising, "It's gonna be okay, Jess. Lucius is gonna be okay. And you're gonna do this today. You *will*."

It wasn't even a matter of doing a great job, I realized. We probably both knew that just getting through the funeral would be a victory. "I hope so."

Min was just letting me go when somebody knocked on the door, and I pulled myself together enough to call, "Come in."

Of course, it would be Dorin and Ylenia, coming to make sure I got to the funeral okay. But after I wiped my eyes again, I saw that my uncle was carrying something in his arms, cradling it like a baby. Feeling even more sick at heart, not wanting to laugh at all anymore, I looked up at Min and, even though I wanted her to stay, told her, "I think you better go now." Because although she was in love with a vampire and had seen me shed and drink blood at my wedding, I didn't want her to see me drink it like *this*.

Chapter 55
Antanasia

"I DON'T KNOW . . . Maybe I should wait until after the funeral."

But Dorin was already pouring thick, almost black liquid into a small silver cup that reminded me of one I'd held under my opened wrist before my wedding so Lucius could drink my blood at the ceremony. I wished they'd brought a different glass. "No, no, Antanasia," he protested in his mild way. But his hand shook as he poured, like he wasn't certain this was right, either. "I don't think it's wise to wait. You need strength for this day." As if I would care, he added, "And this is a wonderful vintage from the cellars. Many would love to taste this!"

I needed blood, but I looked at the cup with aversion. "It's not about the taste."

Ylenia stepped forward then and said to Dorin, "Give us a moment, please? Will you?"

"Yes, of course." My uncle seemed happy to recede into a corner. "Take your time."

Ylenia stepped closer and spoke too quietly for Dorin to hear. "He doesn't understand what you're feeling, because I don't think he's ever been in love."

I kept staring at the cup, filled with a *stranger's* blood. "No, he doesn't understand."

"But he's right about your needing to do this." She rested her hand on my arm. "Don't feel bad, Antanasia. It's not wrong, if Lucius isn't here. You have to do it."

I looked into her eyes—the same shade as mine—and saw not only sympathy but genuine understanding, and I suddenly remembered that question Mindy had raised.

Who bit Ylenia?

Why didn't she have a partner? Because if she was fully a vampire, her fangs released to grow and change by the bite of a male, that moment was as close to sacred as vampires got. My wedding had been a public recognition of Lucius's and my commitment, but our private moment had been even more important. Lucius had told me, before he'd plunged his fangs into my throat, *"This is eternity, for us."*

From that moment on, I was supposed to drink only from him, and he from me.

"It's okay," Ylenia promised again. "You have to drink like this, if you're alone. Lucius will understand. He'd tell you to do this."

The understanding in her eyes gave me the courage to reach for the cup. "I know. I know you're right."

Then she stepped back, too, and I lifted the cup quickly, because I was afraid if I hesitated, I wouldn't be able to do it. And the blood tasted so bitter and sour that I gagged when it touched my lips. I'd heard vampires talk about incredible vintages they'd sampled, and I knew that Dorin had probably picked from the best of the Vladescus' fabled cellars for me, but my shoulders heaved as the blood passed over my tongue. It wasn't just the taste that choked me, or the idea of drinking blood in general, because I did that all the time. It was the feeling that I was breaking my vows, no matter what Raniero or Ylenia or Dorin said.

I'm betraying Lucius . . . again. Betraying him . . .

"Just swallow it," Ylenia whispered, touching my shoulder. "Gulp it down if you have to. It's okay."

I nodded and put the cup against my lips again and did what she told me. I drank quickly, draining the cup, then slammed it down on my vanity and wiped my hand across my mouth. My fingers shook, and I saw the blood on them.

"Get a damp cloth, Dorin," Ylenia directed. "Now."

"Yes, yes," Dorin said. A moment later he was wiping my hands clean, and they both seemed to understand that I didn't want to talk anymore.

We walked to the funeral chamber together and my body did feel stronger, but I couldn't stop thinking that I should have waited until after the burial—trusted my own instincts over my relatives' well-meaning urging—because my head was a mess going into my first appearance before a large gathering of my subjects.

Chapter 56
Mindy

FOR A GUY everybody seemed to hate, Claudio Vladescu drew a pretty big crowd. I was at the tail end of a line of at least a hundred vampires, everybody wearing black and shuffling toward the casket to look at him, like the world's saddest parade.

I turned to check out the guy behind me.

Well, to be honest, nobody looked that sad. Maybe just a little bummed to be stuck spending Saturday with a corpse in a huge, creepy room. The funeral hall was like a church, with a high, pointed ceiling, but there were no statues or anything. Just a bunch of wooden chairs lined up against the walls, and a stone table in the middle of the room, where the casket was, and a little stone platform where I guessed Jess would stand up and talk. There weren't even any windows, so it almost felt like we were *all* getting buried.

I couldn't believe Jess was really gonna take charge of all this.

"Ahem."

The vampire behind me cleared his throat, and I saw that the line had moved ahead without me. I took a step forward, and a second later it was my turn to see Claude. I peeked inside the box, and it wasn't as gross as I expected. He looked pretty much like he'd looked back at Jess's wedding. Pale, and old, and scary. He was all wound up in a black cloth, like a dirty caterpillar that would never turn into anything good.

"Ahem."

I shot the vampire behind me a look and said, "Okay, I'm moving!" Then I went to find an empty seat, and when I sat down I dug in my purse for my phone so I could turn the ringer off, 'cause I didn't wanna interrupt Jess's big moment. Not that anybody ever called me anymore. Jess and Ronnie had been pretty much it. And now it was down to Jess.

I was flicking the switch to mute when all of a sudden everybody around me started making noise. All those bloodsuckers started chattering like either the body had sat up or some huge rock star had stopped by to pay his respects. I got hit with a case of nerves for Jess and looked up, expecting to see Princess Antanasia Dragomir Vladescu walking through the big double doors at the end of the room.

But Jess wasn't there yet, and I got totally confused, 'cause the rock star everybody was still going nuts over, whispering like crazy . . .

It was *my* ex-boyfriend, Raniero Vladescu Lovatu.
Standing right in front of the casket, alone.
In a *suit*.

Chapter 57
Antanasia

DORIN AND YLENIA could only go with me so far before
they had to join the line to view Claudiu, so I stood alone
outside the door that I would use to enter the funeral hall.

My heart had started pounding harder with each step I'd
taken toward that chamber, and it was racing so hard by then
that I was afraid it might explode. A vampire's heart shouldn't
beat that fast. I wiped my mouth again, because I couldn't get
rid of that bitter, sour taste, either, even though my tongue
was dry as a bone.

*I'm not ready . . . I need Lucius . . . Need my mom to tell me
it's going to be okay . . .*

But that wasn't going to happen, and suddenly, from the
other side of the door, I heard the crowd get unexpectedly
loud, and I had no idea what was happening, and no time to
even wonder, because without warning—I still hadn't learned
the secret cue—the door was pulled open and I stood before
a crowd that was bigger than I'd expected.

*This is it. My first appearance as princess since my wedding,
when Lucius was with me.*

The chatter stopped dead as about two hundred vampires
stood up out of respect not for Claudiu but for *me*. I could

sense how curious some of them were—those who hadn't seen me yet in the flesh—as I looked out over a sea of black suits and pale skin, trying to take my time, gather my scattered thoughts, and find familiar faces.

Mindy, who gave me an overly enthusiastic thumbs-up.

Raniero, who stood with his back against the far wall, hands clasped but head unbowed.

And I located Ylenia, who gave me a slight, sober nod of encouragement, and my uncle Dorin, who sat with the other Elders.

I can do this—for Lucius, I told myself. *Step up on the podium, call for a minute of silence, listen for bells to toll, then speak.*

Then I saw Flaviu Vladescu, who managed to scowl and smile at the same time, like he couldn't wait to see me fail, and my mind went completely blank.

Chapter 58
Mindy

THE WHOLE WORLD of vampires was watching Jess, and that was, like, the first time it really hit me: *Holy crap. She is really, honestly a PRINCESS.*

Sure, she'd looked like a princess at her wedding, but lots of girls did. And yeah, she lived in a castle and had servants. But when those big doors opened and my best friend stood alone in a plain black dress and everybody stood up, I honestly got what it meant to be royal.

And for the first time, I had to say that I was one hundred

percent glad she was the princess and not me. I wouldn't of traded places with her for everything in that castle, including the diamonds I was pretty sure she had, even if she didn't wear 'em.

I also kept looking at Raniero, who was standing against a wall in his suit looking hotter than ever, with his hands folded and his chin held high, like he didn't notice that there were still vampires sneaking looks at him, too. And while I finally got who Jess really was now, I kept thinking, *Who the heck do they all think* Raniero *is?* 'Cause I hadn't understood the whispers, but I knew the sound of freaked-out vampires when I heard them. They sounded exactly like freaked-out people.

Ronnie bowed his head, but I saw his eyes moving back and forth like he was hunting for somebody in that crowd, and I started to think about that picture on the Internet, and for the first time since I kissed him, I also wondered, *Am I sure I* know who he is?

Then I looked back at Jess and started to sweat, 'cause it was very clear that she was freaking out, too.

Chapter 59
Antanasia

SOMEHOW I MANAGED to step up to the podium in a silence that was worthy of the mausoleum it felt like we were already in.

And somehow I remembered to call for one minute of silence, using the words that I'd memorized in Romanian. *"Vom respecta acum tacere la marca Claudiu Vladescu trecerea intr-un teren de curcubeu."*

Immediately I heard rumblings, like my pronunciation had been way off, and when I looked to Dorin, his eyes were wide with surprise. And Ylenia had grabbed the arm of the vampire next to her, like I'd shocked her, too.

Hadn't I said the right words? But I'd memorized the script they'd provided. *We will now observe silence to mark Claudiu Vladescu's passage into* eternal *silence.* I was *sure* I'd said it right, but when I looked around, it was clear that something had gone wrong. Some vampires were obviously struggling not to *laugh.* Flaviu was among them, his pale hand pressed against his mouth and his shoulders shaking—although we were there to bury his brother.

Of course Mindy seemed as baffled as me. She turned up her hands and mouthed, "I don't know."

I wanted to ask *somebody* what I'd done, or better yet run out of the room, but I was all alone up there, and all I could do was bow my head and fight to remember the words that I'd speak in English, because there was no way I could have memorized an entire Romanian eulogy.

When I looked down, though—directly into Claudiu's casket—it didn't matter that my carefully memorized speech had flown from my brain. Because Claudiu wasn't in that ebony box.

Lucius was, with a huge, gaping hole in his chest.

And the last thing I remembered was me shrieking so

loudly that the sound echoed off the walls and drowned out the bells that were starting to toll out over the snow-covered valley to announce that a noble vampire was dead.

Chapter 60
Lucius

RANIERO—

Is it the weakness that I begin to suffer which causes me to succumb to foreboding and grim conjecture, or has something truly befallen Antanasia? I felt something tear through me as the bells tolled for Claudiu.

Perhaps my dark intuition is due to lack of her blood, which leaves me fatigued enough that I do begin to coexist peacefully with my rodent cellmate, who curls at the very foot which I once used to kick him. Or perhaps the bond of marriage is truly such that I feel what she feels . . .

Please, Raniero. News.

L

Chapter 61
Antanasia

"SHE'S NOT EATING enough. She's weak."

"She's exhausted from worrying about Lucius."

"What she needs is air! Give her some room already!"

The darkness that had been smothering me started to lift, and I was able to recognize the voices swirling above my head. Dorin, fussing about my diet. Ylenia, sympathizing about my separation from Lucius. And Mindy taking charge in a voice that was more commanding than any I'd used during my entire time as a princess.

"Seriously," Mindy barked as my eyelids fluttered open. "Give her some freakin' space!"

My friends were so intent on helping me that they didn't even notice I was alert, if groggy, until I pushed myself up onto my elbows and cried softly, "Lucius? How is Lucius?"

"He's fine," Mindy said as they all turned to look down at me. I sat up straighter, and she plopped down at my side, elbowing Ylenia aside in the process. "You just had a little freak-out, that's all."

"You promise . . . Lucius is okay."

"I promise." Mindy seemed confused. "Nothing happened to Lucius!"

I relaxed just a little, but my head ached and my thinking seemed clouded. "What *did* happen? I don't remember much, except seeing Lucius in a casket."

Min gave me a weird look. "Jess, it was Claude in the casket. I swear. I saw him."

The fog in my brain seemed to clear a little more, and we shared a look, and both of us knew enough not to say what we were thinking. I'd hallucinated. Again.

Then Ylenia interrupted, explaining, "You were presiding over the funeral, and you suddenly started to cry out for Lucius. Then it seems as though you . . . fainted."

Dorin nodded, confirming the story. "Yes, you . . . you

said something strange in Romanian, then you collapsed. It was terrifying!"

"Yeah, I remember now." It all came rushing back, from stepping toward the podium to the *laughter* to the moment when I'd screamed, and I cried out again, "Oh, no!"

All those vampires whose votes we would need at the congress had seen me lose it. What tiny, tiny shreds had been left of Lucius's dream of coronation were gone, incinerated by me.

Lucius was in prison, but I'd never doubted that if—*when* he was released, he would still have the full faith of the relatives who had watched him grow into his role as a prince. They would still want him as a king. But me . . . They would *never* want me now, and we were a package deal.

"What did I say that made them laugh?" I asked Dorin and Ylenia. Not that it mattered at that point. "I memorized the script."

"You didn't say what *we* wrote," Ylenia gently corrected me. "You committed Claudiu to a 'land of rainbows,' instead of 'eternal silence.' Obviously we didn't write that for you."

"*'Rainbows'?*" I got even more confused. "But I don't even *know* that word in Romanian."

"Who knows what you've heard and stored in your subconscious?" Dorin leaned over me and fussed with my pillow. It seemed like he couldn't even meet my eyes, like I'd humiliated him, too. "Who knows?"

I also noticed that Mindy was watching my relatives with the same expression Lucius often did. One of skepticism bordering on dislike. But my mistake hadn't been their fault.

"Who finished the funeral?" I asked, my gaze darting among the three of them. "How did I get here?"

"Flaviu stepped forward, as was right," Dorin explained. "He *is* Claudiu's successor."

"Flaviu . . ." I rubbed my head where I must have bumped it. *He has to be behind whatever is happening to Lucius—and me. And I don't have the power to fight him. I just don't.*

"How did I get here?" I asked again. "Did somebody *carry* me?"

As if they were puppets connected by the same string, my three protectors turned to the far corner of my bedroom, and I jerked upright as a tall, imposing vampire who I hadn't even realized was with us stepped out of the shadows and announced, "I wish for everyone to leave now. For I want to speak with Antanasia. Alone."

Chapter 62
Antanasia

WHEN EVERYBODY ELSE left, Raniero stood next to my bed, and I saw before me a vampire who really was caught between two worlds. One who looked like *he* was in limbo.

The suit was gone, but so was the taco monster, replaced by a familiar, *expensive* T-shirt. He wore a nice pair of Levi's, too, but his goatee was still a disaster. And his unusual gray-green eyes . . . They seemed almost too still, like the ocean gets right before a huge storm.

"You saw *Lucius* in the casket?" he asked. "You . . . hallucinate?"

I peered up at him from my nest of pillows, and it seemed like my thoughts swirled in a pattern as confusing and convoluted as his tattoos. *He's a damned, damaged peacenik assassin vegan vampire, Lucius's best friend and almost-killer, and second in line for my husband's throne, but he may be the one individual who can help us both if he doesn't go mad in the process—and I have no idea what I should tell him.*

"I'm . . . I'm too tired and confused to talk about it right now," I said, hedging. "I need to rest."

Raniero nodded, and I thought he was going to tell me that it was okay. That I should lie down for a while. I must have expected sympathy because I'd grown so used to everyone offering it as I attempted vainly to be a princess.

And so I was completely caught off guard when he said to me, not unkindly but a little sternly, "I know that this will seem to go against everything which I believe, Antanasia, but if you wish to be a ruler and save your husband—who does grow weaker—now is the time to begin fighting for everything you want, as hard as you are able. There is no more time to be a child, complaining of fatigue and confusion."

While I was still sitting there with my mouth open—*I'm doing the best I can. It's hard*—he added, "And you must decide, once and for all, if you want to ally yourself with me, for I am eager to know if I am about to fight, too. I am happy to lose my worthless existence, but I wish to do so for one who appreciates the sacrifice and is willing to fall by my side, if it comes to that."

Then Raniero drew himself up to his full height and advised me, "And if you choose to fight, I suggest, very strongly, that you begin by getting out of bed."

Suddenly, as I met his eyes, I realized that Raniero was *everything* I'd thought he was—all at once. He was a vegan and a vampire, a Buddhist and a bloodsucker, a pacifist and an assassin. But he was shedding half of those personas, and fast.

He had chosen what he would be, and unlike me, he wasn't looking back, pointlessly wishing he were still in high school when there was a vampire nation to rule and his best friend to save.

I watched Raniero walk out of the room, still speechless and wondering what, exactly, the *old* Raniero would be like when I met him in *all* of his former glory. Because that vampire who was emerging, the one who had destroyed maybe dozens of times and had once nearly staked my husband—he was my new ally.

Chapter 63
Mindy

I WAITED FOR Raniero outside Jess's bedroom, and it didn't take long before he came out. Except the guy who came through the door didn't exactly seem like Ronnie. It was something about the way he walked and the look on his face.

"Raniero?" I asked him. "Is Jess okay?"

"*Si.*" His voice sounded a little different, too. Like . . . harder.

He looked like he was gonna keep walking, so I grabbed

his sleeve and he turned around and looked down at me. Did I used to have to bend my head back so far to look up at him? Or was he, like, honestly getting *taller?* "Ronnie?" I asked again. "Are you sure?"

"*Si,* she will be fine."

We stood there for a few seconds, and I tried to figure out exactly what was different, but I couldn't put my finger on it. I also kept thinking about the way everybody had gone nuts when he'd walked into the funeral, and how Jess kept asking if he was dangerous, so I asked him a question that sounded weird even to me.

"Raniero . . . who, exactly, are you?"

He didn't answer for a long time, and I thought for a second he almost looked normal again. His shoulders kinda slouched, and his eyes got softer, and so did his voice. "Oh, Mindy Sue . . ."

I never thought I'd say it, but I was relieved to see him *not* stand up straight. "Seriously, Ronnie." I watched his face real close. Especially his beautiful eyes, that still weren't exactly like I remembered them. "Who are you?"

He was hiding something. Or, like . . . changing, somehow. But he still sounded like a philosopher—a sad philosopher—when he said, "I am becoming everything you ever wished me to be, Mindy Sue. And that vampire is no one whom you should want to know."

I was trying to figure out *that* puzzle when he walked away down the hall, seeming like he got taller again with each step he took, and suddenly I remembered the thing I really wanted to ask him, and I called after him. "Ronnie . . . You and Ylenia . . . What *happened?*"

He turned around, but he didn't say anything.

He didn't have to. It was written all over his face, just like it had been written all over Ylenia's when she'd kept looking at him standing in the corner—like she couldn't stop looking—and I grabbed my stomach, 'cause it felt like the guy who wouldn't hurt anybody—the one who had that *I am so sorry* look in his gray eyes—had just beat the crap out of me.

Chapter 64
RANIERO

LUCIUS—

I tell you again, rest easy. Your wife does have difficulty at the funeral, but she recovers. I think, in fact, she will be better than ever!

For many years, I believe that I learn nothing good in my time of violent training, but now I (with grudging heart) see the value of what gli Americani *call tough love. The sages, who tell us that no experience is wasted, are proven correct again, yes?*

As we are on the subject of violence, do you object to my borrowing an artifact from your collection of the weaponry of our ancestors? Or do you prefer that I carve a new stake?

R

I add another of the postscripts of which you are so fond. I am taking to wearing pants, as you suggest so often. I suppose that you will not be troubled if I borrow from your closet. Perhaps someday I can repay you . . . such as with my existence! (LOL, very hard!)

Chapter 65
Antanasia

I DIDN'T GET out of bed right away when Raniero left my room. In fact, I lay there for a long time staring at the ceiling while the light faded and deep shadows crept across the walls.

Raniero was too harsh with me. Nobody can imagine how hard it is to be a regular high school kid one day and the married leader of vicious vampires the next. I might honestly lose my husband . . . forever.

The rational part of me said that. The mathematician in me, who weighed and quantified the challenges I faced in a logical way.

But I wasn't really that girl anymore. I was also—had always been—the daughter of Mihaela Dragomir, a powerful queen, who'd faced her own destruction without fear, writing a final journal entry that I'd never been able to finish reading because it started with *"This is my farewell to you."* And I had been raised by another strong woman, Dara Packwood, who'd kissed me good-bye in Romania and gone on to face her own new challenges, telling me, "You can do this, Antanasia. You promised Lucius that you could, and you *will* rise to meet whatever trials come your way."

I heard Lucius's words, too, and understood them. *"Fear is the worst kind of grave, because it buries one alive."*

And last but not least, I heard Raniero telling me to get the heck out of bed.

Rise . . . I had to rise . . .

Without waiting any longer, because it was already almost midnight, I finally rolled off the mattress, changed into jeans, and went to the door. Opening it, I told Emilian, *"Ești demis,"* the same way I'd so often heard Lucius say, "You are dismissed."

I didn't say please, or thank you, and I ignored his look of surprise and uncertainty. After a minute he bowed slightly and agreed. *"Da."*

When he disappeared down the hall—with one glance back, like he really wasn't sure if he should leave—I went back inside and grabbed my coat and tucked my mother's journal into my pocket. Then I headed for the stables, saddled the mare that Lucius and I had ridden to the cemetery, and rode off into the night, ignoring the wolves that howled deep in the forest, too.

I had nothing to fear from a few wild dogs anymore. I lived day to day with much more dangerous predators in my own home. And it was time I stopped hiding from them and started *hunting*.

Chapter 66
Antanasia

THE IRON GATE to the cemetery opened easily, because its hinges had just been used at Claudiu's interment, and the trail of mourners' footprints that I'd followed from the castle continued in the snow, leading to his fresh grave. But I wasn't there to pay my respects to Lucius's uncle.

Pulling the gate shut behind me, I stared across the silent graveyard to where moonlight gleamed off that pale mausoleum I'd barely been able to look at when I'd been there with Lucius. I turned to the Vladescus' crypt, too, and it was almost invisible against the sky, black against black. I could just make out the spiked roofline, which reminded me of the wall of stakes in the *camera de miză*.

"There is nothing to fear in here."

I heard Lucius's words again, and I squared my shoulders and began to trudge toward the Vladescus' crypt. Then I stopped and headed first toward the smaller structure to finally face the vampires who'd given me the existence I'd squandered for too many weeks when I should have been savoring every moment I had with my husband. Some people—and most vampires—never experienced the love we had. I had been wrong to waste a second of that.

My boots squeaked in the snow, and the small gate that sealed the crypt squealed when I pulled it open, yanking harder than I had to. I'd half expected the entrance to be rusted shut, because I couldn't imagine anybody coming here. Not even Dorin, who would quiver in that place, imagining his own demise.

Stepping inside, I lit one of three candles that waited in sconces on the ancient walls, and while I'd expected to be sad, maybe to cry again, I found myself smiling a little, because somebody had been there not too long ago.

Lucius.

Chapter 67
Antanasia

THE NOTE WAS tucked under a small bowl of blood—dried by then—but I could see enough of my name, inked in familiar, distinctively bold handwriting, to realize that the message was for me, so I bent and picked it up, unfolding it with fingers that were stiff from the cold. The paper was brittle, too, maybe from being exposed to the icy air—or maybe because I'd waited longer than Lucius had expected to make the journey.

He'd obviously had faith that I would someday have the courage to stand in that spot with my birth parents—and with an empty place that was probably there, somewhere among the thirty or so caskets inside the walls, waiting for me.

Moving closer to the candle, I read Lucius's words:

Antanasia—I come here often and pour out a cup of blood for your parents. It is a traditional offering among vampires, to show reverence for the deceased. I present this gift in gratitude, too, and as I bow my head, I thank them, silently, for you. I wish that I could offer them more in return for the gift they have given me, but NOTHING could repay that.

L

I was still smiling with a weird mixture of genuine happiness and profound sadness as I tucked the note in my pocket and finally searched the marble walls for the names of my parents.

Mihaela Dragomir and *Ladislau Dragomir.*

And when I found them etched in simple script, I bowed my head and just let myself *feel* for a minute. I let everything wash over me, including the things I'd been struggling to avoid—all my fear and grief and homesickness—and the pride I had in my parents, too. And when I raised my face again, it was like the connection that had been growing between me and my birth mother, especially, was sealed. As I stood there, I knew, for the first time, that I *loved* them. I'd admired my parents, and been in awe of my mother, and was grateful to them for saving my life, but I hadn't quite *loved* them until that moment.

And I suddenly understood why Lucius would visit a graveyard, and what he felt when he was there.

My family is here. This is where I started and where I will likely end and where I belong.

Taking my mother's journal out of my pocket, I moved closer to the candle and finally read her final entry to me. It was surprisingly short and said only, *"It is time for me to say good-bye to you, Antanasia. I want you to know that I am ready and at peace. And if you have read this far—you are ready, too."*

I noticed that she didn't say what I'd be ready for. I was pretty sure she meant *everything*. From marrying Lucius to leading the clans to facing the fate that brought both my mother and me to that place one snowy midnight, almost nineteen years after her destruction.

Closing the journal for the last time, I tucked it into a crevice in the marble that separated my parents' caskets. That was my private offering to them. My way of saying, "I *am* ready."

Then I went out into the cemetery and closed the mauso-leum gate behind me. Standing in the snow, I hesitated again, then took one step toward the crypt whose dark, spiked face was etched with a suitably jagged word. VLADESCU. Some-thing stopped me, though, and I went instead to the shivering mare, climbed onto the saddle, and turned toward home to begin the hard work of saving Lucius.

But when I tapped the horse's sides with my heels, we both jerked to a stop—because somebody had grabbed the reins. I'd sort of known he'd been close by me all along.

Chapter 68
Mindy

I LAID THERE in my huge bed with the MacBook I'd bor-rowed from Jess's office, trying to be interested in surfing Zappos, but I couldn't even care about shoes, or the snack I'd ordered just by picking up the phone, punching buttons, and saying "ice cream" till *somebody* got what I meant.

Jess was right. It was awful in that castle. I was surrounded by great stuff, but it didn't make me hurt any less inside. I woulda gone home if she didn't need me so much—and if my mom still didn't wanna kill me.

I stuck the silver spoon in my mouth, but I hardly tasted the Häagen-Dazs, 'cause how could I care about eating—even chocolate ice cream?

Just from that look on Ronnie's face, and the way he *hadn't* said anything, I was pretty sure he had bit Ylenia Dragomir.

That he'd done something with her that he wouldn't even *offer* to do with me.

I knew I should hate him. But I didn't.

I *loved* that stupid, no-ambition Italian vampire. I couldn't *stop* loving him.

It was HER I hated. There was something wrong about her, from her dweeby glasses to her dumpy shoes, and she'd *done* something to him. I knew it.

With a big frustrated sigh, I shoved aside the laptop and picked up *Cosmo,* 'cause there was nothing I could do that night—not for me or Jess or Ronnie or Lucius—except maybe check our horoscopes to see if there was any good news for *anybody* in the future.

But before I got to the stars, the big feature in "Secrets & Advice" just about stopped me cold. I'd totally forgot that article was in there, but when I saw it then, I read it like there was gonna be a test on every word. It was probably the fastest I ever read anything, and when I was done, I slammed the magazine shut and said the title out loud.

"Keep Your Friends Close, and Your FRENEMIES Closer."

I would remember that. And I knew I'd never forget the last few lines, either—even though I didn't even try to memorize 'em.

"Who knows? Keeping your frenemy close might just win you an honest-to-goodness new friend. Maybe she's not as bad as you thought. And if she is a backstabber, at least you'll probably learn all of her secrets!"

I ate another big bite of ice cream, thinking *Cosmo* always gave good advice.

It sucked, and I hated doing it, but I grabbed the Mac

again and called up Jess's e-mail, where of course there were messages to her new BFF, Ylenia—who it seemed to me should *not* be using the screen name Dragomir1. She was, like, number two—at best.

And even though I had to grit my teeth to get through it, I typed, *"Hey Ylenia it's Mindy using Jess's e-mail. I am getting bored cuz Jess is busy, duh, and she says your the world's best romanian tour guide so how about hanging out? Your friend too—Min."*

I knew it was the right thing to do—I had to know if I was just jealous or if Ylenia really was a bloodsucker-slash-*backstabber*—but I still about puked up all the pricey Dutch chocolate inside me when I hit send.

Chapter 69
Antanasia

"I WAS GOING to come looking for you," I told Raniero, who held the reins while I dismounted. "But I had a feeling you were close by anyhow."

"*Si*, I have followed you." His eyes were trained on the cemetery, and he seemed edgier than me to be there. "I wait for you at the gate."

Was *Raniero* scared that his fate lay inside the stone wall? It didn't seem likely, but he was definitely uneasy. Quite a few moments passed before he tore his eyes away from the grave-yard to meet mine in the moonlight. "Why do *you* wish to find *me?*"

It was probably odd that he didn't first ask why I'd come

to a cemetery alone at midnight, but maybe he knew what I was doing. How *I* was changing. He certainly didn't seem surprised when I told him, "I want us to be partners, and if it comes down to some kind of fight, either in a courtroom or with stakes, I will stand by your side and never run away." I looked deep into his eyes, which were as complicated as Lucius's—and held even more pain. "I made vows to Lucius a few months ago, but I didn't really understand what they meant then. I promise you, though, I understand now."

The guy who was pretty sure that I was asking—ordering —him to sacrifice his existence to save my husband studied me for a long time, like he was deciding whether I might retreat back to bed at some point. Then he nodded and said, "Of course I will help you and the brother who has shown me such mercy. It is my honor."

I knew I'd finally done something right then. I had won the respect of a vampire whom I respected in turn.

But I wasn't quite as bold as Raniero yet, or as bold as Lucius might have been, because when Raniero prompted, "The trial date . . . Do you think of setting it?" I answered quickly, "No. Not yet. There's still no evidence to save him." I kept meeting his eyes, though, so he would see that I wasn't cowering anymore—even if I wasn't gambling everything, either. "But I will find some."

I was pretty sure Raniero would have rolled the dice and set a date immediately, but the love he had for Lucius, however strong, couldn't come close to what I felt for my husband, and I wouldn't take that chance. Not yet. Until I had some proof of Lucius's innocence, it was better to keep risking the possibility of *luat* than to condemn him to certain, outright destruction. To know his existence would end, with no hope of ever seeing him again, touching him . . .

"No," I repeated. "I won't set the date yet."

"Of course." Raniero handed me the reins, and as we started to walk into the dark Carpathian forest, side by side, he asked, "Then how do you wish to proceed, Princess?"

"I need a map of the castle," I told him. "I can't keep getting lost in my own home."

"I can do this," he agreed. "I am good with *mappa*. Can render the estate from memory—including places perhaps you do not even know of."

I wasn't surprised to hear that. Lucius had promised me that Raniero had many hidden talents that would come in handy.

"What else do you wish?" he asked, looking down at me. The surfer really was almost gone, but somehow I was more at ease with the warrior who was emerging. I understood him— because I understood Lucius. And I made another decision, right then and there. If I was going to trust him, I had to do it fully. "I need you to teach me how to use a stake. Lucius was going to do that, before he got incarcerated."

The trees had closed over us, shutting out the moonlight, but I thought I caught a glimpse of white teeth, like Raniero was smiling in the darkness. I hoped it was a grin of approval for the way I was finally pulling myself together and not anticipation at the prospect of touching a weapon I was pretty sure he hadn't handled in two years.

Chapter 70
Lucius

R—

I rouse myself from what seems like endless slumber to ask if there is any news from aboveground since the funeral was held . . . how many days ago? Two? Three? I lose track. Is Antanasia still safe? For I begin to have terrible dreams that too often end in ways which I cannot bear to commit to paper.

I have never gone this long without drinking, and my thoughts when I am awake are preoccupied with thirsting for my wife in so many ways . . . I find that I am unable to even ponder plots and strategies and can focus only to ask, Is there to be a trial? Has a date been set?

I am sorry that I am not able to render more assistance.

L

P.S. I do force myself to clarity, and recall that I would also appreciate news of my esteemed "in-law" Dorin. I know that I should be grateful to him for returning Antanasia to my side, and yet I cannot forgive his toxic, infectious instinct for self-preservation, which I fear influences my wife too much—ironically—to her peril.

Here is one for your philosophy books, brother: is there anything more dangerous than the desire to live free of danger?

You will either LOL at my attempt at profundity—or scratch your head if I already make no sense.

Chapter 7-1
Mindy

I WAS SITTING in the dining room at breakfast, expecting to pick at a loaf of bread alone, 'cause Jess had disappeared since the disaster at the funeral. She'd sent her little servant to me the morning after the mess, with a note asking me to be patient while she was busy for a few days, sorting stuff out.

I was kinda afraid she was hiding in her room and might never come out. So I was totally surprised when the door opened and in walked Princess Antanasia—looking better than she had the whole time I'd been in Romania.

She'd done something with her hair and put on a nice pair of dark-wash jeans and a sweater that didn't make her look desperate to be a princess but was right for a teenage ruler. She didn't look like the girl who used to hang out with me in Pennsylvania, but she didn't look as crushed as before, either.

"Jeez, Jess." I dropped my half-eaten breakfast. "You look better today!"

Like usual when I opened my mouth, I said the wrong thing. But like usual, Jess didn't get all offended. "Thanks." She sat down and reached for a slice of bread. "I feel better."

I was glad to see Jess actually eating, but me . . . I still wasn't hungry. And I got sick again when the door opened one more time and Ylenia came walking in. She still looked like a pale, frizzy Jess knockoff to me, and I didn't get how Ronnie could've . . .

"Hey." Jess seemed surprised to see her cousin. "I didn't expect you, and I'm afraid I'm busy."

"That's okay," Ylenia chirped, in her fake voice. "Mindy and I are actually going to Bucharest." She made a little frown. "Unless you need me to help you with anything."

"No, I'm fine." Jess slapped a ton of butter on her bread. "You guys go have fun."

I stood up, grabbed my tote, and did my best to smile, and I hoped it came out better than it felt. I had a lot of fake stuff, from Gucci bags to Manolo Blahnik shoes, but I had never been very good at being fake myself. "Okay, we're gonna head out, then."

Jess seemed honestly glad that we were doing something together, and I tried to focus on that. At least I was making her a teeny bit happy. "See you guys later," she said.

"Yeah, later." I followed Ylenia out of the room, thinking, *Let's just get this over with.* Every time I looked at her, I saw Raniero bending over her, his teeth changing, and I wanted to scream. It had been bad enough when I only thought she was stealing my best friend.

I stopped short. *Are you just jealous, Min? Is that really why you hate her?*

The door was swinging shut behind me, but at the last sec I caught Jess saying something to one of the servants. *"Ceaiul, te rog."* It was one of the first times I'd ever heard her use Romanian—not counting whatever the heck she'd said at the funeral—and it reminded me of something, so I popped back in, digging in my bag. "Hey!" I found my Amazon gift and handed it over. "I forgot to give you this. Hope you like it!"

"Um . . . thanks." Jess seemed surprised again. I didn't

wait around for her to tear off the plastic, but I did look back real quick to see her smiling when she saw her new copy of *Fluent in Five Minutes: Romanian.*

Then I went out and found my tour guide waiting, and I made myself take her pale, cold little arm in mine like we really were friends. "Come on, Yleni," I said. "Let's go see what you have in store for us, huh?"

Chapter 72
Antanasia

I KEPT FORCING down bread and tea, knowing that I had to eat, and flipping through the workbook to the Romanian-language DVD Mindy had given me.

Good old Mindy. She always knew what I needed. And I was glad that she and Ylenia were trying to be friends. It would mean a lot to me if they could get along.

I turned another page in the book, surprised that so many words in the dialogues seemed familiar. I'd never tried to do more than pick up phrases by listening to Lucius and others speak, but when I saw the words written out, I realized that a lot of them were rooted in the Latin that my mom had drilled me on as a teenager, to prepare me for the SAT I ended up never taking because I skipped college to rule vampires.

Still, as usual, the foresight of my mothers was helping me. I *needed* to learn Romanian.

Had I maybe been not just a coward, but also a little . . . lazy?

"*Scuzaţi-mă?*"

The exact words I was reading in "Dialogue 3: Polite Phrases" were spoken behind me, and I looked up to see the servant who usually brought tea offering me something different on the silver tray.

"*Aceasta este . . . ?*" I made an effort to ask what she was giving me. "This is . . . ?"

"*De La Lordul Raniero Lovatu.*"

I was pretty sure she said, "From *Lord* Raniero." I'd heard him addressed that way at my wedding and laughed at what I'd thought was an overly formal courtesy. I wasn't laughing anymore.

As I took some papers rolled up like a scroll off the tray, I glanced down at my workbook, reminding myself of what to say. "*Vă mulţumesc.* Thank you."

The servant bowed and backed away, leaving me to push aside my plate, pull a rubber band off the papers, and unroll them. And when I saw the drawings in front of me, I realized that Raniero had told the truth. He was *very* good with maps.

He'd even remembered to include a detailed plan to something hidden in the castle. I'd forgotten it existed, but I intended to start using it that very night.

Chapter 73
Mindy

I WAS HONESTLY getting worried that maybe I didn't like Ylenia Dragomir 'cause she had a million things in common with Jess, like living in Romania and seeming to be smart and being a *vampire,* so it probably made sense that over the course of, like, two hundred years—when I was long gone—they would become the world's best friends, and Jess wouldn't even remember me. And maybe I hated Ylenia 'cause she had some kinda past with Raniero.

I really did start to think there was something wrong with *me* while we rode around Bucharest in a car that was so small I half expected clowns to jump out of the trunk every time we stopped at another boring museum or park.

That car—which apparently Dorin used to pick up Jess when she first came to Romania, which was no doubt when she started feeling *not* like a princess—sucked, but Ylenia . . . I had to admit that she seemed okay.

Until we stopped at a building that looked like the White House, if somebody squashed a giant wedding cake on the roof, and she started giving her tour-guide spiel. It was a boring building where boring stuff happened, but by the time we pulled away, I knew I'd finally seen something interesting.

I'd got a peek into the *real* Ylenia Dragomir—and I wasn't the only jealous one in that clown car.

Chapter 74
Mindy

THE ROMANIAN ATHENAEUM was not where the president of Romania lived. It was actually a big theater, and I followed Ylenia and a couple other tourists who were crazy enough to visit Bucharest in the snowy season into the main part, where all the seats were.

"This is really pretty," I said, rubbernecking around. "Like, wow."

"Yes, it is 'wow.'" Yleni was gawking, too, like she'd never seen the place either, even though I knew she had. "It's considered the most beautiful building in the city." She pointed to the ceiling. "Look at the brilliant red color, like blood, and the gold leaf. And when it's filled with the sounds of the orchestra, and the people and vampires dressed in their finest clothes . . . It's just amazing to be here on a summer night, even if you're only sitting in the least-expensive seats, watching from far back."

You could never go anywhere without a vampire bringing up blood, so that didn't seem weird to me. What seemed weird was the way she got very dreamy and sort of drifted off, so we both stood and just stared at everything—way after I was ready to go. It was a fancy, nice place, but I was getting depressed, 'cause even if I didn't wanna hate my new frenemy, I still did, and I wanted to go back to Jess's castle. I wasn't learning anything from Ylenia except communist history.

Maybe for once *Cosmo* was wrong. Maybe hanging out with a frenemy just made your head—and your heart— kinda hurt.

I was just about to tap her arm, 'cause she seemed *really* lost, when all of a sudden she pointed to some seats on the second floor—the kind of box seats where rich people sit— and said, real soft, but in a way that about made me jump out of my skin, "That is where I first saw Lucius . . . and Raniero."

Why had I ever doubted *Cosmo*?

Chapter 75
Antanasia

I STOOD IN front of the huge mirror that hung on the wall of my dressing room—but I didn't look at the pale young woman reflected there.

Instead, I reached behind the top right corner of the heavy wooden frame, searching blindly with my fingers.

Lucius had shown me the hidden door when we'd first gotten married, and he'd directed me to it more recently when he thought I might be in danger. *"You know where to go."* But I hadn't known what he meant. I'd forgotten all about that door until Raniero drew his map—and included the network of tunnels that Lucius had promised were waiting behind the walls.

"Of course we have an elaborate system for escape concealed within the stones," he'd said, guiding my hand to the latch. *"We are vampires, and we never seem to slake our thirst for deception."* I'd met his eyes in the mirror, and he'd smiled. *"Not that I would run from danger!"*

We'd only been married a few days, and everything was so perfect that even the mention of emergencies couldn't stop me from smiling. Not when we were alone, hands touching, my husband's powerful body at my back. *"And me? Do I ever run?"*

Even in our first blissful days together, Lucius had of course understood the risks we faced, and his hand around mine had stopped while he'd seriously considered his answer.

"I do not know. In theory, princesses do not flee. But if you

were ever truly in danger, I cannot imagine myself not forcing you to run to safety." He'd paused, eyes softening, and added, *"And should we ever be fortunate enough to have children, I would compel you to protect them while I remained behind. Just as our parents protected us at the expense of their own existences."*

I still felt way too young to think about babies, but Lucius always thought in terms of family, and something about hearing him mention, for the second time in our brief married life, that we might actually have children together . . .

I'd felt an intense rush of emotion for my new husband, who would be an amazing father, and I'd turned around and kissed him . . . and that must have been why I still couldn't find that latch with my fumbling fingers. We'd never finished the lesson.

"Come on," I mumbled, growing impatient and digging deeper under the wooden frame. It seemed impossible that the mirror, sized to reflect kings and queens in full regalia, would ever move. But then I found it. A little metal bump, like a button. I pressed it, and that huge mirror released from the wall so quickly that I almost yelped, because I was sure it was going to fall and crush me. It must have weighed over a hundred pounds.

But it didn't come off the wall. It just swung back a few inches on invisible hinges to reveal a black passageway. Just like Lucius—and Raniero's map—had promised.

Peeking into that dark, musty tunnel filled with dust and cobwebs, I almost changed my mind. After all, I was starting to get better control of Emilian, and I could dismiss him if I wanted to go somewhere alone.

But the new princess who was emerging inside me . . . she wasn't even sure she trusted her guard anymore. I wanted to be able to use these passages whenever I preferred to move in complete secrecy. Like I did that night.

And so with the route I'd memorized from Raniero's map in my brain and a flashlight in my hand I stepped through the looking glass. Taking a deep breath of the stale air, I turned around and pulled the mirror-door closed behind me, even though I wasn't sure the latch could be undone from the inside—or that the exit at the other end hadn't been sealed up generations ago as the rambling castle evolved. For all I knew, Raniero had never really set foot inside these passages and knew them only in legend.

Glancing over my shoulder, I considered testing whether I could return that way—then decided I wasn't going to start this journey by turning back.

I was *done* with looking back.

Chapter 76
Mindy

"RANIERO?" I KNOCKED real soft on his door, 'cause it was late by the time me and Ylenia got back from Bucharest. I couldn't wait till morning to talk to him, though. I *had* to know what had happened with my ex-boyfriend and Jess's cousin, even if it killed me.

I could still hear Ylenia talking about Lucius and Raniero,

and how she'd watch them from the cheap seats, drooling over them—and hating them at the same time.

"Every head would turn to see Lucius, with his black hair and dark eyes that seemed to know everything, and Raniero, with his olive skin and smile that made the debutantes shiver, because you knew he was so wicked. . . . They looked like they ruled not just the vampire kingdom, but the world, *and you could hear everyone whispering, 'Vladescu . . . Vladescu . . .'"*

I didn't wanna, but I'd had to ask her. *"Did you ever, like,* hang out *with them?"*

She'd given a creepy smile that said way too much about her and Lucius and Raniero—and Jess. *"Oh, no! That was before Vladescus* fell in love with *Dragomirs . . . back when even a* European, educated, noble Dragomir was just dirt under their feet!"

Oh, she'd about burned up with jealousy, to think of an American farm girl coming over and winning the prince's heart. . . .

"Raniero?" He still didn't answer, so I knocked louder, 'cause it suddenly seemed weird—even weirder than somebody describing his smile as "wicked"—that Ronnie had closed his door. He never did that. Supposedly, he didn't even have one on his beach shack. Just an old shower curtain.

I turned the knob, which rattled but didn't give. And Ronnie *never* locked anything. He practically wanted people to steal his stuff.

All of a sudden I was not just upset but really worried about him, and I dug around in my bag till I found a nail file, which I jabbed in the old lock, just like I'd seen on a million TV shows when I shoulda been studying.

For once, though, TV paid off. Or maybe the lock was just so old it was easy to pick. It looked like it was from the Revolutionary War or something.

Either way, the door opened after about five jabs, and a second later I was in the room. It was dark in there, and at first I didn't move, 'cause that room . . . It smelled like Ronnie. Like *surfer* Ronnie, who had somehow smelled like the beach even when he lived in Pennsylvania. His skin and hair always smelled like coconut and salt water and . . . sunshine. It was stupid, but the creature of the night I loved really used to smell like sunshine to me.

I knew I was acting like a stalker, but I started walking toward his bed, thinking I'd just sniff his pillow. Just for a second.

Something stopped me, though. Something on the floor that tangled up my feet, and the next thing I knew, I was sitting on my butt and trying not to yell, 'cause I got jabbed when I fell. I didn't know what the heck happened, so I started feeling around—and it was like I was sitting in a pile of *dust*.

I sniffed and smelled something different, too. Like . . . *wood*.

The floor of Ronnie's room smelled like the wood shop at Woodrow Wilson High.

I felt around a little more, and my fingers hit that sharp thing. A *bunch* of sharp things.

Tapping the floor with my hand, I tried to count 'em. *One, two, three, four, five* . . .

With a sick feeling in my stomach, I gave up and picked up just one and said out loud to nobody . . .

"Raniero Vladescu Lovatu—why the heck are you carving all these *stakes?*"

And why did somebody call you wicked?

Chapter 77
Antanasia

AS FAR AS I could tell, the tunnels did match the map that Raniero had drawn, which was reassuring. Yet it was still hard not to be uneasy as I followed the route I'd memorized deeper and deeper into the heart of what felt like a true labyrinth, straight out of mythology. I stumbled a few times on the uneven floor and tried to keep that math-oriented side of myself trained on counting small deviations from the main path.

I needed the thirteenth tiny branch to the left. That would take me where I wanted to go.

"Don't be afraid," I said out loud, when my flashlight flickered like the battery was dying. "Don't be scared."

That had to be my mantra now. I would chant it aloud if I had to.

But it was almost impossible not to be nervous as the ceiling lowered and the beam from my flashlight started to get dimmer. I must have walked a mile, and it felt like I was heading straight into the mountain.

Is that possible? No, of course not . . .

Then, just as my flashlight sputtered again and went out, plunging me into blackness, I found the thirteenth exit from the main path, and refusing to hesitate—because the way was tight as a grave, so my shoulders would brush the walls—I squeezed into the darkness. Seven steps later, I felt the very thing I *had* feared.

A dead end.

But when I put out my hand to feel in front of me, coming very close to a claustrophobic panic, I felt not stone but wood under my fingers. Damp but smooth wood.

Although I knew there was probably some hidden mechanism to release the door, I needed to get out of there, so I pushed hard—and nearly tumbled through, because it gave way without the slightest effort.

Probably because Raniero had opened it from the other side and was waiting for me—along with a box of freshly carved stakes.

Chapter 78
Antanasia

THE *CAMERA DE MIZĂ*—the room of stakes—seemed to make Raniero as uneasy as the narrow passage had made me. He paced while I lit the two candles, because he'd been waiting in the dark, and when the light flared, I saw him glance around warily . . . without coming even close to looking at his own stake, encased in glass.

He hates being here. Hates being in the presence of all these weapons and his own stake.

"This was a bad place to meet," I said. "I chose here because this is where Lucius keeps his stake, but you're upset."

"No, I am fine." But he kept pacing like a lion desperate to get out of its cage.

"We should go somewhere else," I offered. I glanced at the box of stakes, which appeared newly carved. He'd set it on the table next to Lucius's weapon, which had been returned to its usual place after his detention. "Especially since I guess we don't need Lucius's."

Raniero slowed down then and met my eyes, speaking more calmly. "I am sorry that I am agitated. I ask you to be brave—and then I act cowardly myself." He took a deep breath. "We should stay, Antanasia."

I watched his face, trying to judge whether that really was a good idea. Each time I saw him, he seemed less like the surfer I'd first met. He never slouched anymore, the blissful smile was gone, and the shorts and logo tees had disappeared. He seemed to raid Lucius's closet at will, and stood before me in one of my husband's many pairs of Levi's and a gray shirt that matched Raniero's eyes, which never seemed green anymore. But when I looked into those eyes, I didn't see anything that terrified me. I saw a vampire who was powerful and dangerous in the way that Lucius was, but not one who was about to snap. Not yet, at least.

Maybe that was why I took a risk and pushed *him* a little, like he'd pushed me. Stepping to the glass case, I said, "Raniero, before we go any further, I think you should tell me why your stake is kept here like either a precious artifact or a virus that needs to be contained. And I want to hear the story of the day you almost destroyed Lucius, too."

When I said that, and he finally looked at the case, I did see something scary flare in his eyes—but he got it under control and agreed. "You are correct, Antanasia. I suppose it is time that you know the whole truth about the vampire who stands with you—an arm's length from the weapon which nearly makes *him* the next king-to-be."

Chapter 79
Antanasia

RANIERO DIDN'T START his story right away. He spent a few moments looking down at his bloodstained stake, like he was getting used to seeing it again.

"Which is it, Raniero?" I prompted softly. "Enshrined—or contained?"

"In truth, I believe it is both," he said. "The Elders removed my stake from my possession, as is customary for those condemned as *blestemată,* but it was Lucius's decision to provide it with this special place." He traced the glass case with a finger inked with a small peace sign. "Although I have expected never to touch this again, Lucius believes that it waits for me and is different from the others—not because it has caused perhaps more destruction than any other here, but because its owner is still with us. And for a long time, Lucius believes."

He raised his face then, and I saw that familiar shadow of pain. Vladescu pain. But although his eyes were stormy, his emotions were still in check. "I think Lucius also wishes to memorialize the day when *he* comes closest to destruction."

It was hard to even hear those words, and I had to remind myself that the story had a happy ending. "What happened?"

Raniero dragged one hand through his long hair, clearly pained to relate the tale. "One day, Lucius and I were training in the dungeons . . . it was near the end of our time as partners in combat, and we fought the contest viciously, hand to hand. There was much blood, for we were growing stronger. No longer boys, but men." He smiled wryly. "I suppose we had been men for very long and did not even know it."

Knowing that the story ended with Lucius alive didn't stop my mouth from getting a little dry. "So . . . ?"

"We are given a rest," he said, slipping into present tense, this time like his memories were too vivid to be contained in the past. "And the ones who oversee our fighting—Claudiu and Flaviu—pull us aside to tell us, as always, what we do wrong." He rubbed the back of his neck, hard, and I wondered if I had made a mistake by asking for this story. But it was too late to go back. It was like he was taking his own first steps into a mausoleum or a dark tunnel, like I'd just done. Facing things Lucius believed he could handle, too.

"It is Claudiu who speaks to me," he continued. His mouth turned down and his eyes got like flint. "He tells me that Lucius is the victor that day. That he is sorry they bother to take me from my beloved home in Tropea and waste precious efforts on making me a warrior."

"That must've been awful," I sympathized. "To be told your lost childhood was pointless . . ."

"*Si,*" he agreed. "And then, when I am so angry, Claudiu whispers in my ear, '*Why do you not prove yourself now? Take down the prince, rise to the throne and make your sacrifice worthwhile?*'"

I stood stiffly, rapt and horrified.

"I did not need to be urged twice," Raniero admitted. "Lucius is still speaking with Flaviu—his back to me—and I cross the floor and grab his shoulder, and when he turns to face me, he sees the look in my eyes and grasps *immediatamente* that we are no longer playing at war."

A chill ran down my spine as Raniero's fingers clenched like he held an imaginary stake, and the look in his eyes . . . He wasn't playing in memory, either.

"I strike without hesitation, because I have one moment of advantage as Lucius grapples with the change in our contest." I saw a flash of fangs. "And my aim is good."

I took a step back, sickened—and aware that he was lost in the past. *I've pushed him too far. Made a mistake. And how close did he come . . . ?* "But?" I said loudly. I was suddenly desperate to hear the end of the story—the happy end—and to call Raniero back, too. "What happened?"

My voice did seem to reach him. He met my eyes, and I saw that he was in the present again, although his shoulders heaved like he was still in the heat of battle. "We are evenly matched enough that Lucius steps back, perhaps an inch, and it is that small move which saves his heart."

NO! I wanted to cry out. I hadn't expected that Raniero'd come *that* close to ending Lucius's existence. *How many times will my husband come close to destruction—and survive? How many chances does one vampire get?*

"Lucius lies upon the floor," Raniero added, sounding spent of his anger. His fingers unclenched, his shoulders drooped almost like they used to, and his fangs were gone. "I am above him, and I kneel down, prepared to be the victor that day. The victor for all time." He hung his head and looked at that hand he hated. "But as my fingers wrap around the stake to press it the inch deeper which will give me the throne, your husband, who is always brave, even when suffering, somehow manages to smile while his blood drains out upon the dirt, and says to me, through many gasps, 'Raniero, my brother! I would almost think you mean to destroy me, if we were not engaged to have dinner this very night. You will not make me miss a hare that I have looked forward to all day, will you?'"

Raniero raised his eyes, and I saw that he was laughing at the memory. Horrified and laughing, just like I was.

When Lucius is released, I will order sixty-five thousand euros' worth of rabbit for him, for being brave enough to joke in a way that almost certainly saved his existence, so I could meet and marry him.

"Lucius calls me brother—and smiles." Raniero kept looking at his fingers, which were trembling. "My hands begin to shake like this, and I pull the stake from his flesh and press my fingers to the wound, telling him to close his eyes. That he is safe, and I am sorry that my hand slipped." He raised his eyes to meet mine again. "But we both know that what I have done was no mistake."

I understood everything that had passed between Raniero and Lucius that day. The strange mix of anger and brotherhood and jealousy that had led to that moment. But there was something important that I didn't get. "Why wasn't Claudiu punished for inciting you to do that? He used *you* as a weapon. I don't know much about our laws, but that *must* be treason."

Raniero shrugged. "Lucius and I do not speak more of

the incident, and soon I am dispatched as an assassin, and it is not until much later that we even mention what nearly occurred—and never directly."

"I see."

But Raniero wasn't quite done confessing, and he dragged his hand through his hair again. "I think you do *not* see the most terrible part of the story, Antanasia. No one ever does, for I never confide it before."

I got chills again, because he spoke very strangely. Yet I had never trusted him more than when he showed me his eyes, full of self-recrimination, and admitted, "As I prepare to destroy your husband, there is a part of me that acts not out of child-ish anger, but from a genuine desire—a powerful hunger—to take away *everything* that he has and make it my own."

Raniero and I faced each other across his bloody stake, that confession hanging between us. *The vampire who once swore he needed nothing had really wanted EVERYTHING. Lucius's power—and his life.*

I let that sink in; then I told him, "It's getting late. Hand me a stake."

Chapter 80
Mindy

I SAT ON Ronnie's bed eating vanilla Häagen-Dazs and thinking about Jess and Raniero and Ylenia and Lucius, and the whole mess we were all in.

"Connections, Min," I told myself. My Critical Thinking

professor always said that anybody can memorize stuff, but a smart person makes *connections*. "Connect the dots."

A dead vampire in a foyer. Blood on a stake. Raniero being treated like a scary rock star—and carving weapons. The way Ylenia looked when she talked about both guys—and Jess. Not to mention that picture on the Internet, which showed Ylenia at some vampire party . . . with Ronnie. And my best friend, who was the sanest person I knew, *hallucinating* at the most important moment of her princess-ship.

"Oh, gosh." I took another bite of ice cream and slammed the container down on the nightstand, mad at myself. "I'm not smart enough to put all *that* together."

Giving up, I flopped back on the bed that smelled so much like Ronnie—and like incense, too, the kind he always burned when he meditated. The little marble thing he used to hold the incense cones was next to my ice cream, and I rolled over to look in the bowl. The ashes looked old and cold and didn't smell that much, like he hadn't blissed out in a few days.

The first time I smelled that incense, I got on his case, 'cause I'd thought he was smoking pot. But he didn't do that. That was those stupid guys he crashed with, who were always getting high with anything they could get their hands on, from cough syrup to cactuses and herbs and little bags they bought on street corners.

"Do not let it bother you," Raniero said, when the guy named Dirk had an honest-to-god bad trip and freaked out. *"To induce visions is part of many religions, many cultures, and is not for us to condemn. Live and let live, yes? This is just a place for me to sleep and be near you."*

I leaned over the mattress and checked that pile of stakes again. I guessed "live and let live" wasn't the philosophy in this castle. Not even for Ronnie, who would have some explaining to do . . . if he ever came back.

I rolled over, and even though I was scared and mad and had a broken heart, too, after a while I got sleepy, and right before I dozed off, I thought I was either gonna have amazing dreams, 'cause I could smell the beach—smell *Ronnie*—on his pillow, or I was gonna have nightmares from eating ice cream right before going to bed with a bunch of stakes all around me.

And right then, when my eyes were shutting, I finally felt the tiniest start of one connection shaping up in my brain. It was a *crazy* connection, but I was in a completely whacked-out place where vampires who quoted Gandhi carved stakes and the world's sanest girl had visions, and I kinda left it alone to glow like Raniero's incense, to see if it might just catch fire in my head.

Chapter 8-1
Antanasia

RANIERO WRAPPED HIS hand around mine, guiding my fingers like Lucius had done when he'd shown me the latch behind the dressing-room mirror. But while the warrior I loved had been offering me an escape route, the pacifist was trying to show me how to fight.

"This still doesn't feel right." I pulled out of his grasp and set down yet another stake, rejecting it. "Are you sure I shouldn't try Lucius's?"

"No." Raniero's grip had been soft, but his tone was firm. "Lucius's stake is much too big for your hand. I have carved these to fit you. They are the best of perhaps fifty I create." He lifted probably the tenth stake from the box. "Try this one."

I accepted yet another piece of sharp wood and wrapped my fingers around it, already shaking my head. "I'm sorry. It just doesn't feel right."

"Antanasia."

I raised my eyes to find Raniero frowning. "Yes?"

"Is it that the weapon feels wrong in your hand—or in your mind? Your conscience? For you cannot reject them so quickly."

I paused with the stake in my grasp. He was right. I was being squeamish again, in spite of my promises to stop cowering. "I'll try again," I said more resolutely. "And try harder."

"Good." His tone softened as he took one more stake from the box. "You must take time and understand the weapon. You grip it too tightly, and do not allow yourself to feel it against your fingers. Do not be afraid to let it rest in your palm and find its own place."

It was strange how he brought a touch of the philosopher to even that setting and lesson. I watched as he tossed the stake in his hand, allowing it to fall naturally into his palm, clenching and reclenching his fingers around it, but gently. There was a look of concentration on his face, but it was obvious that he was very familiar with the motion, too. "Here!" He found what he was looking for. "This is the way to hold this one."

"How?" I still didn't get it. The stake looked perfectly smooth, uniform all the way around. How could there be a "right" place to grasp it?

Raniero opened his palm and bent so our heads were nearly touching. "See this?" He drew his index finger down the wood, close to his thumb. "There is a slight groove and a notch."

"Yes." I saw it. A very subtle concave sweep, which ended in a slight bump that was just enough to delineate the "blade" from the "hilt." "That's for . . ."

"Keeping your fingers from slipping, yes, when the weapon meets flesh." Before I could get squeamish again—I refused to get squeamish—he added, "Here." And without seeming to move his fingers, he spun the stake so the wider part faced me and the point faced his body. It reminded me of gunslingers in the Old West who spun their weapons and then fired off six rounds with deadly accuracy. "You try it, yes?"

Feeling even more like a novice after watching that, I gingerly plucked the stake from his palm, using my thumb and forefinger.

And he snatched it right back.

My head jerked up. "What?"

Raniero held out the weapon again. "Take it like you mean it, *Princess*."

It was probably wrong for him to taunt a sovereign, but I'd asked him to teach me, and I understood what he was doing. I wasn't like Cinderella, trying to learn to hold a teacup without breaking the china. I was a *vampire* princess and needed different skills.

He held his hand out, waiting, and I nodded. "Okay." Then I pressed my palm against his and grasped the stake with my whole hand, without hesitating—with confidence—and to my surprise it slipped into place like it really was meant for my fingers.

Raniero saw the expression on my face, and for the first time since I'd joined him in that room, he smiled with genuine pleasure. "That is good. You do well." Then he seemed to catch himself, like he didn't think he should grin about anybody's proficiency with a stake. "I think that is enough for one night, yes?"

"Yes. It's getting late."

"I will return with you through the tunnels, for you are correct that we should work in secret. Surprise is an excellent weapon, too. It is good when your enemies underestimate you—and we do not yet know who are they are, yes? It is best to keep everyone complacent."

He was full of surprises and secrets, too. I knew the biggest ones by then, but I was sure he had lots of other tricks up his sleeve. He hadn't drawn that map of the passages from distant memory—and had very likely omitted something important. As we reached the door, I stopped him with a hand on the arm. "Raniero . . . you've seen Lucius, haven't you?"

He hesitated, then admitted, "I watch over him sometimes. I think it is not quite breaking his beloved law if I do nothing more than observe from the shadows as his guard sleeps—under the influence of the wine I send to him, almost every night."

I squeezed Raniero's arm, and although I was getting better at issuing orders, I heard a touch of pleading in my voice when I said, "Take me to see him, too."

Raniero's eyes got very troubled, like he was going to

object—but he *was* my subject. "Of course. You are the princess, yes?"

My heart started pumping too hard again as I followed Raniero into the tunnels, into passages he hadn't marked for me, and which grew damper and more stale, until I felt like I was suffocating. It seemed like we walked forever—like we really were headed into the heart of the mountain, or maybe to hell—before Raniero finally opened a small, secret door that had to be the lowest in the castle, and I stepped out after him, crying softly, "Lucius."

As Raniero grabbed my arm, stopping me from running to the cell where my husband lay on a wooden plank, I understood why he'd been reluctant to bring me there.

Chapter 82
Antanasia

WHEN I STOPPED pulling against Raniero, he released me and stepped back, like he was giving me a private moment with the husband I couldn't even touch, and who was breaking my heart from across a dirty dungeon.

Lucius lay on his side on the wooden cot, without even a pillow, and his left hand dragged on the floor, the way it sometimes hung off the bed when we slept together. He always seemed to be reaching for something, like he was ambitious even in dreams.

His black hair gleamed by the light of the single oil lamp that did little to illuminate his cell—because the Vladescus didn't really want electricians snooping in their dungeons—and although he'd only been incarcerated for about nine days, I thought his hair already seemed to be longer. It reminded me of how he'd physically shifted into the role of a warrior the first time I'd come to Romania. He'd worn his hair long, carelessly tied back, when he'd declared war on my family.

But he'd looked powerful then. He *still* looked powerful, but also like he was fighting for survival. A part of me had braced for the worst, but I must have secretly expected to find the indomitable Lucius Vladescu pacing and alert, maybe even joking with his guard. *Not like this . . .*

I dared to take a few steps forward, needing to see his face better, and although I didn't want to wake up the guard, who was snoring in his own hard wooden chair—next to an empty bottle—I spoke his name softly again, hearing the dismay in my voice. "Oh, Lucius . . ."

I'd seen him sleep many times. I *liked* to watch Lucius sleeping, because that was the only time I could study him without getting distracted by his ever-changing eyes—or teased for daydreaming over him.

"You find your husband handsome, don't you?" my wonderfully arrogant prince liked to joke, whenever he caught me gawking like I was Mindy in the bleachers back in high school. *"I've no idea why it took you so long to love me, as I loved you even in your worst horse-themed T-shirts!"*

I almost broke into a smile, but it died on my lips as I watched Lucius stretched out on the rigid slab. Even on our soft mattress he was a restless sleeper, but that night he didn't move.

Is he entering that place of terrible dreams that drives vampires mad? I took another step forward, thinking, *Screw rule of law. I'm going to him.*

But before I could run, Raniero stepped up behind me and took my arm again. "No, Antanasia," he quietly ordered *me.* "It is time for us to go now."

I looked up at my imposing escort and almost protested. But I knew he was right. Lucius wanted everything to happen according to law. He wouldn't want me to ruin his grand design on impulse. Wouldn't want the guard to wake up and tell Flaviu and the others, "His wife comes to see him." Which would leave them all wondering what other, bigger laws we ignored, when it suited our purposes.

I turned to Lucius again, hoping that he would move—but he didn't.

"Come." Raniero kept his hand on my arm and led us back to the tunnels, with me still looking over my shoulder at the husband I was so desperate to talk to and touch.

I kept watching him until Raniero reached past me and sealed us in the narrow black passageway that was obviously as familiar to him as the feel of a stake in his hand.

"Does he ever move?" I asked. The words caught in my throat. "Ever?"

"He does," Raniero confirmed, and the rush of relief I felt nearly made me cry out in a different way. "He still speaks, even. But you see that he is growing very weak."

We started to walk into the darkness, but after about fifty feet, I reached for Raniero and stopped him again. I felt and heard him turn around. "*Si?* Yes?"

"I'm going to summon the Elders and set a trial date," I said. "I'll do it tomorrow."

Raniero paused, then said, "It is still risky. There is still no evidence to exonerate him."

I knew that. But I also admitted to myself then that I had been selfish to play it safe. I'd known all along that Lucius would rather be destroyed outright than fade away in a cell, slipping into a netherworld that was neither death nor life. He would never want to exist by half, and would choose the crypt over a fate that diminished him or left me to care for a shell of his former self. I couldn't let *my* fears dictate *his* existence. Or my own existence anymore, for that matter.

"Then we better find some evidence," I said. "And fast."

The passage was pitch black, but even that profound darkness wasn't enough to hide the incredibly white teeth of a vampire when he smiled with approval. I knew then that Raniero had never seriously intended to discourage me from seeing Lucius. Maybe he'd even planned to take me there all along, when he judged that the time was right.

Chapter 83
Lucius

R—

Thank you for removing Antanasia before she could approach me. (You will not be surprised to know that I have been aware of your frequent presence in those shadows, too.)

It took all of my self-control not to displace the rat which now always sleeps curled at my foot, rise, and call for her to come closer so that I could see her face more clearly, touch her through the bars.

It is strange how love is a source of power—can spur the desire to fight to the death, or to fight back from something that seems like death for long enough to write a coherent note—but also of weakness. I nearly abandoned everything upon which I intend to base my kingship, not to mention my best (only?) defense, just to share a few moments with her.

And now I cannot think, except to recall her face . . .

L

I am not mistaken and dreaming, am I? She WAS there, correct?

Chapter 84
Mindy

I SLEPT THE whole night in Raniero's room. It was light when I woke up to find that he never did come back. I was sure I was alone.

Then I rolled over and saw that I was wrong.

Raniero wasn't just in the room, he was *on the bed.* Sitting right next to me and not moving a muscle. Just watching me.

I rubbed my eyes to see him better.

Well, I was kinda right. The Raniero I used to know hadn't come back.

And the guy who was sitting there, who had carved all those stakes and who was wearing Lukey's clothes—a gray tee that cost at least two hundred bucks, 'cause I could *smell* the Prada label—I shoulda asked that guy a million questions. Like, What have you done with my ex-boyfriend? Where did you lock him away inside this vampire with the cold eyes and the hot clothes? And why did Ylenia Dragomir say you were wicked?

And he probably had a million questions for me, too, like, Why are you here after you pushed me away for months? Why are you in my bed after I finally agree to leave you alone?

We probably shoulda had a talk that ended in a big fight and a flood of tears, 'cause it was like there was a time bomb sitting between us.

But this was me and Raniero, and right before that bomb blew up, I caught a little glimpse of the old Ronnie—the one that used to love me—in his awesome gray eyes, and we exploded in a different way, when he moved closer to me, and I put my hands on his face—his stupid, scruffy beard—and his mouth pressed against mine like he was starving for me, just like I was for him.

We kissed for a long, long time, and it was like we said a million different things to each other that we couldn't say in words, like *I'm sorry* and *I'm crazy about you* and *This is so wrong* and *Let's never stop* and maybe it woulda gone on forever if I hadn't changed everything by whispering in his ear the one thing I thought I'd never say, when his fangs—his incredible, sexy teeth that used to scare me—started brushing against my throat, again and again.

"Bite *me*, Raniero," I begged him. "Bite *me* and stay with *me* forever."

Chapter 85
Mindy

HE PULLED AWAY, and I was so glad that the old Raniero was still with me. The sweet one. I wasn't sure I liked the new one, even if he dressed better and took charge of things. "You know, don't you?" he said, very quiet. "You have guessed at one of the worst things which I have done. Equal almost to destruction, in my culture."

I was starting to guess that Raniero Vladescu Lovatu had done a lot of bad things in his life. Stuff I probably didn't even wanna know about. But I'd heard Ylenia talk about him and seen the way she looked at him—and he *didn't* look at her. And I'd seen that photo in the Romanian *Enquirer* with the screaming headline that was, like so much stuff in Europe, printed in two languages—*"Partidul Vampir Expus! Vampire Party Exposed!"*—and where she was *holding his hand . . .*

"Yeah, I think I know."

He stroked my cheek, and I wanted to shove him away, but I couldn't. "I am sorry," he said. "Of all the acts for which I despise myself, it is that one which causes me perhaps the most remorse."

I believed him. He looked a million miles past sorry. Which didn't make it any easier to ask, "Then why did you bite her?" I sounded pretty bleak, too. Like I was gonna cry. "Why?"

Raniero rolled onto his back and stared up at the ceiling,

like he couldn't tell me to my face. I wasn't sure I wanted to look at him, either. There was a good chance I was gonna have to hate him soon.

"It happens at the congress of vampires when everything falls apart," he said. "I am such an angry vampire then. I have been on the road for many months, doing terrible things, and when I return to Romania, Lucius is the only vampire who greets me with warmth. My own parents, who give me away years before, look at their child, the *assassin,* with something like fear in their eyes. I am no longer even a bitter but powerful son of wealth and privilege. I am a *pariah* who has lost everything but one friend, whom he does not deserve."

There was so much wrong with what he was saying. Like . . . he was an *assassin?* I needed him to explain that, and hoped he was using English wrong, like he did all the time. But I didn't ask questions yet. I wanted to hear the rest of the story first. The part that might kill *me.*

"I am alone at the biggest party, watching the uncles whom I despise smiling and plotting their evil for the coming year, and from the darkness, Ylenia approaches me. I know her right away as a Dragomir, and I am pleased in two ways. A small, sad part of me is happy that someone other than Lucius even speaks to me, for most avoid the vampire who may one day destroy them." He finally turned his head to look at me. "And I know that it will horrify my uncles to see me with a Dragomir girl, for I have been raised to loathe all Dragomirs."

When I saw his sad eyes, I couldn't hate him. Not yet. "Yeah? And . . . ?"

"We talk, and she suggests that we share something to

drink." He added, real quick, "Only to share blood in the way many young vampires do. Drinking from the stores in the cellars. And she is very sweet. Seems to understand that I am not happy and offers to find something for us, too, although the estate is my home." His jaw twitched, which I'd never seen before. "Or, it was where I lived once. Never a home."

That little flame in my brain flickered again. "So *Ylenia* got some . . . blood and you drank it?"

"*Si,* and we walk to speak privately." He must of known better than to say much more, sparing me the gory details—maybe 'cause he'd asked me to take a walk like that once, too. Either way, he skipped to, "I did not intend to drink from her, Mindy Sue. Never. But she urges me, again and again, and it is like everything changes, and I lose restraint. . . ."

He sat up and buried his face in his hands, and I sat up, too, so I could hear when he said, very fast, like he had to get it out, "All of the anger inside of me rushes out, and I am sinking my teeth into her, and the strangeness I already feel . . . it becomes *molto peggio*—much worse."

"Ronnie?" I kinda choked on the words. "Did you ever—ever—think seriously about being with her, forever? 'Cause that's what's supposed to happen, right, if you bite a girl?"

He kept his head down. "I do not have a chance to consider that. For that very night, soon after I taste her blood, I destroy a vampire for no reason, and I am marked for destruction on my hand—a mark which no one has carried long. There is no chance to even speak with her again—and there could be no future for her with a doomed vampire, regardless. It is a mistake best forgotten."

He had lost me with half of that, but I was pretty sure I'd

heard the worst of his "wickedness" spilling out of him in one gushing, messy rush. He'd bit Ylenia, like I'd thought, and done a bunch of other awful stuff, too. Stuff *nobody* could forgive.

"Show me the mark," I said, real soft. I took his hand with all the tattoos and he lifted up his head, and I saw that he had been *crying*. Just a little. Just, like, one tear down his face.

All I'd ever wanted was a tough guy, but I never loved him so much as I loved him when he cried. Even though I hated him, too. I *had* to hate him, not for biting Ylenia, but for keeping so much stuff from me. Like the fact that he was a killer and it sounded like, *doomed.*

"It is the Cyrillic 'b.'" He traced it with a blank finger. "It tells other *vampiri* that I am dangerous and will be destroyed if I commit another act of violence. And that is why I cannot fight, even for you, because I fear that I will lose control again and cost even more lives."

I found the mark and kept holding his hand and leaning against him, feeling his hard body that was so soft and busted up inside.

That's why he didn't wanna come here. And why he shouldn't *be carving stakes. But he came for me and Lucius and Jess . . .*

"I have kept so much from you, Mindy Sue." He sounded sorry for that, too. "I try to make myself believe that the old Raniero does not exist and you do not need to know him, but I have lied to us both. Buried the lie in philosophy, even, which says that only the present matters."

Even though I believed him, we both knew he'd kept way too much from me, so I didn't even say anything. We just leaned against each other and held hands, and I tried to keep myself from crying by blowing on that little flame that was lighting up in my brain. That little connection.

Ylenia Dragomir, super jealous one-time member of the stoner-loser clique at a boarding school. Jess, freaking out. Raniero, being extra "wicked" . . .

I didn't know anything for sure, but I squeezed his hand and asked, with the tiniest bit of hope for his future, even if his past was awful and our present was done, "What if that really wicked Raniero never actually existed? What if somebody, like, *created* him?"

Chapter 86
Mindy

"MELINDA SUE, I do not think that Ylenia Dragomir poses any kind of threat to Antanasia or anyone else," Raniero said. He got up out of bed and started pulling on the gray tee that had come off while we were kissing, so he started to look like the new Raniero again. His head popped through, then the arms I could still almost feel around me—and wouldn't again. "She is timid by nature, and sweet."

"She was brassy enough to come up to an *assassin* at a party," I reminded him.

"She felt sorry for me, Mindy Sue. And she was afraid of me, but her pity overcame fear. I remember how she approaches me, as if she is a nervous bird approaching a wounded lion!"

I didn't know why a bird would ever approach a lion,

wounded or not. "And then she begged you to make her a full-fledged vampire. That's pretty gutsy!"

It still hurt so much to say that, and to picture Jess's cousin with the guy who was sitting down on the bed again to put on Lucius's cool Euro sneakers, which had come off, too. He shoulda been mine, but never would now. That was both my fault *and* his.

"It was a strange evening, Melinda, and I believe that she was hurting, too." He tugged hard on the laces. "She is like me, that night. Alone. I think she has always been a lonely girl. I see her at the Athenaeum, and always she watches Lucius and me from her seat far in the back—and always she is alone."

My eyes got wide. "You remember her? 'Cause she sure remembers you being there."

Ronnie just shrugged and started tying his other shoe. "I am an assassin and trained to watch a prince, Melinda Sue. I notice everyone. Especially those who watch Lucius and myself, in crowds." He sat up again. "I think you are good to wish to help Antanasia, but what we deal with here has nothing to do with an unhappy schoolgirl. It is an attempt to overthrow a government and destroy a prince." His voice got quiet. "What is happening is almost certainly the work of Flaviu Vladescu. It is just a matter of trapping him."

I crawled to the edge of the bed and sat next to him. I probably shouldn't of touched him, but I took his hand again. "Ronnie, you think like . . . royalty, and you know about plots to bring down princes. But I know hurt, jealous high school girls, and I am telling you that even if she didn't outright kill your uncle Claude, Ylenia is messed up in this somehow. And if you wanna help Jess and Lucius, you'll start taking a closer look at her."

I could tell he still didn't buy into what I was saying, but he looked me in the eye. "You honestly believe this?"

"I do. I think she's got all kinds of secrets and anger bottled up inside her little body, and if they ever spilled, they'd blow you away."

"And how do you suggest that I expose these secrets?" he asked. "For I do not think that she is likely to tell me anything. Not after what I have done to her."

I didn't wanna say it, but I had to. And me and Ronnie were done. It didn't matter what he did with another girl. "Maybe," I said. "Maybe you should just . . . get to know her better. Ask her to do something . . ."

His one eyebrow shot up. "You are saying . . . ask Ylenia Dragomir on a *date?*"

No, I didn't wanna say that. But I nodded. "Yeah. Kinda."

He shook his head, hard, and pulled his hand away. "Mindy Sue, I have already wronged her. I cannot play with her like a toy." He looked down at those stakes we weren't talking about. "Especially when I am damned. Especially when I do not believe that she has done anything worse than be lonely!"

"Look, Raniero . . ." I kinda gagged on my own words, 'cause suddenly I knew I was saying something that was completely different from my original idea—but probably true, too. "Even if you don't believe that she's scary, like I do— *especially* if you don't believe that—maybe, just to do the right thing, you oughta at least apologize and let *her* decide whether she wants anything to do with you." I couldn't look at him anymore. "Maybe, given how important what you guys did together is . . . maybe, just maybe, you owe it to each other to at least *talk*."

"Mindy Sue . . ." He seemed shocked by what I was saying.

Was it 'cause I was *really* pushing him away then? Not like when I used to break up with him, expecting him to come back, or even telling him to hang out with a girl so he could get the lowdown on her evil schemes, but honestly suggesting that if he didn't believe Ylenia was a conniving bitch, he probably owed her something. Maybe a chance to be together.

All of a sudden, it wasn't just a plan to help Jess that we were talking about.

It was eternity. *Forever.*

"You truly believe that I do the wrong thing by never bringing up this terrible evening again?" he asked. His voice was very low. "That I am wrong to keep distance between myself and Ylenia—and give her freedom from *me?*"

I kept staring at the floor. "Yeah. Probably." I felt the tears starting in my eyes, but I made myself look at him. "If you'd bit me like that, I woulda at least wanted you to try to get to know me. To give us a chance and not make it like the world's worst one-night stand."

He shook his head. "There is no 'chance.' No future. Especially not in this place."

"If you really believe she's innocent and sweet," I said again, "then you gotta give her a chance to decide that, too."

Raniero's eyes went through a million changes. I couldn't

even tell what he was thinking, but all of a sudden he seemed to make up his mind, and he said, "If this is what you believe to be right—for whatever reason is in your heart—then I will do as you ask. I will at least speak to her, and see if she has any wish to take the mistake which we already make and drag it even farther, together."

He stood up and walked to the door, kicking through the sawdust. I couldn't tell if he was mad at me, or mad at himself—or not mad at all. He just seemed . . . cold. Totally shut off.

"Where are you going?"

"*We* are going to your room," he said. "It is time that this transformation I begin reaches its conclusion. There is no turning back now."

I followed him out the door, and it was a long, long time before I realized I never asked him about those stakes on the floor, even though I almost tripped over 'em again, 'cause of the tears that were still in my eyes.

Chapter 87
Antanasia

"*VA MULTUMESC.*" I pulled the earbuds out of my ears and pushed aside my workbook and iPod, which I'd loaded with *Fluent in Five,* to make room on the vanity for the tray the servant carried. "*Vă rog. Sticla. Masa.*" I only used a few words, "please," "bottle," and "table," but I also did some pointing, so she understood and placed the blood and small silver cup where I wanted them.

"Vă mulțumesc." Lucius might not have thanked her twice, like me, but I was definitely getting better about giving direction. The servant used a tarnished pewter tool, like an ancient corkscrew, to open the bottle, but before she could pour, I dismissed her with *"Ești demis."*

Bowing silently, she left the room and I took over, pouring a liberal dose of the blood I'd ordered. I still didn't want to do this, but I needed to be strong for the meeting I'd called that afternoon. I lifted the cup, sniffing the contents. The thick liquid wasn't as pungent as the blood Dorin had brought for me, and I could smell the mix of herbs that were used, along with the tight cork, to keep it from coagulating in the bottle. But while this blood wasn't as offensive to my nose, it didn't have the heady, delicious smell of Lucius's, either, and I didn't drink right away. I was a little relieved when someone knocked on the door so I could set down the cup.

"Come in. *Intră!*"

"Antanasia, you look lovely." Dorin slipped into the room and closed the door. "Very regal!"

I stood straighter in the dark suit I'd chosen. "Thanks. I want to look like I mean business."

"You do, you do!" He frowned. "But why are you assembling the Elders? The whole estate is buzzing with curiosity." He twisted his hands. "Is there some news? Have you discovered anything about Claudiu?"

I wanted to tell my uncle everything, but Raniero's words about surprise being a weapon held me back, just like his hand had done in the dungeon. It wasn't that I needed to surprise my own uncle, but he had trouble keeping secrets. "I just think it's time to move forward," I said vaguely. "And show that I'm in charge."

"Well, I suppose that's good." Dorin crossed the room to join me and frowned again when he saw the bottle on my vanity. "But what is this?" I noticed then that he carried a bag tucked in the crook of his arm, and he opened it and pulled out a bottle of his own. One that was dark green and labeled by hand. *Franța 1977.* He bent to peer closely at the blood I'd ordered—which was also labeled, *România 1872*—then straightened and shook his head. "No, Antanasia. I have brought you something better. You don't know how to order yet. This blood will not taste good. Romanian blood from that time is legendarily bad." He started to move the cup away, but I stopped his hand, and was surprised to find that even just dealing with me, when Lucius was nowhere around, he was a little shaky.

Did he *always* tremble?

"I'll just drink this," I said. "I don't really care how it tastes. But thanks anyhow."

But Dorin went ahead and opened his bottle with a twist of his right hand, still shaking his head. "No, no . . . This is much better." As soon as he yanked out the cork, I could smell the strong, bitter, sour scent that apparently marked "good" blood, and I cringed at the thought of drinking it. Dorin seemed oblivious, and he started to reach for my cup again, like he was going to pour out my Romanian vintage. "I told you long ago, Siberian is best! Fit for a princess!"

I stopped his hand again, suddenly frustrated. If I really was a princess, why couldn't I have what I wanted? "No, Dorin. I ordered this. And I want this. If I can't have Lucius, I want blood that doesn't make me gag."

It was one of the few times I'd come close to treating Dorin like anything but an advisor—as an equal, if not a superior—and the dismayed, almost panicked look on his face didn't help me get down the mild Romanian blood I poured over my tongue. I still wanted to choke when I drank it, but I didn't feel as guilty. I wasn't betraying Lucius. I was saving him.

At least, I hoped I was, because as of that afternoon, the clock would start ticking toward his trial.

Chapter 88
Mindy

ME AND RANIERO didn't talk at all while I got ready to cut his hair.

He got the chair from the little vanity in my room, like a mini version of Jess's, plunked it down in the middle of the floor, and pulled off his shirt again, like he knew there was gonna be a lotta hair falling. Then he straddled the chair backwards and crossed his beautiful tanned arms over the back, while I shook out one of the Vladescus's thick white towels and put it around his shoulders, knowing it was probably the last time I'd ever touch them.

Then I got the kit I usually used to make Jess gorgeous, found my professional-quality scissors, and dug my hand into his thick waves.

Just do what you always wanted to do, Min. Give him the cut you always dreamed about.

"I'm gonna—"

"Do as you wish," he interrupted me. "I am certain that it will be good, for you have a talent for this. And I know that you always wish to cut my hair."

That was all we said.

I always did want him to have shorter hair, so why did it hurt so bad when I made that first cut, taking off about six inches, so his hair was above his ears? Why did it suck so bad to make him even more beautiful?

Because you're not making him beautiful, Mindy. He was beautiful to begin with.

I got this choking feeling in my throat, but I kept cutting. Taking off more and more of the brown waves that were highlighted by the sun, and it was like I was cutting away the beach that he loved. Throwing the waves and the sun right on the floor, so they were just . . . garbage. More stupid sawdust. I was carving *him* into a stake. Finishing up making him an *assassin* again. Making him somebody he didn't wanna be— for some other girl.

He sat very still, but it wasn't like he was meditating. I could tell he was all tense inside, even though I couldn't look in his eyes. I just focused on his hair and the way I was tapering it in the back to show off how strong his neck was. He wouldn't be able to hide that anymore, or make a ponytail . . .

When the basic shape was in place—a tight cut in the back, a little longer in the front, so what was left of his waves would frame those eyes I couldn't look at—I got my straight razor and made everything . . . perfect.

Perfectly *awful.*

I had never cut anybody's hair without being able to look at their face, but I didn't need to see him. He looked hotter than any model. And it was *hideous.*

"I think that's it." I stepped back and stared at the floor. "You're done!"

But he grabbed my hand, so I almost dropped the razor. "No. Not yet."

I finally looked into his eyes. His wonderful gray eyes, which were getting so hard again. Even harder than they'd been when I'd stopped him outside Jess's room and he'd pushed me away. "What else?"

"Shave my face."

"No . . ." He wasn't going to lose his goatee, too. And he could do that himself, if he really wanted to. If I shaved him, I'd have to hold his jaw and look at every inch of the face I'd never touch again, either. The one I was helping to totally ruin. "I don't wanna."

He gripped me harder, and it was the closest he ever came to hurting me—like, in a physical way. "Please. Just finish what you start."

I stared at him for about a minute and he stared back till I gave up and tugged free from his hand. "Okay."

Then I went into the bathroom and I couldn't look at my own ugly face while I got a cup of water and the little tube of shave gel I brought for my legs. When I went back into the bedroom, he was still sitting very still, and I dipped my fingers in the water and put a little bit on his cheeks, feeling the stubble. Then I squeezed some gel onto my fingers, too, and I stroked it over his whole face. His skin was so rough, and it felt so good under my fingertips. I wanted to touch him like that for hours. Throw away the stupid shaving cream and just touch him . . .

I couldn't help looking at his eyes again, to see if he felt it, too, but he had closed them. Shut himself off from me *totally.*

I grabbed my razor again. "This might hurt."

Hurt *me.* Hurt us *both.*

"I am used to pain," he said, without opening his eyes. "This will be nothing."

"Okay." I took his jaw in my hand and started to drag the razor down his cheeks, and my fingers shook so bad I was terrified I would slice him to bits. But somehow I did it. I made line after line in the lather, and before long the goatee I'd always hated was gone. He hadn't even cringed the couple times I'd tugged at the hair and left nicks on his skin.

I stepped back and looked at the floor again. "You're *totally* done."

Out of the corner of my eye, I saw him yank the towel off his shoulders, flip it to the clean side, and start wiping away the little patches of foam that were still on his face. He stood up while he did it and then pulled on Lucius's shirt.

"How do I look, Mindy Sue?"

I didn't have any choice but to finally really look at him,

head to toe. And what I saw almost made me sob. I shoulda been an Italian Renaissance artist, 'cause the vampire that stood before me was way more incredible than any statue. His body had always been perfect, but when he finally really stood in a way that showed off just how powerful he was, it made me suck in a big breath. Knocked the wind out of me. Without his scruffy beard, I could see his jaw, and even that had muscle. And his short hair showed off his cheekbones and shoulders and his eyes . . . His eyes . . .

"Oh, Raniero!" I kinda gasped in admiration—and cried at the same time.

"It is good, yes?" he asked. "You create in me the vampire of your dreams? The Raniero you always wish for?"

No, I didn't do that at all. I wanted the old Ronnie back. This new one . . . I didn't like his eyes at all. They were hard but filled with pain, and he was mad, too. "I don't know, Raniero . . ."

He knew how he looked, though. He knew that every girl in a fancy concert hall would turn and look at him again.

Had a part of him always hated me for wanting him to change? As much as I hated myself now?

"Thank you, Mindy Sue," he said, like there had never been anything between us. Like I'd totally cut that away, too.

"You're welcome." I couldn't think of anything else to say.

He tossed the towel on the floor, leaving the mess for the maids, and headed for the door, and right before he left, I had to know.

"Raniero?" I could hear the stupid tears in my voice again. "Why . . . why didn't you ever offer to bite *me?*"

"I loved you too much to bring you into this world that I

am reentering," he said. "I did not wish to force it upon you, when you were clearly uncertain how you felt for me. I wait for *you* to ask, at the time that is right for you. But of course, that time never comes, until too late."

Raniero always mixed up tenses, but I noticed he was very clear about saying "loved," not "love."

All along, he was waiting for me. But now it really is way too late.

"Thank you, Mindy Sue," he said again. "Thank you for the haircut, and for showing me that I have been wrong in my treatment of Ylenia. I have not seen from her perspective."

I couldn't say "You're welcome" again. I just let him leave, then got down on my hands and knees and started sweeping up the hair, 'cause I couldn't wait for the maids, either. I had to get that mess out of there, 'cause what had started out as a plan to catch Ylenia Dragomir doing something bad had turned into me handing over the guy I loved to a girl who already had a claim on him, forever.

That hair really did feel like sawdust in my hands.

Chapter 89
RANIERO

LUCIUS—

It is my pleasure to bend your rules farther than you intend and to look in upon you now and then—if only to see how the rat fares. And I did bring your wife, too. Do not worry. You are not seeing things . . . yet.

I know that you struggle to think clearly, but is there anything which you can recall from the night upon which I become a damned vampire? Any detail which you have not shared with me, specialmente *regarding Ylenia Dragomir?*

In the meantime, know that the trial date is to be set today. Your wife, who gains power as you weaken, has called a meeting of the Elders to make the announcement.

Stay strong, brother.

R

Chapter 90
Antanasia

THERE WAS A part of me that wished Dara Packwood could be there to hug me, like she'd done before every one of my math and 4-H competitions, but I shook that off and squared my shoulders. And as always happened, the doors opened on a cue that apparently I didn't even need to know, and I found myself facing a long table flanked by vampires who'd seen me do nothing but fail.

But that was going to change. Or if I did fail, I would go down fighting, like I'd promised Raniero.

Stepping into the room, I looked at them one by one, and as I met their shrewd, cold eyes, I was suddenly keenly aware of a mistake I'd made, ever since joining their ranks.

This small part of me had wanted them to *like* me, as if I'd transferred to a new high school instead of become their ruler. Or if I hadn't exactly wanted them to like me, I'd at least hoped they'd accept me into their clique, even as the lowest girl, kept on the margins.

As I locked eyes with Flaviu, though, and saw his disdain for me and his hunger for power, I knew that of course we would never like each other. He was a vicious vampire from a line of vicious vampires, and he was almost certainly trying to ruin, if not end, Lucius's and my lives.

A queen has few friends, my birth mother had tried to warn me in her journal. *If she has many, she is almost surely doing something wrong.*

As I continued to meet Flaviu's eyes, I also recalled how Lucius had strode through the cafeteria on one of his first days at high school. I'd felt bad when students edged away from him, but he had seemed gratified by what he perceived as deference to his superiority.

It's all about perception, I told myself. *Mine—and theirs.*

And without taking my eyes off Flaviu's, I made my first impromptu change of plans, walking not toward my usual seat at the foot of the table, but directly to Lucius's chair at the head, where—without sitting down—I announced very clearly, "I have convened you here to set Lucius's trial date—for two days from today."

My words set off a chorus of muttering—hopefully nervous on Flaviu's part. And Lucius's uncle did look a little pale. But I knew that most of those vampires were excited at the prospect of seeing a prince almost certainly get destroyed.

I took my seat then, and although I was tired of his endless fear, I looked out of habit at Uncle Dorin—and I probably shouldn't have been surprised to see that he seemed even whiter and more shocked than Flaviu.

Chapter 91
Antanasia

"ANTANASIA, ARE . . . ARE you certain you wish to do this?" Dorin sputtered. I knew he was terrified that I was risking losing the love of my life, even if *he* didn't like Lucius. "Is there some pressing reason? Has something changed?"

"I don't wish to explain anything right now," I told them all. But the comment was directed to Dorin. I didn't like speaking almost harshly to my uncle again, but in his effort to protect me, he was inadvertently undermining my authority by questioning my motives.

Of course, Flaviu smirked and undermined me on purpose, addressing all the Elders. "Nothing has changed! She acts out of fear! She knows that Lucius grows weak without blood, and she gambles on a trial to save him from the state of *luat*—although she almost certainly dooms him, anyway. Lucius's stake tells us all that we need to know!"

I rose again, just like Mihaela Dragomir would have done, and although my knees shook, my voice was completely steady. "You will not address me as if I'm not even here—unless you want to join Lucius in the dungeons. And then we'll see how long *you* last without blood, because you are two hundred years older and nowhere near as strong as my husband."

My words surprised even me—I'd gone farther than I'd expected. Flaviu was clearly taken aback, too. His eyebrows shot up, and he almost started to laugh, like I was a little kid who'd suddenly thrown a tantrum. "You are joking. You wouldn't dare."

I raised my eyebrows, too. *Wouldn't I?*

And suddenly I was so pissed at all of them that my knees started shaking with *anger,* and I knew that I had to be careful not to lose control in a new way. I wasn't about to pass out or hallucinate, but all at once I wanted to scream at them. Months of frustration and fear, everything I'd felt since my wedding, since I'd started to crumble, came close to rushing out of me.

They'd beaten Raniero until he was broken and on the brink of destruction, at least one of them was responsible for Lucius's current state, they laughed at me—and they were the worst bunch of gossiping, conniving backstabbers I'd ever met, just in general.

I might not have transferred to a new school, but it was still like I'd joined the world's oldest, grayest, least peppy cheerleading squad, and I was sick of being stuck in a castle like a prisoner myself with the whole lousy bunch of them.

"Gardă! Vin aici!" I heard myself growling in a voice I'd never used before.

I wasn't sure where the words came from, either. They weren't on my DVD, but I must have heard Lucius summon the guards often enough that when I really needed to use the phrase it just came out, and both of the vampires who were posted at the doors stepped to my sides.

I didn't look around at the Elders—I wasn't about to stop glaring at my new worst enemy—but I heard murmurs again, like everybody was more surprised by my flawless Romanian than by my announcement about the trial.

I narrowed my eyes at Flaviu. "Well? Do you want to see how long you can last without blood?"

Our stares stayed locked, and the smirk that had been on his face gradually faded, replaced by a new anger that I knew was dangerous. But Flaviu had always been dangerous. It was better to face him head-on. It *felt* better.

"Well?" I repeated.

"Continue with your meeting," he finally agreed, looking away again. "Set your trial date and save—or more likely doom—your husband."

There was still a disrespectful edge to his voice and his words, but not enough for me to make a big deal over it. I was lucky I had won a small victory, and I jerked my head to send the guards back to their places. Then I said again, "I propose that we establish the date of Lucius's trial for two days from this one, meeting in the *Sala de Justiție* at dawn."

Most everyone started nodding, and so I added, "All agreed, raise your left hand."

Dorin nearly raised his right—by accident again, or not? Then he joined the others in raising his left. I watched all of their faces carefully as I counted the votes. Was there a clue, a sign of guilt in someone's eyes? Did they look too often at Flaviu?

I wished I could have studied them more, but I could only delay for so long, so I announced the count as unanimously in favor, then said, "Meeting adjourned."

I didn't move, acting like I was setting a new protocol by letting them leave first again—but only because my knees began shaking like *crazy* and I was afraid to try to walk. Apparently, I had been pretty scared, deep inside. But I'd mastered it for as long as I'd needed to. It was a start.

As the Elders filed out, I looked to Dorin for congratulations, but he didn't meet my eyes, like he was suddenly afraid of me. He only managed to smile for a second and say, "You did well," as he left the room with the others.

When they were all gone, I slid down in the chair and exhaled with a whoosh as everything I'd just done sank in.

I might have just taken my first tiny step toward securing the future that Lucius dreamed about for ourselves and our families. I had seen, if not the guilt and nervousness I'd hoped for, respect on a few faces. Maybe, just maybe, I had won my first votes of confidence.

I closed my eyes, trying to regroup.

Or maybe I had just doomed to destruction the vampire I loved more than my own existence.

Why didn't Flaviu seem more nervous?

Chapter 92
Antanasia

RANIERO—THE LATEST incarnation—was waiting for me in the *camera de mizǎ*, and I nearly gasped when I saw him.

The transformation he'd been making from surfer back to assassin was complete.

It wasn't just the way he stood, with no trace of his old slouch, but not stiffly, either. He was drawn up tall but at ease, like Lucius stood. Like nobility. And it wasn't just the clothes he wore, or even the haircut and shave that I assumed Mindy had given him, because I knew her handiwork, knew how she liked guys to look, and Raniero Vladescu Lovatu looked like the culmination of every fantasy she'd ever described. A guy whose strong jaw and high Vladescu cheekbones, which you could finally see, looked like the culmination of *a lot* of girls' fantasies.

But it wasn't even the sum of all those things that made him look like the royal, dangerous vampire he'd been raised to be.

No, it was mainly the freshly carved stake that he was tucking in the back of his jeans as he asked, "Are you ready for your second lesson, Antanasia? Do you bring your own weapon?"

Chapter 93
Antanasia

"RANIERO, ARE YOU sure you should be carrying that?" I didn't have to say *what*. "Is it even allowed?"

"*I* do not work within the restriction of laws," he said. "Not anymore. But if you directly order me to be without a weapon, of course I will bow to your decision."

I watched him for a few seconds, trying to gauge his expression, but his eyes seemed closed off. "Are you sure you need a stake right now?"

"Antanasia, there is one vampire already destroyed, and a prince about to go on trial. I am foolish not to be armed when I am asking questions about the murder. Very often, those who ask questions find themselves the next with a hole in the chest, yes?"

I didn't want to agree, but he was right. And like Lucius had been when he'd first summoned his cousin back to Romania, I was a little worried that Raniero would ultimately disobey if I did order him to forego carrying a weapon. Not to mention that I probably owed it to him to allow him to protect himself . . . "Okay, keep it, if you want."

But please don't use it. Not unless you have no choice.

He dipped his newly shorn head. *"Grazie."*

"You said you're asking questions—"

"And learning nothing. I ask everyone on the staff if they see anything the morning of Claudiu's death." He gave me a level look. "Including a prince who should not have been about."

My heart skipped a beat, not because I distrusted Lucius, but because I realized I never had learned where he'd been that night. "And?"

"No one sees anything. They can tell me nothing unusual."

"Oh." I was relieved and disappointed at the same time.

Raniero's eyes softened, just a little. "Do not worry, Antanasia. We will discover the truth. And of course I listened from the antechamber, and you do well at the meeting, when you set the trial date. There are Elder vampires who will see you in a different way now."

I looked down at the stake in my hands. "I hope so."

And in that second when my eyes were averted, Raniero chose to begin our lesson—so the next thing I knew I was pinned against his chest, the same way I'd once been pinned against Lucius's, with a stake to my breastbone, as he advised me, "It is never wise to express doubt in front of an armed and dangerous vampire, especially if it causes you to bow your head like a sacrifice—and drop your own weapon."

Chapter 94
Antanasia

"RANIERO . . . WHAT ARE you doing?"

I fought to quiet my breathing and not succumb to panic. Raniero was incredibly strong. His chest was hard against my back, and his hand was firmly planted against my stomach, right under my breastbone. I could feel the point of the stake.

"Raniero!" I said a little louder.

He had both my wrists trapped in his one formidable hand, and he tightened his grip. But his voice wasn't threatening—just clearer than usual—when he said, "I am showing you, in one quick motion, almost everything you will need to know if you are ever to truly use a stake."

"Okay, show me." He sounded calm, but I fought hard to control my voice, which wanted to shake.

"You will remain still and listen carefully, yes?"

"Yes," I agreed. I had no choice. "I will."

"You are small, and therefore it is to your advantage to act first," he said. "To use the element of surprise, if possible. You see how easily I took you, because you were not ready."

I hadn't even seen him move. "Okay, I understand."

"And this . . ." He squeezed his arm against my chest. "This is the best position to inflict serious harm. Your own body provides the resistance, so there is more power when you thrust the stake. It is a principle of leverage, and especially important for someone small, like yourself."

I nodded, my head tapping his chest. "I get it."

"If you cannot trap your opponent like this, try to make sure his back is against a wall. Otherwise, you may find yourself stabbing several times, which is dangerous. A weak fighter too often ends up lunging several times in panic, during which time his opponent begins to fight back. You cannot afford that."

I nodded again, trying to focus in spite of the pressure of the stake, which he was still pressing close to my heart. *I trust him.* "I will . . . I would try to use a wall."

My trust wavered when he pressed the stake more firmly, causing me to wince. But his words made sense. "This is the spot where the point *must* enter. Remember it, yes? Otherwise—again—you may not destroy the first time. And then you will find yourself in a struggle."

"I'll remember." I *did* remember that spot, from the time Lucius had nearly destroyed me. I would never forget that spot.

We stood in silence, and I waited for him to keep talking—or let me go. But he didn't do anything else. We stayed locked in place, and I could feel him breathing against my ear, and I finally said, in a voice that I hoped projected authority that would reach him, if he really was spinning out of control, and this "lesson" was nothing more than a ruse to make me vulnerable, and he was at that very moment trying to decide what would happen next . . .

"Raniero, I order you to let me go. Now."

Immediately, he released me, and I turned around and

saw that he was nodding with approval. He tucked his weapon back into his jeans. "This is the last point that I wish to make. A lesson which you are learning on your own, and can only learn on your own."

I stepped away from him, still wary. "I don't understand."

"You are royalty," he said. "That carries with it a special power, and if you believe that, you enter any battle with an advantage. You see how I step aside, upon your order, the moment when you remember who you *are*."

"I don't think somebody who's trying to destroy me will listen to my orders."

Raniero smiled, but not warmly. It was a warrior's smile, maybe sparked by some remembered triumph. "No, perhaps not. But your opponent may hesitate, just for a moment—and that is when the battle is won."

Is he thinking of that momentary advantage over Lucius? I nodded. "I understand."

"I am sorry for frightening you," he added. "But your fear will help you recall everything I have taught you. I promise that you will remember every moment we have just shared."

"Yes, I definitely will." I bent to pick up the stake I'd dropped—without taking my eyes off him. "And I think that's enough for tonight."

But when I straightened, Raniero grabbed my wrist, stopping me again. "With your permission, I would also like to administer a small test to you. A challenge. And if you pass this—if you can do as I ask—I think you will be ready to carry a weapon with assurance."

My gaze darted to my hand and he let go. "What kind of test?"

"You are becoming very courageous, and very quickly," he said. "But do you have the nerve to actually *use* the stake?"

"Use it? Like stab something?"

He nodded. *"Sì."*

I wasn't supposed to look away from an armed vampire, but I gave a quick check around the small room. "There's nothing here but more stakes. What would I use?"

"We can use this."

"What?"

I looked over to see that Raniero wasn't holding anything. He was just pointing to his chest.

Chapter 95
Antanasia

"YOU'RE JOKING, RIGHT?"

For a moment I wasn't sure if Raniero was teasing or actually offering to let me *destroy* him. Then he held up his hand and said, "I will place my hand upon the table, and you will drive the stake through. This is how you learn what it feels like to cause a wound."

"You can't be serious."

"I am very serious. You cannot imagine how it feels to cause harm until you actually do it. If you are not to hesitate at a crucial moment, it is best to have the experience safely first. And soon, like many other things, causing harm becomes easy with practice."

I heard the wistful, bitter quality return to his voice, and once again, it made me trust him more. He regretted what he'd done in the past. "But I can't even imagine how much it would hurt you if I actually *staked* your hand."

He didn't seem concerned. "Enduring pain is like causing pain. It, too, becomes easier with practice. And you know, of course, that vampires heal quickly." He spread his tattooed hand on the table and indicated the fleshy part between his thumb and forefinger. "There is no bone here. The wound will last a few days, at most."

I shook my head, appalled. "No . . . I couldn't."

Raniero smiled at my horror. "The Buddha himself says, 'Life is suffering.' Pain cannot be avoided, only fully faced and accepted. A moment of discomfort is nothing to me."

"I don't think Buddha would approve of my deliberately *stabbing* you."

The smile slowly left his lips, and I knew that I had accidentally brought his new philosophies crashing into his old life, where they didn't fit quite as well as they did on the beach. Which was precisely why he didn't want to be here.

"This is how Lucius and I trained," he said. "And while I cannot order you, as you are a sovereign, I strongly suggest that you do this if you wish to have the skills you will need to survive in your new role."

I drew back. "You and Lucius deliberately *staked each other's hands?*"

He didn't answer, but I could tell from his expression that they had done it. Had been forced to do it. And maybe more than once—which was probably why he'd been able to stake Lucius's *chest.*

He leaned against the table, watching my face, and

grew reflective. "Have you ever hurt anything or anyone, Antanasia? I do not speak of stepping on a spider, but of causing true pain."

"Well, I did stab Lucius's foot with a pitchfork once."

Raniero's lips, no longer hidden by his goatee, twitched with amusement, like he knew that story and didn't think it counted.

"No. I guess I haven't really hurt anyone," I conceded.

"You left the courtroom, unable to even vote to destroy a vampire," he surprised—and embarrassed—me by saying.

"How do you know that?"

He shrugged. "News travels even to vampires who live on beaches."

Even Raniero knew what had happened, and he deliberately kept himself away from the gossip. I leaned on the table, too, my new bravado taking a small hit. "If *everyone* knows I ran away, how can I even dream of being elevated to queen?"

Then the vampire who thought he'd shed his philosopher persona gave me another profound thing to reflect on—and this time, it was a quote from Raniero, not the Buddha.

"If you cannot destroy a vampire who deserves such, in accordance with law, perhaps you should not *wish* to be queen."

I took a few moments to let that sink in, and suddenly it was like my eyes were opened.

What I'd *wished* for was to be Lucius's wife. That was what I'd really wanted when I'd agreed to be a princess. And I had accepted the idea of building a better kingdom for the subjects I'd gained when I'd slipped on my wedding ring. I did want to do that—for Lucius, mainly.

But it struck me then . . . had I ever really, honestly, *wanted* to *be* a ruler?

And I knew the answer was no.

Being a princess had always just been an unhappy circumstance of my birth and the unfortunate door prize that came along with being Lucius's wife. I hadn't just been failing as royalty because I didn't try hard enough to read Romanian or study the old law books or learn my way around the castle—although those were pretty big mistakes on my part.

I had been failing because my goal had only been to *act* like a ruler.

I hadn't wanted to be a monarch in my gut, like the vampire who was lying in a cell, and who craved the chance to be king—a good king—with every weakening beat of his heart.

I owed it to him to *want* to rule by his side—not because it was the price of being near him, but because *I* believed in being a leader. Had to have that scepter in my hands. To give anything less wouldn't just be cheating my subjects or myself—or my birth parents, even. It would be cheating Lucius.

And I wouldn't do that. Somehow, I would change not only my actions, but my attitude. Somehow, I would *will* myself to want—and claim—my birthright.

I had fallen so deep into thought that I'd almost forgotten Raniero was at my side until the very perceptive vampire whom I was slowly coming to understand—even as he felt he was losing himself—said, "Well, Antanasia? What do you wish to do?"

I met his eyes for a long moment, then shifted my stake

in my hand until it sat the proper way and told him, with conviction that I *would* feel—was in fact already starting to muster—"I *wish* to be Princess Antanasia Dragomir Vladescu, ruler of the world's most venerable vampire clans."

Without hesitating, Raniero placed his hand on the table, and I drove the stake into his flesh with every ounce of strength I possessed.

Chapter 96
Mindy

"YOU'RE GONNA LOOK great," I told Ylenia.

And she would look awesome, 'cause I was doing her hair, and I didn't do bad work, even for a girl I hated—maybe for the right reasons or maybe for the wrong ones. I could hardly tell anymore.

"Thanks, Mindy," she said. "It's nice of you to help me." Her pale cheeks got a tiny bit red. "I know I'm not so good with hair and clothes."

"You do okay," I fibbed. "But I helped Jess win Lucius, so I do think I got the touch."

"It's not a date," Ylenia said, way too quick. "He just asked to talk. And I couldn't even believe he did *that*."

"Yeah, well, you never know with Raniero, right?" You really didn't anymore. I tugged a little too hard, trying to get the boar-bristle brush I'd bought specially for Jess's curls through Ylenia's frizz. "And it never hurts to look good."

She smiled and looked honestly shy, like Raniero said she was. "No, I guess not."

"So . . . where are you going?" That was what I really wanted to know, and why I'd volunteered to fix her up in the first place.

"I told you, it's no big deal." She shrugged her bony shoulders. "Just for a walk in the formal gardens."

"Oh." I tugged way too hard—not 'cause I hated her. It was just that my fingers got shaky.

Maybe I was keeping my frenemy too close. I *wanted* to hate her, and I still didn't trust her, but right then I felt sorry for her, too. Raniero had bit her and then left her, and no matter what she said, she was excited that he wanted to talk.

Or was it her fault that he was damned? And that Jess and Lukey were in trouble?

Or was I the crazy one, seeing stuff where it really wasn't? 'Cause I was almost insane with jealousy right then to think about her and Raniero walking around a beautiful garden, just like him and me used to walk around a stupid park in Lancaster.

The whole time I was thinking, my fingers were moving, and I got lost in my head and her mess of curls, and my box of makeup, and when I finally stepped back from my second makeover that week so Ylenia could stand up and do a little twirl, I just about screamed to see her glossy curls and her big, bright eyes, 'cause she'd ditched the glasses for once . . .

Jeez, I did *way* too good a job.

Even though her skirt was totally out of date, the rest of her looked almost like . . . Jess.

Almost like an honest-to-goodness vampire princess.

Chapter 97
Lucius

R—

Yes, I recall many things from the convocation which resulted in the mark upon your hand. I venture more and more into the past, or what seems to be the past, until memory is clearer than reality. And on that night, I recall that you were angry—but sane. You rebuffed even my attempts at conversation, seeming to prefer to remain aloof—until Ylenia Dragomir approached you.

How strange that seemed to me . . . A girl who was always at the margins, and a Dragomir, at that . . .

I recall thinking, as you walked off together, too close to one another, "This is a mistake." For the look in your eyes was dangerous, Raniero—because, to me, you appeared not threatening, but rather vulnerable. (It is strange to use that word to describe you—but it is accurate.)

And when I saw you next, your eyes were unfocused and wild—different even from how you appeared on the day that you nearly destroyed me—and you stood in a pool of blood with a newly bitten vampire at your side—and a dead vampire at your feet.

As one who slips slowly toward madness myself, Raniero, I know—with even more certainty than I knew on that night—that the change you experienced in minutes usually happens in hours or days or years. I knew, even then, that Claudiu must have done something to alter you, hoping to get you destroyed by a mob, because it was not enough to send you away for months at

251

a time. Even that could not ease his worry that one day the truth about how he incited you to destroy me would come out.

And of course I have always known that it was Claudiu who prompted you to attack. I have ALWAYS trusted you, Raniero. It was not the jest I made that day that spared my life. You were never truly as close to ending my existence as you have come to believe.

It takes all of my energy to write this, and to remain focused, but if it helps you to realize that you are not only fit to rejoin our society, but to reclaim your place among royalty . . .

This is perhaps my last missive, and so before I rejoin my dreams, which grow darker and longer, I issue one final command. When I am gone, as seems likely, either by destruction or into the realm of mad imaginings, claim your place as regent and rule by Antanasia's side, for we both know that there is no restriction against a bleste-mată vampire ruling. No precedent, and so no restriction.

Do this for ALL of us, brother—best man—protector of the bride . . .

With gratitude as eternal as I hope your existence is,
L

Chapter 98
Antanasia

"'*IN CAZUL IN care acuzatul nu poate vorbi,*'" Raniero read aloud, his finger tracing the words, and because I was nowhere close to understanding the complex sentences in the law books we were poring over, I found myself fixating on the bandage on his hand.

I did that to him—and it felt terrible. But powerful, too.

The stake hadn't gone all the way through, but I'd done some damage. Much more than when I'd struck Lucius's foot with a pitchfork. And Raniero believed I'd done well.

"This is the passage we seek," he said, jolting me from my thoughts. "A case from 1622, but relevant. *In realtà,* the Elders will respect such a venerable precedent. Some may even recall the trial."

"What does it say, exactly? I need to know the precise wording."

Raniero took a slip of paper off Lucius's desk and began to write. "In the event that the accused is unable to speak . . ." He finished and slid the note to me, and when his hand moved, Lucius's laptop sprang to life for the third time that evening. And for the third time, I saw my husband's e-mail messages. All those exchanges with Raniero, some dated right before Claudiu's destruction.

What did they discuss? Soccer and surfing? Or secrets and statecraft?

"If you have what you need for now, it grows late, and I have an appointment," Raniero hinted.

I wanted to study those law books all night. Lucius's trial was less than a day away. But I had already asked enough of Raniero for one day. Probably for one lifetime. I didn't even have the right to ask him what who his "appointment" was with.

Does it involve Mindy? Because she is not ready to handle the emerging Raniero.

"I will not see Mindy Sue," he surprised me by saying. My concern must have been obvious. "Do not worry for her." He smiled sadly and bitterly, combining the only kinds of smiles he had anymore. "I have told her *everything* about my past as she uses her scissors, and whatever is left between us disappears with my hair. I promise you."

I started to stand up. "I should go see her. She must be upset."

But he put a hand on my shoulder, pressing me down. "She is fine—and has plans, too, I believe."

Plans? Late at night in a lonely castle?

But I took Raniero at his word, because I couldn't help Mindy much anyhow. Not until I saved Lucius. Then I would give her a shoulder to cry on for eternity, if she needed it. "Okay, if you're sure she's fine."

"You should go rest," Raniero suggested, heading for the door. "You need strength as much as knowledge."

I sat back in Lucius's chair. "No, I'll keep working. I can sleep when Lucius is free."

"This is a good attitude." Raniero opened the door. "Even better than your husband's, I think." Then he left before I could ask what he knew of Lucius's outlook—or his sanity.

I knew I needed to work, but when I was alone, I wasn't sure what to do. I was running out of time to exonerate Lucius, and I had . . . nothing. As I struggled to think, I absently reached for the mouse to his laptop and shook it, so the computer woke up again, and this time I gave in to temptation and clicked on his e-mail.

I wasn't really snooping, I was just looking for any kind of information that might help him. I wanted to know more about Raniero, too, because the conflicted assassin was part of *my* life now. And part of me craved even that little contact with Lucius. Wanted to read his long-winded, witty, sarcastic prose, which was so . . . him.

With just the slightest twinge of guilt, I opened the last message between the two powerful, mysterious vampires and scrolled to the bottom of correspondence that started weeks before my wedding and continued, sporadically, up to the morning Claudiu had been destroyed.

The e-mails were, of course, meant for Raniero, and I did get some insight into their friendship—and their suspicions. But I also found something else scattered through the messages, and it was almost better than clues.

A love letter to me.

At least, it started out that way.

Chapter 99
Mindy

I SHOULDA KNOWN Raniero would meet Ylenia in a garden. He always liked to be outside and said buildings suffocated him, and no matter what he thought about himself, I knew he wasn't really changing. He might have better clothes, and a new haircut, and even look mad sometimes, but he was still sweet, do-no-harm, nature-loving Ronnie.

If he wasn't a good guy, he wouldn't of agreed to do the right thing by Ylenia, who was already sitting next to him on a bench under the stars. I got there late, 'cause I had to ask directions from two different servants, but it didn't seem like I missed much. From where I stood in the shadows, it seemed like all the worst, most painful stuff was happening right then.

"Ylenia," Raniero said, sounding very sorry. "I think that I have been wrong not to speak with you before now. I believed, at first, that I am doing you a favor, because I cannot imagine who would want a *blestematǎ* vampire, but perhaps that choice should also be yours, yes? For our tradition says that what we have shared together—blood—is binding for eternity."

I stood like one of the marble statues I could see in the bushes around me, like the Italian Renaissance was still going on, and I couldn't move, either. I was like made of stone, too.

I shouldn't have come there to spy on them. I wasn't really there to catch Ylenia doing or saying something wrong. I was there 'cause this part of me wanted to watch the guy I'd thrown away—and who I wanted back—leave me forever.

I, like, *wanted* to hurt. And I got what I wanted.

"I understand why you acted like you did," Ylenia told him. "That whole night went so wrong . . ."

"*Si.* It did."

I saw her reach out and touch him, like I woulda done, and my heart shriveled up in my chest.

"But Lucius obviously believed that you didn't really mean to destroy anyone that night," she said. "And I believe it, too. I don't know what happened, but you didn't mean to do it."

"I still do not understand that, either." He shrugged, almost like he'd given up caring about that bad thing he'd done. "But I do know that we have shared something sacred to vampires, and if you do not despise me—if you wish to begin, somehow, to know one another more slowly, and to determine whether you do, perhaps, want a vampire who is troubled and almost certainly doomed—I will court you, as you deserved and still deserve."

She sat there staring at him, and my shriveled-up heart stopped. *Say no! Tell him no! Tell him to get lost!*

But, duh, she'd been crazy about him for years—totally hated and loved him—and she said, "I'd like that, Raniero. It would mean a lot to me. Just like that night meant a lot to me."

Neither one of 'em said it in so many words, but I knew what had just happened. She'd basically told him, "I accept you as mine, forever." A lot of vampire life was a mystery to me, but I knew that a girl who'd been bitten had a claim on a guy forever. As a girl who *hadn't* got bit, I knew that WAY too well.

I pretty much got "destroyed" right then, and the only thing that kept me from screaming was knowing that Raniero hadn't said that night meant a lot to him, too. I was glad for that, at least.

Till he leaned over and *kissed* her.

It wasn't like the kisses we used to share. It wasn't like Raniero fell on her, and she fell on him, and they couldn't pull themselves apart if the world ended around 'em. It was just a kiss on the cheek—but it was the final big, ugly stake in *my* heart.

I started to turn around, knowing I'd made a HUGE mistake coming there.

I shouldn't have seen that. It will haunt me forever . . . even if I don't have *forever, like they're going to, 'cause she will NEVER let him go.*

My breath started getting all raggedy and hysterical, and it was a wonder I even heard her whisper to him, "I'll be good to you, Raniero. I promise. And you'll need someone, if . . . if the worst happens to Lucius, and you rise to become Antanasia's regent. I promise, I'll be ready to help you rule."

I had my back to them, and I froze again. My fingers clenched so tight my nails dug into my skin.

Bitch. She WAS a conniving bitch.

She didn't give a damn about Jess.

And what the hell did *Raniero* mean when he said, "Thank you, Ylenia. I believe that you will do well by my side if I take my place as regent, ruling with Antanasia in Lucius's absence."

One of my nails snapped against my hand.

That was all wrong. He shouldn't act like there was any chance Lukey wouldn't be okay. Friends didn't talk like that. And he shouldn't be talking about ruling anything. He didn't want that. He always swore he didn't . . .

So why did he sound like he was *drooling* over the chance to take Lukey's place?

All of a sudden, I wasn't sure I'd been right about my ex-boyfriend after all.

I stood there in that garden that got very silent, like maybe two people were kissing some more, and for the first time I actually wondered if Raniero hadn't just hid some very important stuff from me. I wondered if maybe he'd outright *lied* to all of us all along, pretending to be a good guy and a good friend.

258

Chapter 100

Antanasia

ALTHOUGH LUCIUS didn't talk about Raniero very often, there were times when they e-mailed quite a bit. Their correspondence was one of those things he kept private even from me—maybe in part because that was where he talked *about* me. I was sure it was the only forum, outside our bedroom, where Lucius Vladescu came even close to expressing *feelings.*

"My wife grows weak, Raniero . . . I worry for her . . . Cannot bear to see her struggle . . ."

"I'm sorry, Lucius," I muttered, ashamed. "Really sorry."

Scrolling up higher, I realized I'd reached the end of the string of messages, and I sat back in the chair, angry at myself and seeing even more clearly how I'd cowered behind him since our marriage. How I'd let him down and added to his burdens.

Almost all of Lucius's early messages had included—hidden inside the guy banter about sports and stakes and the merits of wearing or not wearing pants—some kind of compliment to me. *"Antanasia is brilliant, Raniero. You must come to my wedding, if only to see the woman who has the power to render ME speechless."*

Raniero had written about Mindy, too, and while I'd skimmed those parts, not wanting to pry, it was clear, even with all the the LOLs about her shoes, that he cared about her very much, and maybe saw what she needed more clearly than Mindy did. *"She attends college, because her mother wishes this, but I tell her there is a very excellent school of beauty not far from my home upon the beach."*

Unfortunately, over time both relationships seemed to disintegrate a little. Raniero's LOLs ended more often with *"but sadly,"* while Lucius began to express regret not for marrying me, exactly, but for dragging me into a life that was slowly crushing me.

I reread one of the last messages, in which Lucius asked Raniero, again, to come help him manage the kingdom so he could focus more on protecting me.

"I'm so sorry," I repeated, raising my finger to close the program.

But just before I clicked, I noticed the time and date stamps on the last few messages, which had been exchanged during a brief period when Lucius mentioned me sleeping nearby, because he sometimes did bring the laptop to our room and work in front of the fire.

Scrolling back down, I followed the trail again, getting excited as images of clocks, and Lucius waking me, and *bright red blood* suddenly started to dance in front of my eyes.

I forced myself to calm down and think clearly, using both sides of my brain. *Think like a vampire—and a mathlete, Jess. Use your rational side and your new familiarity with blood, too.* And gradually, the question formed in my mind:

Given the rate at which blood coagulates, could a vampire who was sending messages at 6:47 a.m.—and next to me in bed at 7:15—have been in the foyer at the proper time to drive a stake three times into his foe?

Chapter 101
Antanasia

LUCIUS'S TRIAL WAS looming, and I only had one small bit of evidence in his favor, so I didn't think I'd ever be able to sleep that night. But I'd recently run a stake through Raniero's hand and read up on the law and done my usual study of Romanian, and I guess I was exhausted enough that when my head hit the pillow, I fell asleep almost immediately.

Or maybe I didn't really fall asleep, because as I was drifting off, I started to have a dream that was almost as vivid as the hallucinations I'd suffered. Except this time—maybe fueled by Lucius's e-mails—I had a *good* dream.

It was a memory, really. One that started on the night I got married, when Lucius closed the door to our bedroom, so for the first time since we'd spoken our vows, we were alone.

Chapter 102
Antanasia

"I WOULD HAVE taken you anywhere in the world, you know," my new husband teases, pulling me close. *"We did not have to stay here, in our own home, on our wedding night!"*

I smile at him. "I didn't want to travel. I just wanted to be here with you."

He smiles, too, and kisses my throat, then says, "I have no objection to that, wife of mine. I would much rather carry you to our bedroom than drag suitcases around airports!"

I laugh—but a little nervously. I've waited for this moment for so long . . . but suddenly I'm also keenly aware of my inexperience.

Lucius is experienced.

It shows in the way he shrugs out of his jacket without stopping the gentle, insistent brush of his lips against my throat. And a second later, he undoes his cuff links behind my back, so I hear them clatter to the floor.

I don't even know how cuff links work. Am I supposed to help him? Undress myself?

Of course, Lucius senses my tension, since I've gotten stiff in his arms, and he says softly, "Do not be nervous. I love you."

"I love you, too." I pull back slightly and reach for his bow tie, yanking on it—which does nothing but make us both practically fall over. I put my hand on his shoulder, trying to catch us. "I'm sorry. Shoot!"

I didn't mean to say that lame, juvenile half-curse or almost drag us into a heap on the floor. I'm embarrassed and ruining the most special night of my life . . .

"Let me, please." I expect Lucius to laugh at me, but he doesn't. And with one quick tug, the tie is undone and hanging around his neck. Then he kisses me, his lips hard but tender against mine, and shifts to whisper in my ear again, murmuring one of the sweetest things he's ever said to me. Words I'm sure I'll never forget, any more than I could ever forget his proposal or the vows we've just spoken.

"Someday, Jessica," he says quietly, "you will stand before me in this very room, as we prepare for some function which we both dread, for we have been to so many in our years together, and you will smile and reach up to adjust my crooked tie, as you always do. And one of our children—perhaps our first son—will tug at your dress, demanding our attention. Then I will kiss you, and reach down to lift our child, thinking, How did I come to be so happy?"

I love this little story. The warrior prince I've married has imagined this scene of a family. The family we will create. He sees us long after this first night, together and happy and familiar with each other, but still thrilled, like we'll always be . . .

And suddenly, I'm not nervous at all. "And if we only have daughters?" I tease him, because I know that his comment about a son wasn't just offhand or a joke. He's been raised to believe that having a male heir is incredibly important.

I wrap my arms around his waist, feeling his crisp white shirt under my fingers. I've had dreams, too, of having his children— someday. I'm only eighteen, and I've never told anybody that. But I do think about it sometimes. "And if we only have girls, what then, Prince Lucius?" I ask again, laughing.

He grins and presses his mouth closer to my ear—and my body closer to his, so I can feel all of the power, the good tension building in him, because although we're talking about our future, we're falling more and more under the spell of the present. "If we have only daughters, I will be the happiest vampire alive," he whispers. "For I have come to learn—from you—that a princess can be as powerful as a prince!"

Then he sweeps me off my feet for the second time that evening, *and carries me to our bed, and I can't imagine why I was nervous for even a second as we are together—completely together—for the first time, and soon the fangs that I've felt brushing against my skin again plunge deep into my throat . . .*

I woke up in the middle of the night and rubbed my neck like the dream had been true. Not like it was another hallucination. Just a vivid, wonderful dream that *would* come true. He'd seen our future, and it would happen.

I would *make it* happen.

I wanted to be the one who adjusted the king's tie, and went to boring functions, and watched him swing our children up to his shoulders. And I wanted more than that. I wanted to regain that power Lucius had first seen in me, and which I'd lost, and use it to lead a kingdom of vampires with the same strength my birth mother had shown. I wanted all those things, deep, deep in my gut, more than I'd ever longed for anything in my life. As I lay in Lucius's and my bed, the desire to rule, which I'd started to feel when I'd first used the stake and experienced that power in my hands, hardened into a fierce resolve. A *craving*.

I didn't just want to be just Mrs. Lucius Vladescu, or a princess, even. I wanted to be *queen*.

I suddenly understood how Raniero must have felt in that moment when he'd been tempted to seize power. But I wasn't about to pull my hand away and step back, afraid to give a final thrust to take what was mine.

I had just hours left, and I would make the most of them, to get everything I *had* to have.

As I swung my legs off the bed, I thought about Lucius and the image of the stake that was always so important to our life together, and I could still feel the strength and authority in his hands, left over from the dream—and something else clicked into place for me. Something that was again a combination of rational math and the irrational sphere of vampires—and so glaringly obvious that I couldn't believe I'd never realized it before.

Hurrying to dress, I left my room, not even bothering to say anything to Emilian.

I felt him trailing behind me while I raced to Raniero's room, which I entered without knocking. Closing the door behind me, shutting out my guard, I went to the bed and shook Raniero awake, jolting him, so he sat up fully alert, and asked, "Raniero . . . Have you ever exhumed a body?"

Chapter 103
Antanasia

THE NIGHT WAS very cold but the moon was bright, and we didn't even need a flashlight when we got to the cemetery, where there were no trees to block the light. Through the bars of the iron gate, I could already see the mausoleum where my birth parents were buried—and where maybe someday I would rest—like a gray smudge on the expanse of white. And in the distance I could see the Vladescus' much grander crypt, where a place waited . . .

I looked at Raniero, who was hanging back, a shovel balanced on his shoulder like a surfboard, while I shoved up the latch.

"You are certain that we need to do this?" he asked.

"Yes. I remember something from the day Claudiu died. Something I didn't even think about until you taught me how to use a stake." I stepped inside and quickly found Claudiu's grave again. The brand-new marker gleamed whiter than those around it, and the snow was higher on top of him, because the earth was still freshly turned and mounded under the drifts.

I took a few steps forward, then turned back, because Raniero still wasn't following me. He was standing at the gate, seeming edgy, like the first time I'd met him there. "Don't tell me that *you're* nervous to be here?" I asked.

He shifted his feet. "No, I have told you before that I am lazy. The ground will be hard."

"If you don't want to help me, I'll do it myself."

"I merely try to make a joke, Antanasia." But he still didn't move. He took a moment to survey the cemetery, and even by moonlight I could see that his jaw was tense. "I do not like to be here. I am responsible for more than one of these graves. To walk in here is to step into a minefield—and to wonder if the sight of one headstone will be enough to make me explode. I only joke to fend off darker thoughts."

I wrapped my coat tighter around myself. "I'm sorry. I didn't think about that. I only want to help Lucius."

He gave me a skeptical look. "And you think that raising the body of Claudiu Vladescu has the power to help anyone?"

"Yes."

His fingers flexed around the shovel's handle. "I still do not understand."

"And I don't understand why vampires still investigate

266

crime like we live in the Middle Ages, relying on torture and whispers and one vampire's word against another's," I told him. "I want to bring *evidence* to Lucius's trial." I scanned the expanse of snow dotted with gray headstones. Somewhere under the ground lay a vampire I hadn't been able to sentence. "There were eyewitnesses, but no real evidence, when Ylenia's father's killer was tried." I met Raniero's eyes. "And did anyone besides Lucius try to defend you at your trial?"

"No. No one." He shuffled his feet again. "So you wish to make vampire justice like that on American television shows, yes?"

He was still sort of joking, but I was deadly serious. "Exactly. And while we might not have liquid chromatography equipment or even a fingerprint kit, we can collect facts. The Elders can be compelled to make more rational, measured judgments."

Raniero nodded more thoughtfully. "Lucius says that your logical American way of thinking will benefit our clans."

We stared at each other across a few feet of snow, then I said quietly but firmly, the way he'd spoken to me now, several times, "If I can get out of bed and face the things that terrify me in the future, you can face your past."

The wind gusted, and I glanced at the Vladescus' crypt again. *Am I a hypocrite . . . ?*

When I turned around, I found that Raniero had stepped closer. I hadn't even heard the gate swing shut or the snow squeak under the heavy boots that had replaced his flip-flops. He jerked his head toward the new marker. "Let us go, Antanasia, and be done with this."

Without another word, I led the way to Claudiu's grave.

When we reached the plot, Raniero lifted the shovel off his shoulders, tossed Lucius's coat to the ground, then bent and jammed the blade into the snow and earth.

While the dirt probably was hard, it was still loose in the shallow hole, and Raniero was strong. He didn't even breathe heavily as he worked, and it only took a few minutes before the blade struck wood. Within a half hour, he had the casket cleared.

Kneeling beside the narrow hole, he wrapped his fingers under the lip of the ebony lid and raised his face to mine. "Are you ready, Antanasia? It is cold, and not much time has passed, so there will not be much decay. But the sight will not be pretty."

I knew that. And I knew what had happened the last time I'd peered into that coffin. But I needed to make sure. "Go ahead."

His hand jerked hard, and I jumped, because the lid gave easily, opening to reveal the body. Leaning over, I forced myself to look inside. "Undo the shroud so we can see the wound," I directed.

Raniero wordlessly began the awkward process of uncovering Claudiu's chest, and I turned away—not because I was too freaked out to watch, but because, although I'd despised Claudiu, it seemed disrespectful to look at his bared, bony shoulders. I was almost embarrassed for him. "Tell me what you find."

Raniero's voice was muffled because his head was bent into the grave. "Perhaps you can tell me what you wish me to look for." But I didn't even have to answer. Before I said anything, I heard him mutter, softly, an Italian expression of surprise. *"Mavalà."*

About an hour later, we had reinterred Claudiu Vladescu, and Raniero put his coat back on, concealing the freshly carved stake he still had tucked in the back of his jeans.

We tromped through the white drifts, and as he swung the iron gate shut, I glanced at the sky, hoping that it would snow even more, because I wanted the grave to look like we'd never touched it . . . just in case I needed to open it again.

Chapter 104
Antanasia

"WHY ARE WE HERE?" I asked Raniero. I felt for the stake in my coat pocket, where I was trying to get used to keeping it. "I thought my lessons were done."

We had headed directly from the cemetery to the *camera de miză,* and Raniero had been quiet the whole time. As I lit the candles, he paced, but not like he'd done the first time I'd met him there. This time, he still looked like a lion, but in the way Lucius did when he strode back and forth while deep in thought.

Raniero looked like he was on the prowl, with his prey in sight.

"Raniero?"

I woke him out of a reverie that seemed even deeper than the sleep I'd interrupted earlier. *"Si?* Yes?"

"Why are we here?"

"I need to see . . ." He moved to the box that held Lucius's stake and flipped open the lid with fingers still dirty from digging up a corpse—and probing Claudiu's wounds. ". . . this."

He lifted Lucius's weapon and held it up to his face, then ran one finger along the layered bloodstains, like he was testing them. Or *measuring* them.

I could still faintly smell the stench of Claudiu, and like always, I wanted to back away. But the assassin who knew so much about wounds and stakes and blood didn't avoid the rank odor like he'd avoided the cemetery. He wiped his hands on his jeans, cleaning off some of the filth, and held the stake closer to his face, breathing in the scent from point to hilt.

Then he turned to me and declared, very solemnly, "This stake is stained with Claudiu's blood. But it is not the weapon which destroys my uncle."

My heart skipped at least five beats. "How do you know?"

"Claudiu's blood, which is pungent, is only upon the very tip of this stake."

"Which means . . ."

"Someone weak has used it—and failed to penetrate deeply enough. Or the blood was added later, by someone who does not understand how deeply the point must enter to pierce a heart. It is either a forgery or part of a failed attempt—and we have established that Lucius would not fail."

My heart started *adding* beats. "This is good news. Right?"

We'd already established at the cemetery that my memory had been right. Claudiu had been stabbed *three* times, while Lucius would have destroyed with a single thrust. Moreover,

Raniero had determined that the first two blows had been struck by a *right-handed* vampire. He didn't need any special lab or equipment. Just his personal expertise in how wounds were inflicted in fights to the death.

"So you're saying not only that the *number* of wounds, and their angles and placement, help to exonerate Lucius, but that his weapon didn't even cause the fatal wound?" I asked for confirmation, because this was so important.

"Yes—but do not get too excited, Antanasia," he cautioned. "It was still a *left-handed* vampire who pierces Claudiu's heart."

But I was excited. "Lucius would never need help in a fight," I reminded Raniero. "It will be obvious to the Elders that he wasn't involved at all."

"*Si.*" Raniero wasn't really listening, though. I could tell that the wheels were spinning in his head—and there was something he wasn't telling me. I knew that guarded expression. He was getting angry, too, for some reason. "I am sorry that I did not look at the stake, and the body, earlier."

"It's okay. We know more now, and that's all that matters."

He shook his head, though, seeming even more preoccupied. I didn't press to know his thoughts, because he was like Lucius and wouldn't reveal anything before he was ready. "I have lost some of my instincts, after leaving this place." He met my eyes. "I am sorry."

I wasn't sure if he was sorry for not thinking to check the stake earlier—or for what he did next. Which was walk over to the case that held his own, even bloodier, weapon and bring his fist smashing down on the glass so it shattered and liberated the stake, which he lifted up with incredible assurance and tucked into his jeans, in the valley of his spine, after taking out the other, smaller, newer one and tossing it to the ground.

"It is almost dawn," he noted, when he saw me watching him, speechless. "You should go to prepare for the trial, for I believe this will be a long day."

Chapter 105
Mindy

I GOT TO Jess's room real early with my whole makeup kit, thinking I'd need to do one more makeover before I put my scissors away forever. After getting Jess through this trial, I was *done* with doing hair. I was sick of beautiful people—and vampires.

When I knocked and opened her door, though, Jess wasn't there.

Princess Antanasia Dragomir Vladescu was.

"I guess you didn't need me today," I said. "Wow!"

She had looked beautiful at her wedding. But she looked *powerful* now.

That was, like, the only word for it.

"I'll always need you, Min," she said—and somehow, even though the love of her life was about to go on trial for his life, she smiled. "Always."

But she wouldn't need me. Not the same way. Something

had changed inside her, like, overnight. We would always be best friends, but something was different. It didn't make sense, but it felt like I was letting her go when we hugged. "Good luck, Jess. I'll be watching."

"Thanks." She grabbed my hand before I could go. "And when this is over, I'll be there for you, too. You know that, right?"

I guessed she saw I was hurting pretty bad right then, too. Not as much as her, maybe, but enough, in my own way. "Yeah. I know."

I thought about telling her that I was confused about Raniero, and didn't know if she should trust him, and that I was a mess about Ylenia, too, but in the end I just shut up. Today was her fight, and I could see in her eyes that she was determined to win it, and me confusing her about vampires she probably saw way clearer than me wasn't gonna help at the last minute. I might just shake up everything she'd somehow managed to pull together. And I knew from a million articles I'd read about confidence that believing in yourself was half the battle.

If that was really true, Antanasia Vladescu was at least ninety-five percent of the way to winning her first trial. So all I said was, "You watch your back, okay? You know who your real friends are."

She gave me a look that said I was still number one. "Yes. I know."

Princess Antanasia turned to look at herself in her mirror, but there was nothing to fix in how she wore her dark red suit or her black curls, or especially how she just . . . stood so she looked about ten feet tall. So I grabbed my carryon and left her alone.

As soon as I closed the door, I bumped into Emilio, who was carrying a bottle—and a note. "Gimme that." I held out my hand.

He pulled back. *"Este pentru prințesa."*

I didn't know what that meant, but I kept holding out my hand. "Give. Me. That."

Emilio was used to being told what to do, and he handed over the bottle, and I opened up the note and read, *Please, Antanasia, drink this before the trial. You will need your strength. D&Y.*

Emilio held out his hands. *"Vă rog, trebuie să duc asta."*

I didn't understand a word of that, either, so I wasn't really lying when I said, "Sorry. Don't speak Romanian."

I could feel him gawking after me the whole time I walked down the hall with the bottle.

Maybe Princess Antanasia did still need me, just a little.

I stopped in one of the gazillion rooms that hardly ever got used in that too big castle and dumped all of my makeup onto a rug, 'cause I wasn't taking any of it home, and the maids might as well get a nice surprise gift. Some of that stuff was Sephora and not even opened. I used the empty space for the bottle full of disgusting blood, feeling a lot better for Antanasia, and a little better about myself, too, 'cause I was pretty sure I'd just saved her butt one last time.

Chapter 106

Antanasia

THE ELDERS WERE already gathered when I arrived in the courtroom, and I paused on the threshold to face the substantial crowd that had come to see Lucius's trial. The room was packed, and there were more vampires waiting in the halls and outside the castle walls.

I'd heard a soft, persistent noise outside at dawn, and I'd gone to my window and looked down to see a steady stream of my relatives shuffling up the icy road, in the quiet way that vampires had, thanks to centuries of trying not to attract attention. At first I'd been surprised, before I'd realized that of course this trial was of interest to the whole kingdom. I hadn't sent out word that it was even happening, and had been too preoccupied to think about how curious our subjects would be. I'd imagined news getting out later, after the verdict, but naturally, even without organized media, the date and time had spread throughout the clans.

As I stood in the courtroom, I took an extra moment to meet some of their eyes.

The same vampires who saw me collapse at Claudiu's funeral are here.

Even more *vampires are here.*

Without hesitating longer or looking around at the Elders to see if anyone objected, I went straight to Lucius's chair again—the seat of power—and sat down.

I kept my chin high as I claimed my spot, and then I looked slowly to the left and to the right, meeting the eyes of all the Elders, too—passing quickly over Dorin, because I didn't want to see his fear, which was contagious—and locking my gaze with Flaviu's, because I wanted him to see exactly what I was projecting.

Power.

He didn't look away first, and he smirked a little, but that was okay. I knew that one small victory in a council meeting wouldn't be enough to undo the damage I'd done by cowering for months. It was enough that I'd seen a small measure of respect on several of the other Elders' faces.

Without wasting more time, I turned to the crowd again and announced, in a clear voice that completely concealed the terror I'd locked away deep inside, knowing I could never let it show again in public, "Bring in the accused."

I didn't even waver—didn't even blink, although a part of me *screamed* inside—when Lucius was escorted to that pale gray circle on the floor.

Chapter 107
Mindy

I WASN'T SURE how Jess held it together when Lukey was led into the packed courtroom, with his hands in chains in front of him. I didn't know where the guards thought he was gonna go, 'cause it looked like he could hardly make it to the middle of the room, which I'd wriggled into by shoving about a hundred vampires out of the way. When I got a spot, though, I almost wished I hadn't.

"Poor Lucius!" I kinda whimpered. Jess had told me he would be almost dying from not drinking blood, but I guessed I couldn't imagine what that would look like. Which was *bad*.

Jess didn't even flinch, though. She just faced her husband, who was trying so hard to be his old self but looking more like Raniero used to look when he was a surfer. It was like they'd traded places. Lucius's shoulders were slumped over, and his beautiful black hair was messed up, and he needed a shave, and his clothes were dirty, and when he finally opened his eyes to try and look around, like he wanted to tell everybody he was still in charge . . .

I looked at Jess again. How could she not cry, to see him fighting so hard to still be . . . Lucius?

But Jess was fighting, too. Fighting for him, and her eyes were like ice. They were like *black* ice, like all the brown part was gone. I'd never seen her look like that.

"It is clear that Lucius Vladescu is not prepared to speak for himself," she said, then stopped to give one of the uncles—the one I thought was named Fabio—a look that shoulda killed him on the spot. *I* shrank down a little. "Because he has been held in solitary confinement without sustenance. And so, because I am his wife and not eligible to render a verdict, I will speak on his behalf, call for his witnesses, and present his case."

That seemed to shock everybody, and the old vampire who looked just like the one I'd seen in a casket not too long ago shot out of his seat and started sputtering like he was having a stroke.

"This is unprecedented! Lucius must speak for himself! And your role is to preside, *Princess.*"

Uncle Fabio shoulda been in chains for talking to her like that, but Jess didn't even bat an eye. She just turned to him and said, very calm, "There is precedent." Then she stood up, taking her time, and spoke to everybody like she was on the Supreme Court.

"*Vladescu versus Vladescu,* 1622," she said. "Queen Sorina Vladescu both presided over the courtroom as a nonvoting judge and spoke for the accused, her husband, Alexandru, who was close to the state of *luat* due to deprivation of blood. The cases are identical."

All around me, I heard vampires translating everything Jess said, and I saw some of the Elders bobbing their gray heads and saying, *"Da,"* like they agreed.

"Princess Antanasia is correct," one of 'em piped up. "I attended that trial, as did Horatiu Vladescu, and it occurred as she relates. There is precedent. She should proceed."

"Da. Da." Everybody—except Fabio—nodded. "Proceed."

Holy crap. I was about knocked over for two reasons. Jess had totally won round one. And there were guys there who'd been *alive* in 1622?

Would Lucius and Jess and Raniero—and Ylenia—really live that long just 'cause they drank blood? It had never seemed real before, but now I realized that at least some of them honestly would still be walking around when I was long gone.

I started looking for Raniero and Ylenia, who I had been trying not to see, and I found Ylenia sitting close to the front, like she was already creeping toward Jess's spot, and I hated her even more right then. I wasn't just jealous anymore.

I hated her like I'd never hated anybody else in my life.

And Raniero . . . He was nowhere to be found. What did *that* mean?

I looked back at Jess and Lucius . . . and that was the first time I saw her eyes get soft, for just a second, when Lucius raised his face to look at her. He seemed so tired, like he'd been sleeping on his feet, but the weird thing was I coulda swore he *smiled* at her, and got that Lucius Vladescu gleam in his sleepy eyes, right before Jess got tough again and said to the guards, "*Intoarcerea la prizonier în celulă.* Return the prisoner to his cell. His presence is not needed now."

Lucius was beaten down, but he was still Lukey, and I got a little lump in my throat when he shook off the guards and walked by himself out of the room while everybody watched in complete silence.

He was freakin' Lucius Vladescu, and I didn't think anybody would ever have the guts to whisper, even when he was half dead. Even then, he looked like a king.

Somehow, fighting to stand up in chains, he looked *more* like a king than ever.

When he was gone and the door slammed behind him, I started hunting around again for the guy I was afraid wanted to steal the throne—but I didn't have to look long, 'cause Jess sat back down and said, "I wish to summon Raniero Vladescu Lovatu to present the first evidence."

Oh, gosh, did the crowd go crazy, gasping and muttering, and then my heart stopped when Raniero walked in the door Lucius had just gone out and took his best friend's place in that circle on the floor.

Chapter 108
Mindy

HOW COULD SEEING somebody so strong and gorgeous, who I didn't even know how I felt about anymore, hurt me even more than seeing a good friend who was sick and broken?

I guessed it was 'cause Raniero looked more ruined to me, standing there in a tailored suit, than Lucius did struggling in chains. It didn't help that Raniero's eyes got very black, too, when that creep Fabio and the other old vampires started squawking right away, "But he is *blestemată* . . . condemned himself!"

Yeah, there was a pretty big uproar while the Elders decided if they could—or should—listen to testimony from a vampire who was, like, the worst criminal ever.

I watched Raniero stand very straight through the whole argument and saw that they might as well have been punching him. I could tell he was trying hard not to duck every time somebody said, "But he is damned. . . . His testimony is not valid."

Jess kept punching back for him, though, and she told them all, still very calm, "*You* trained Raniero Vladescu Lovatu to be what he is: the world's most skilled assassin—an expert in destruction, wounds and blood—and in his own way, the most credible witness our clans could produce." That was when she started to win round two.

There was this big moment of silence, then old Fabio said, very slow, like we were idiots, "He will lie to protect his friend."

Jess took a sec to let everybody think about that. Then she gave the knockout punch—by saying the very thing that was making me a little sick right then. "Raniero has much more to gain by seeing Lucius Vladescu sentenced to destruction than he does by saving him. He is in line to rule as my regent. Thus, if his testimony exonerates a prince, it is more credible than any other, for it comes at great cost to himself. He will lose the chance for wealth, privilege, and power that most only dream of."

Jess sounded like a different girl—a different *woman* then. Like she was channeling her birth mom and using a whole new vocabulary that was even better than Romanian. She was speaking *royalty*.

There was more silence. You coulda heard half a pin drop. Then somebody finally said, talking for all of 'em, "Let the *blestemată* vampire speak. There is no rule against it."

I watched Raniero cross his hands in front of himself, standing like Lukey had just done, but without chains—at least not ones you could see—and with his head held high and his feet planted wide apart. And while I thought I'd seen Lucius smile when he stood on the spot, I was *sure* Raniero's eyes flickered like they were on fire in a way I'd never seen before—and wasn't too keen to see then.

I looked at Ylenia, and she was kinda smiling, too, as that trial got under way for real.

Chapter 109

Antanasia

FOR A VAMPIRE who once claimed that he wanted everything Lucius had, Raniero did an impressive job of defending the very prince who blocked his path to power—even though just showing up at the trial really did cost him. If not the chance at a throne, in terms of pain.

"He's an assassin . . . Damned . . . Condemned himself . . ."

As we'd heard the Elders—especially Flaviu—speak those words, I'd known that Raniero was finally being pushed to that place he'd feared going. His eyes had grown black and dangerous. And yet he did his best for his friend.

He produced Lucius's stake and showed everyone how the bloodstain was all wrong. And he got the servants who'd prepared Claudiu's body for burial to confirm that there were three wounds to the destroyed Elder's chest.

"Two are shallow, and made by a right-handed vampire—and one final thrust is made by someone who attacked with the left," he told everyone. "It is very easy for myself—as one who has destroyed often—to see the pattern. And we all know that Lucius Vladescu would destroy with a single left-handed thrust. He would *never* use his right hand—or *miss.*" Raniero actually smiled a little. A grim smile of appreciation for Lucius's nerve. "And Lucius Vladescu does not ask for help when he does battle. If Lucius did this act, there would be *no* right-handed wounds."

Most of the Elders, and everyone in the courtroom, agreed that Lucius would always use his dominant hand—and destroy more efficiently, and certainly without any pathetic assistance from some weaker, right-handed vampire. Everyone knew his reputation, and his power had been apparent even when he'd walked into the courtroom, shackled but fighting to stay upright, still every inch a sovereign.

But unfortunately, it still didn't seem like he was going to win his trial.

I could tell that nothing Raniero said was enough to counter their repeated, almost confused, refrain. "But Claudiu's blood is upon the stake, and Lucius cannot explain it."

Even my time-stamped evidence of e-mail messages, exchanged when Lucius would have *had* to be in the foyer if he'd really destroyed Claudiu, didn't sway them. If anything, all the information I presented about computers only seemed to baffle and raise suspicions among the older vampires.

They understood that it was strange that Claudiu's blood had still been bright red when Lucius had been dragged from bed and we'd all convened in the foyer, but they didn't see how a computer could prove that he'd been busy in our room for a long time before that, too, so that the blood would have *had* to coagulate and darken if he'd committed the act.

I had been so certain that we would win—that my new attitude would carry the day—that I thought Raniero and Mindy, who knew me so well, must have seen the disbelief in my eyes as I brought down a gavel and said, "We will adjourn for the day and reconvene tomorrow." Because by late afternoon, I had run out of ideas to save Lucius, and felt like the best I could do was hope for a miracle that night. And if I didn't get one . . .

I wasn't sure what I would do.

As the Elders and the spectators shuffled out, I finally did meet Dorin's eyes, and for once he didn't meet mine, even for a second. He was looking at Ylenia—and they both looked more perplexed than I felt.

Chapter 110
Mindy

THEY MET IN a different garden the night after the first part of Lukey's trial. I followed Ylenia right to the tiny secret courtyard where Jess and Lucius got married.

Back on Jess's wedding night, the wild, twisty vines that crept up all the walls had seemed romantic, but that night it felt like they were choking the life out of that little place. Like they were gonna sneak around my arms and legs and squeeze the life out of me, too. Out of *everybody* in that castle.

Lucius was in big trouble.

Those vampires were too old to understand real evidence, like from computers. Or maybe they just wanted to see a young, strong, up-and-coming king go down hard 'cause they were old and had never been anything but weaklings themselves. I'd about got sick of watching even Jess's uncle Dorin fretting away like he was gonna pee his robe.

And I about threw up in the shadows, too, when the guy

I'd been in love with, who stood just about on the spot where I'd first seen his unbelievable eyes, whispered to Ylenia, "You are certain that you wish for this life? For you see how Antansia suffers. If I were to achieve power, it could be dangerous for you, too."

Her little eyes, no longer hid by glasses, glowed even brighter than before. "Yes, I would be ready. I could handle it."

I tried real hard to understand what Raniero was doing, 'cause I coulda swore he fought hard for Lucius back in the courtroom.

Or had he? Was that why Jess had lost, in the end? Because Raniero hadn't really tried hard at all?

I honestly couldn't tell. It had *seemed* like he said the right stuff, but then again . . .

"It is good that we have come together again," he told Ylenia. He spoke soft, but not like he used to talk to me. He didn't sound sweet. Hot, yeah—but not sweet. "It is good to have a second chance."

I turned around and left 'em alone, and went back to my room and made sure that bottle I'd snatched was safe and sound. I even stuffed a few extra shirts around it in the carryon, just to make sure it wouldn't accidentally break when I took it to the sentencing the next day.

I was gonna let Jess keep doing her thing, 'cause I wasn't one hundred percent sure I was right about that bottle, or Ylenia, or especially Raniero. He seemed like two vampires in one, and I couldn't figure out which was the real thing.

But if it all went down wrong in the end . . . Well, I was no vampire, but I was gonna uncork that bottle and spill some blood myself. I was gonna raise a little hell in a place that already seemed pretty darn close to there, if you asked me.

Chapter 111
Antanasia

I SUPPOSED BY that point I could have roused the drunk, sleeping guard and just demanded the key. But as I stood in the shadows of the dungeon, part of me clung to the small hope that the Elders would still find Lucius innocent, based in part on his continued insistence on obeying the laws that were sending him to a world of mad nightmares. So ultimately I stepped quietly toward my husband, who was stretched out on his plank bed already looking like a corpse, and whispered, "Lucius."

He remained completely still.

"Lucius?"

At my second, slightly louder call, his eyes opened, and even by the weak light of the oil lamp, I saw so many emotions course through him. Surprise, and disapproval, because I shouldn't be there, both because the law forbade it and because he would think it was risky for me to wander alone. But above all I saw the love that I needed to see.

He didn't move right away. I thought he was too exhausted, and I had to tell him, softly, "I can't come to you. I don't have a key." I stole a glance at the snoring guard. "And I can't risk waking him by hunting for one."

It hurt so much to be separated from Lucius, and it had hurt more to see him struggle in the courtroom. But nothing hurt as badly as watching him fight, hard, just to rise and come over to *me*. He sat up on the cot and paused for about thirty seconds with his head hanging down, and I almost told him just to stay there. That it would be enough for us just to look at each other.

But I wanted to touch him, and he wanted to touch me, too—enough that he managed to stand and walk the few steps to the bars which were spaced just widely enough for me to slip my arm through and reach him. He leaned against the wall, but soon we both sank to the floor, holding on to each other in the only way we could. Which wasn't half as much as either of us needed.

Still, he told me, "You should not be here, Jessica. If the guard awakens, *you* will be punished for breaking our laws, too."

I knelt next to him, and for the first time since we'd gotten married, when I'd pretty much let Lucius take control, I reasserted my authority with him. "I don't care, Lucius."

He had closed his eyes, but opened them again, and I saw an incredibly precious trace of amusement there—along with the admiration that had been draining away since our marriage. "You have changed, wife of mine—of whom I often dream as I lie here," he said. "*One of us* is getting stronger." He managed a smile. "You were very brave to choose to preside at Claudiu's funeral, when you did not have to, and you were a force to be reckoned with today at the trial."

I didn't remind him that I'd had to preside over the funeral, but it scared me that Lucius would forget even a small detail of royal protocol. The books I was struggling to decipher were burned into his mind.

"I dream about you, too, all the time," I told him, shoving aside my worry. I clutched his arm with my hand, and we tried to rest our foreheads against each other's through the narrow gap. "I miss you so much." My voice cracked, but I got control of myself. "It's over tomorrow, though. You'll be free."

Lucius might have been losing touch with reality, but he still chose to face the truth head-on when he recognized it. "I do not think that I will walk free, Jessica. I understand that you and Raniero did admirably today, but my guard reports the rumors honestly. The Elders do not believe in my innocence."

"They will, Lucius. I'll think of something else. I promise."

He lifted his head away from mine and met my eyes. "You have done well, Princess. You took a risk, and you must never regret that. I would have done the same."

"It's going to pay off."

He didn't believe it. "If it does not, know that I have faith that you will be an incredible ruler . . . already *are* an incredible ruler. And always remember that you were the love of my existence."

That was too much for him, and he couldn't say any more. I couldn't seem to say anything, either.

I sat with him quietly, not wanting our time together to end. Eventually, though, the guard shifted, and Lucius mumbled, "You should go now."

"No, not yet. Not before you drink."

He shook his head, seeming confused. "No, Jessica . . . We already break enough laws, and there is no way for me to reach you. I will not hurt you or try to drink desperately through bars, like an animal." I saw regret in his eyes. "You could not offer me enough to sustain me for more than a few hours, anyway. It would take weeks of rest and much, much blood before I was strong again." He continued to meet my eyes, and I saw the truth in his. I saw just how close he was to . . . disappearing. He was only there because he loved me enough to come back from the place of nightmares long enough to say good-bye. "I do not want you to remember me hurting you, or acting in—fruitless—desperation."

I couldn't accept that. He had to keep fighting, and I pulled back my arm, rolled up my sleeve, and slipped my hand through the bars again. I was being selfish, too. If he really was vanishing from me, I wanted him to take a part of me with him. And I wanted to feel him drink from me again. To connect with him that way. "You can drink like this, Lucius. From where I cut myself at our wedding."

He looked from my arm to my face. "I do not think so, Jessica."

Oh, my frustrating, brave, wonderful husband. I was trying hard to be brave, too, and starting to succeed, but tears pricked at my eyes. "I love you, Lucius. And I'll die without you, and you *are* going to drink my blood tonight." Suddenly I sounded like Raniero back in the *camera di miză*. "Do you think I care about a few minutes of physical pain? Do you think I care about *law?*"

He hesitated, and I added, "Do this for me. Please, Lucius. I can't live if something happens to you. I *won't* live."

I knew I wasn't playing fair. I was asking him to break his code of honor using the only temptation I knew he couldn't resist.

Me.

He wouldn't break the rules to save his own existence, but he would do anything to save *mine*.

"Lucius," I whispered, seeing him weaken in a different way, "if you drift into limbo and never return to me, not only will I join you, but you won't have any chance to create a better kingdom for hundreds of thousands of vampires who need a king like you. So tonight we're going to break one law, in the interest of saving ourselves, and ultimately for our relatives, most of whom probably don't even deserve the life we want to give them."

He paused for just another second. "I forget sometimes how strong your will is. How strong *you* are."

Yes, because I'd forgotten it, too, for too long. I stretched my hand farther into the cell. "Here . . . do it."

"As you order, Jessica." I could've sworn he was smiling faintly—just like he'd smiled with pride at the trial. An almost imperceptible lift of his lips. "As you *insist*."

Then Lucius took my arm into his cool hands and bent his head over me, and I immediately felt his fangs graze my skin, because he was starving. I was drinking blood sometimes, but I was starving, too, for him. Even though of course I couldn't take a drop from him, my own fangs ached as his lips brushed against the pale inner part of my wrist, and it did hurt when his teeth broke through my flesh. The spot was sensitive, his fangs were much thicker and blunter than the knife I'd used at my wedding, and what we were sharing right then was different from the passion that usually made being bitten feel *good.* This was a new feeling, and everything about it was painful. Just loving the vampire who was so desperate for sustenance, but trying to be gentle as my blood coursed into his mouth, *hurt.*

"Drink more," I urged when he started to pull back. "Please. Drink as much as you can."

But of course he was Lucius Vladescu, and while he might have destroyed vampires and rammed a stake through his best friend's hand, he was also my protector, and a prince, and he didn't believe that he could be saved by draining me on one desperate night, and before I even felt dizzy, he raised his head and tilted it backward, eyes closed, like he was satisfied— although I knew he wasn't. His fingers didn't feel any stronger when he wrapped them around my arm, staunching the flow of blood.

"You should have more, Lucius." But I knew he wouldn't.

"I love you, Jessica," he murmured, seeming to get very drowsy. "But you should go now . . ."

"Yes, Lucius. I'm going. I love you, too." I didn't leave, though. I sat with him, watching his face, while he slept right there on the floor, with his back against the wall and his head resting against the bars.

When the guard finally got too restless, and I couldn't bear to see Lucius's eyes, no longer mischievous and happy, twitch beneath his lids as he returned to a place of torment, I crept off to my room—and out into the darkness, one final time.

Chapter 1-12
Antanasia

THE CEMETERY FELT even colder than before, and I knew I really was alone that night. Raniero had done his part for Lucius, and he seemed to have other things to preoccupy his new life now. I hadn't seen him since the trial and didn't know where he'd gone.

Pulling open the iron gate, I went first to my parents' crypt, where I poured my own offering of blood into the small bowl, and said quietly, "I hope that in the end, I've made you proud. And I hope that you'll be happy, and not disappointed, if I'm not laid to rest here next to you—although it would be an honor to be by your side."

Then I left the Dragomir crypt and went to the soaring, spiked Vladescu mausoleum, which I had avoided even looking at for so long, and where I was going to insist that *I* be entombed.

Chapter 1-13
Antanasia

I LIT A row of five candles that waited on a marble shelf inside the Vladescus' tomb, and first poured out another offering of blood into the bowl that Lucius used for his own parents.

"I should have come here earlier to thank you for Lucius," I told them, bowing my head. "You can't imagine how incredible your son is, and I thank you, too, for signing the pact that made him my husband, linking me to him for eternity."

When I said that word—eternity—I raised my head and finally faced the thing that had made me avert my eyes from that crypt for too long. I finally faced . . . the future.

Unlike the Dragomirs, who left blank spots in their mausoleum—one maybe reserved for me, or maybe not—the Vladescus were realistic about the prospects for even their favorite sons. I read the words, etched in marble.

LUCIUS VALERIU VLADESCU, A.D. 1993–

I stared at his name and refused to tremble. I wouldn't do that anymore. Lucius stood in that same spot and faced this every time he came to see his parents. Maybe that was part of the reason he was able to face the end of his existence at other times, too.

And in that grim, terrible place, I made a new promise to Lucius.

I would be destroyed with him before I took any part in sentencing him to destruction. I would commit treason myself by defying the Elders' ruling, break some of our biggest laws and die with my husband if it came to that.

I had made a vow to Lucius on our wedding day to be with him for eternity, and I was going to keep that, if not in the way I hoped, in any way I had to. I would either be destroyed outright, or if Lucius was somehow exonerated but already lost in that realm of nightmares, I would follow him there, and find him, and we would suffer together, because I would never drink anyone else's blood again, and I would rather spend immortality in torment by his side than five minutes alone in a castle with every comfort all our money could buy.

Snuffing out the candles, I left the mausoleum, and on the way back to the estate, as I walked through the woods filled with wolves, I wondered who would bury me, if it really came to that.

Would it be Dorin, whose whole existence was spent in a shallow grave of fear, batting at shadows that weren't even there yet?

I thought more and more about my own funeral, and as I did, I started to walk faster and faster, and although Lucius insisted that royalty never hurry, by the time I was almost home, I was in a dead run.

I needed to see the *Carte de Ritual.*

The book that dictated, down to the smallest detail, the way our clans conducted the rites related to birth, marriage . . . and destruction.

Chapter 14
Antanasia

MY FINGERS TREMBLED with excitement and rage as I ran them down the proper page of the *Carte de Ritual,* painstakingly comparing the words I saw on its pages to those in my Romanian-English dictionary, which was finally starting to get suitably dog-eared.

Inmormântarea . . . Pentru . . . Conducător . . .

Over the course of three hours, I translated the whole section on funerals for Elders to make sure that there was no way I was wrong. I took special care with the intonation before the ringing of the bells. *"Acum vom respecta un moment de tăcere pentru a marca trecerea lui Claudiu Vladescu în tăcerea veșcnică."*

And when dawn arrived, I slammed the book shut with a thud that must have rocked the castle's foundations.

Everything I read in there, and other things I remembered, too—a word on a bottle, a cork pulled a little too soon, a shaking right hand . . .

It all translated to . . . *betrayal.*

Chapter 1-15
Mindy

I TRIED TO find Jess before the second day of the trial, but she didn't even sleep in her bed that night. I waited for hours, like I'd waited for Raniero, 'cause I did feel like I should warn her about what I believed about Ylenia, and Ronnie, too.

I sent texts and tried to call her cell, but she never answered. Even little Emilio didn't know where she was, so I ended up taking my carryon to the courtroom, clutching it like a baby and waiting with everybody else—a bunch of vampires who looked at me like *I* was crazy.

And maybe I was a little intense. But not as much as the princess who marched into that court in a very unprofessional pair of jeans and a T-shirt, looking like she had gone to hell and back—and was about to drag the rest of us back there with her, just like I kinda planned to do.

I knew in a split second—and everybody else knew it, too, even old Fabio—that we weren't just seeing a princess standing there in a pair of jeans and boots.

We were all getting our first glimpse of the next *queen*.

Chapter 116
Antanasia

I COULD TELL that everyone in that courtroom knew that I meant business, even if I wasn't wearing a suit and heels. I could've been wearing the nightgown I'd put on when I'd run out of my first trial and the look in my eyes would have been enough to silence the whole chamber.

The atmosphere was tense and nervous and excited as I marched into the room, and I knew that this was how a princess—or a queen, even—was supposed to be received.

Even Flaviu stopped smirking, and I imagine he thought he was going to be the target when I walked not behind the table of Elders to take my place, but in front of all those vampires, who eyed me warily until I found the one I wanted. And when I did, I rested my hands on the table and watched him quake as I announced, without the slightest hesitation—and in the same low, soft, menacing tone I'd heard Lucius use to intimidate so many vampires, making it my own—"Dorin Dragomir, you have betrayed your sovereigns and committed treason, and you will pay with your existence."

"I DIDN'T . . . I didn't do anything, Antanasia," Dorin sputtered. He held up his hands. "Nothing!"

I wasn't having any of it. His ashen cheeks and his terrified rabbit eyes gave everything away.

I narrowed my own eyes and leaned closer to him. "You mistranslated the *Carte de Ritual* to force me to preside at Claudiu's funeral when I didn't have to, and you made me a laughingstock by teaching me the wrong thing to say, so I would commit his body to a land of rainbows instead of eternal silence. I didn't say 'rainbows' randomly. You *scripted* it for me. Then you *drugged* me . . . gave me blood that was tainted so I would hallucinate in front of everyone. You *wanted* to see me fail."

The other Elders were all rearing back in their chairs, and the spectators who'd come to see Lucius's fate unfold rustled and muttered as those who spoke English translated my words for those who couldn't understand.

"Why . . . Antanasia . . . I wouldn't . . ." But he was rattling in his seat. "Why would I . . . ?"

"I don't know . . . yet," I growled. "But you tried to drug me again before my last meeting with the Elders. You gave me blood that was already opened—and that smelled wrong even to me. You wanted me to hallucinate *again*, in front of them!"

"Of course I opened it . . ."

"You called it Siberian, because you were desperate to

make me drink it, but that was a lie. I saw the word *Franța*—
'France'—on the label. For whatever twisted reason, you were
panicked for me to drink it—scared like you always are—and
you *made a terrible mistake.*"

Lucius always said Dorin's fear would be his undoing.

"You've been drugging me all along, making me, and
everyone else, think I was losing my mind—and you destroyed Claudiu, too," I accused him. "Raniero said the weakest wounds were made with a right hand, and you are one of
the few right-handed vampires in the whole kingdom. You always raise the wrong hand at meetings, although you are
nearly one hundred years old. You can't stop using your right!"

Of all the things I'd said, that one really seemed to reso-
nate with the Elders. Vampires were like the mirror opposite
of humans when it came to dexterity. A right-handed member
of the undead was uncommon indeed. And a right-handed
vampire with access to the castle and Lucius's stake . . .

Even rarer.

I really did have no idea why a feckless weakling like
Dorin had done these things, but I knew that he had.

He was such a coward, though, that he still couldn't
admit it.

Not until Mindy, the only non-vampire in the room,
stood up and said, "Excuse me?"

I turned around to see her clutching a small suitcase that
I thought contained makeup and hair spray, which had saved
me so many times before, and I didn't understand what she was
doing until she said, "I think it's over, Dorin. I got the last bottle of tainted blood in here. The one you sent Jess yesterday."

He broke then. Broke like the pathetic excuse for a vampire—for a *Dragomir*—that he'd always been and said, with tears starting to run down his face, "Have mercy on me, Antanasia. She made me do everything. It was her plan, and I was scared of her. She's bitter and twisted, and she hates you. Wanted to destroy everything that you and Lucius have! She can't bear that Lucius actually loves you, when she couldn't even keep the Vladescu nobleman she drugged to trick him into biting her. It's her fault that Raniero is damned, and she still doesn't stop!"

It was hard to follow a finger that was shaking so badly, but I turned around again to see that he was pointing to my only other *friend* in vampiredom.

Ylenia Dragomir, who was already standing and pushing to get out of the room.

"She made me lure Claudiu to the foyer and help her destroy him, to ruin Lucius and you, too," Dorin kept babbling as Ylenia broke free of the seats and started to run. "She made me get Lucius's stake and call for a meeting with Claudiu at dawn. . . ."

I didn't bother to chase after my cousin. I was royalty, and royalty didn't run. At least, not in public.

More to the point, I'd seen a trained assassin step from the shadows where he'd been watching everything, and I decided to let him do what he did best. Track down and bring the worst vampires to justice.

He wouldn't snap—because he never really had.

I turned back to Dorin, who was sobbing as he spoke. "And *she* was the one who really destroyed Claudiu. I struck at him, but she pierced his heart with a stake she carved herself, in case I couldn't do it. And I couldn't . . . I couldn't . . ."

He might not have struck the fatal blow, but his crimes were unforgivable, and I announced his fate without pity, but without cruelty, either, because I had spent the worst of my anger. And a part of me would always know what it had been like to be weak, too. "Dorin Dragomir," I spoke resolutely, forcing myself to meet his eyes. "You have committed treason, and you will be tried in two days and face the penalty of destruction."

Then I turned to the guards who watched the doors and said, "*Duceți-l la temniță.* Take him to the cell that Lucius Vladescu will no longer occupy."

I messed up the Romanian, but I didn't care. I'd said the words the right way—with no room for contradiction—and that was all that mattered. I looked at Flaviu to see if he would dare protest my liberation of Lucius, but for once he seemed like the confused, ridiculous old vampire he really was. Like he wasn't sure what was happening, because he'd so expected me to fail.

And Dorin . . . I heard him weeping the whole time I walked slowly and regally out of the room. I didn't look back, and I didn't run until I was sure no one would see me, and then I tore toward the dungeons ahead of the guards and Dorin to see if Lucius could still be brought back, or if we were both going to wander together in a realm of nightmares, trapped forever between life and death.

Chapter 1-18
Mindy

I FOUND RANIERO and Ylenia right outside the court-room—she didn't get very far—but by the time I muscled my way through the crowd that was watching, he already had her trapped against a wall and was clutching a stake, warning her in the deepest, scariest voice I'd ever heard anybody use, "Because of you I am marked for destruction, and today *you* will be destroyed, too."

"You don't understand," she was blubbering. "I just wanted you to bite me that night. I just put a little salvia in the blood I gave you, because I'd heard of guys doing that to girls. . . . I thought if you bit me once, we'd be together, and I'd make you happy. If you just got to know me, you'd like me, but you'd never even *looked* at me . . ."

I watched Raniero's hand start to shake, and I'd never felt worse about being right about anything in my life. I'd known she'd drugged him—and Jess. I'd made *that* connection, 'cause I'd seen Ronnie's roommate freaking out, and it had looked just like Jess's meltdown. I'd guessed days ago that Ylenia'd borrowed some kind of trick from her stoner boarding school friends and messed with them both.

Too bad she didn't read the in-depth *Modern Girl* maga-zine article "Barely Legal: What Your Friends MIGHT Be Using to Get High." Maybe if she'd read that, she woulda stuck to giving him a little cough syrup, instead of salvia, a plant that was like LSD and could make you get *violent*.

Maybe then she wouldn't be trapped against a wall by a vampire whose hand, holding a bloodstained stake, was shaking harder when he *snarled,* sounding even *scarier,* "It is your fault that I destroy a vampire and become *blestemată.* It is YOUR FAULT that I am marked for destruction and believe myself to be even worse than I am. Because of you, I live every day for two years wondering if I might destroy wrongly again! I *despise* myself!"

I didn't know if I should run forward and grab his hand or if that might just make him slip and do something terrible, but before I could decide, Ylenia's face twisted up in a weird way, and all of a sudden she wasn't crying anymore. She was *yelling.* "You don't think you're anything but perfect! You and Lucius both think you own the world!"

Raniero still had her pinned against the wall, but she balled up her little fist and stamped her foot like a spoiled brat, like she hated everybody so much she didn't even care if she got herself killed. "I hate you all, and I hope Lucius spends eternity twisting in limbo so she's miserable forever, too! She's a Dragomir and can't even speak Romanian or find her own room, and he *still loves her*—while you never even *looked at* me! I hope they both rot away and suffer forever—and you get destroyed, too!"

It was one thing to ruin Raniero's life and get him marked for destruction, but it was another to insult his friends and mess up *their* lives, and I guessed that was what made him finally really snap like he'd been afraid would happen for years. It wasn't a semilegal drug that sent him over the edge and made him crazy, it was a jealous, loser, teenage vampire-princess wannabe who was gonna ruin *all* our lives if I didn't say something, 'cause for the first time since I'd known him, Raniero actually looked ugly to me.

He pulled back his hand with the stake and his face got so I could hardly even recognize it, and I guessed that's why I closed my eyes—so I could picture the Ronnie I wanted back—when I cried out to him, as loud as I could, like I was a queen myself, "Stop it, Raniero Lovatu! Stop it right now, you stupid Italian vampire! Stop it, 'cause I love you, and I wanna live with you on the beach, and I want you to grow your goatee back and find your dumb taco shirt and *get out of here with me on the next plane* before we can't have *anything* together! I'm sorry I ever wanted you to change or fight anybody and just . . . STOP IT! NOW!"

All the noise in the world stopped. Even the vampires who were translating everything into a bunch of Euro languages shut up and didn't move.

And when I had the guts to open my eyes, I saw Raniero's shoulders shaking, and his hand shaking, and I thought I would die before I could find out which Ronnie I'd see when he started to turn around to face me.

Chapter 19
Antanasia

THE GUARD WHO was preparing Dorin for incarceration had left the key to Lucius's cell in plain sight, and I mastered my fingers to undo the lock, then slipped inside the bars and ran to my husband, who lay on his side, eyes closed.

"Lucius." I shook him gently. "Please. Open your eyes."

Epilogue
Antanasia

I LAY DOWN next to Lucius and watched him sleeping in the sunlight that streamed into our room. His face looked so peaceful. He always looked serene now, and that comforted me.

"Wake up," I shook him. "The sun is out."

His eyes opened, and I saw once again that he had changed since his imprisonment.

He wasn't worried and sorry that he'd brought me into *our* world, and he considered me a true equal again. Was *proud* of me.

Edging back, I gave Lucius room to prop himself up on his strong arms—it hadn't taken him long to recover at all—and he looked over at the clock. Then he fell back on the mattress and grinned at me. "Why do you allow me to sleep so long on such an important day? Do you not want your husband, the future king, to look his best?"

"I still like you to rest."

He reached out and pulled my arm so I tumbled on top of his chest, and I could feel his muscles, which did seem just fine. Back to perfect form. "I have been well for months now, Antanasia," he said. "You need not baby me any longer."

It was hard to stop, though. He'd been so weak when he'd been carried to our bedroom that I'd barely been able to coax him to drink. I'd had to cut my wrist again and let the blood drip into his mouth. And when I'd first looked into his eyes, back in his cell, I'd sworn he would never come back.

But he was Lucius Vladescu, and of course he'd fought to return to me so we could have that dream he'd whispered into my ear on our wedding night.

"Do you really think we'll get the vote of confidence?" I asked, staring into his black eyes, because I knew I would read the truth there. "Do you think all these vampires who are milling around inside our house trust us enough?"

"I think we have a fair chance," he said. "Better than I had at my trial, and I won that."

"*I* won that," I reminded him. "Me and Mindy and Raniero."

"Yes, yes," he agreed, laughing. "I know. So you often remind me."

I got serious. "Could you really not speak, that first day in the courtroom?"

He tucked one of my curls behind my ear. "You were doing well enough on your own. I had nothing to add."

I asked him that now and then, just to remind myself exactly how much faith he had in me. And the answer was always the same. Then I posed another question, just to see the mischief it always sparked in his eyes. "Where were you that night, when I tried to find you in your office and you came to bed so late?"

He gave me the look I'd hoped for. The arched eyebrow. "Jessica, do you really wish to know all of my secrets?"

Maybe . . . Maybe not.

That look—and thoughts of that night—reminded me of someone else. "Is Raniero coming today?"

Lucius shook his head, and his short, neat hair gleamed in the sun. "No. He has done enough for us. I excused him from voting, although he offered."

We didn't mention the absence of my cousin Ylenia or my uncle Dorin, although they were never far from my mind. I was a princess, hopefully about to be queen, but I still suffered at the memory of handing down their sentences of destruction. It wasn't exactly guilt that I felt for presiding over their trials while Lucius recovered. It was a deeper, conflicted sadness, but one that I had to learn to live with.

Lucius must have seen me growing somber and didn't want that, because he suddenly and easily rolled me onto my back, and although *I* was already dressed for the biggest day of the summer convocation, our vote of confidence, he kissed me in a way that told me that he might be strong again, and not desperate for blood, but that he was still, and always would be, very thirsty for me.

Mindy

"DO YOU WANT, like, a taco or a burrito for lunch?" I asked my surfing vampire boyfriend, who ditched his board in the sand next to my cheap lawn chair and shook a bunch of water out of his long hair—right onto me.

"Hey! I'm paying for lunch, so don't make me mad!"

"I will buy you lunch today," Raniero offered. He bent down and kissed me, which helped make up for getting me wet, then plopped down in the sand. "*Il mio trattare—* my treat!"

"And you will use *what* to pay?"

"I win two hundred dollars for taking second place in the *competizione,* do you remember?"

I looked over at him and rolled my eyes. This was apparently how we were gonna live. Following surfing competitions from beach to beach, with me cutting hair when I got the chance. I really hadn't thought I'd do that again, but we needed cash, and I kinda had a reputation among the traveling surf circus already.

Then I looked out over the ocean, which was super rough that day, and I got reminded of the way Ronnie's eyes had looked when he'd turned around, just about to stake Ylenia Dragomir through the heart.

He *hadn't* lost control, but he'd been a lot closer than was comfortable for anybody.

And I never asked him if he'd known all along that Ylenia was evil . . . or if he'd started to slip a little, for real, and dream about power and riches in those castle gardens.

"Better, for me, sand running through otherwise empty fingers than blood on hands full of money."

My surfer–practically prince–philosopher said that sometimes, and I had to agree.

All of a sudden, I remembered something I hardly ever thought about anymore, which was *time.* "Hey . . . Isn't today Jess and Lucius's big vote?"

"*Si.*" Ronnie nodded. "I offer to attend, but Lucius insists that the surfing is too good now for me to leave California. They will win or lose without my vote."

"They'll win," I said. And I hoped they lived happily ever after in their castle. Maybe we'd visit now and then.

Maybe not.

Maybe they should just come visit us. We could make room, now that I only owned, like, six pairs of flip-flops. All my sort-of-designer shoes were still in Pennsylvania, where my mom was holding them hostage till I wised up and came back to college or something—which wasn't gonna happen.

I reached down and grabbed Raniero's hand in the sand. He let me take it, and it felt good and cool against mine. "So, what is it? Taco or burrito?"

"I would like a *vampiro*," he said, grinning at me like an idiot. He was always bugging me about becoming undead now. "When do you allow me to make you mine forever? It is a good life, if you stay away from the violence."

"I don't know," I told him, yanking my hand free. "There's no rush."

I knew I'd do it someday, though. The more I was around him, the more I got used to the idea of drinking blood.

Okay, maybe I kinda wanted it.

But I wasn't gonna let him know that yet.

First he had to prove that he really was gonna take me to Tahiti. *Then* we'd talk eternity.

"Come on." I stood up and brushed the sand off my butt, then held out my hand for Raniero to pull him up, too. "Let's go eat lunch."

The jobless guy with the shaggy hair, and the goatee, and the Goodwill swim trunks—and the killer abs that I got to see all the time now, since shirts were completely optional—grabbed onto me again, and kept his fingers wrapped around mine the whole way to Terrible Taco, and I was really proud that he was mine.

Acknowledgments

Like all books, this one is the result of collaboration with and support from a lot of wonderful people—way more than can be credited here. However, I would like to take a little space to thank, in particular, all the readers who asked for this novel. Without you, it definitely wouldn't exist.

And special thanks, too, to my editor, Margaret Raymo, whose guidance and insights always amaze me. Not to mention her patience.

Thanks, in fact, to everyone at Houghton Mifflin Harcourt—and to Cliff Nielsen, who's created the beautiful covers for all three of my books, as well as Lieucretia Swain, who maintains my website and went above and beyond the call of duty to make Jess and Lucius's wedding happen.

I'm also incredibly grateful to all the e-mailers, bloggers, booksellers, and YA librarians who supported *Jessica's Guide to Dating on the Dark Side* and helped to ensure a sequel. I wish there was room to acknowledge you all, especially those of you who've become genuine friends.

I also want to again credit my agent, Helen Breitwieser, for always making me feel like I'm the only author she has to handle, and for doing such a great job on my behalf.

Finally, I have to acknowledge my friends and family—including my Pilates pals; Patti and the Lewisburg, Pa., McDonald's crew; the stylish women at the Styling Nook; as well as everybody in our little town who cheers me on.

And the biggest thanks to my husband, Dave; my parents, Marjorie and Don Fantaskey; and my in-laws, George and Elaine Kaszuba, all of whom not only support my projects but help to watch my fantastic kids, Paige, Julia, and Hope—a trio who still only vaguely get what I do, but who encourage me with boundless enthusiasm.

Without all of your help and guidance and good wishes, this book wouldn't be here. Thank you!